IS BARRY STRANGE

IS BARRY STRANGE
A Transformative Journey

BILL DAVIS

Charlottesville, VA

Is Barry Strange/Bill Davis—1st ed.
ISBN 979-8-9990613-2-4

This is dedicated to the ones I love, especially Emily, Alex, and Will, Millie, Sarah, Donna, Mom, Dad, Karen, Susan, John, Tim, and everyone else!

And whether I come to my own to-day or in ten thousand or ten million years, I can cheerfully take it now, or with equal cheerfulness I can wait.

Walt Whitman

CHAPTER ONE

Nervous about the whole thing, Barry Strange takes a deep breath and enters the hotel. With way more volume and bravado than necessary, he demands to know the location of the ballroom where the damn "YOU BEING YOU!" workshop is taking place.

The 20-something smartly dressed staff member, nametagged "Malcolm," clasps his hands Buddha-like and bows slightly. Without a word, as if revealing a great mystery, he gestures slowly toward a doorway above which hangs foot-high calligraphy displaying the name of the very room just mentioned.

"Oh, thanks!" Barry says in that voice of complete innocence and cheerfulness for which, in his own mind at least, he is justly famous. "Barry Strange!" he says shaking the clerk's hand. "Famous celebrity."

"Welcome to the Regency, Mr. Strange! I hope you enjoy the workshop. I have never heard of you but that does not mean a thing. There are lots of people I have yet to hear of."

"A good day to you, Malcolm!" he says squinting comically

(he hopes) at the clerk's name badge. "Have a blessed day!"

He turns away from the desk thinking, '*Good God, Barry! Calm down.*' He is not a religious person but wonders about his smart-assed blessing. Is he employing the reflexive departing word of a Christian as a kind of decoy whereby Malcolm can attribute Barry's odd behavior to theology, or is it mythology?

Before reaching the ballroom, a strong physical necessity turns him back to the clerk.

"One more thing—where is a restroom?"

Another polite bow and gesture direct Barry's attention to a huge sign with stick figures representing a man, a woman, a human figure wearing both skirt and pants, a baby, a person in a wheelchair, an alien, a human figure with two heads, and the words, "WHATEVER just wash your hands!"

Although Barry grasps the message well enough, he feels like playing the fool one more time. He flashes Malcolm what he thinks conveys a look of total bewilderment.

Gratefully, the clerk laughs this time. "It... is... a... Gender Neutral... *toilet*," he says as if explaining the basics of life to the village idiot. "Anyone, regardless of gender identity or mental competence, is welcome to use it, even you."

Barry smiles and laughs as if to reassure the clerk that he is only joking after all. After a jaunty, care-free wave he is safe inside where he releases a huge audible sigh along with an unseemly and involuntary burst of pent-up intestinal gas.

"Oh, Lord, save me from this torment..." sings a woman's voice behind the door of the first stall reserved for 'Accessibility.' Barry thinks her song is a kind of announcement of her presence. A warning perhaps? Certainly, no hint of an invitation. In any case, he thinks it quite beautiful and considers it a useful bit of information. The musical lilt confirms that this is an all-gender facility. Also, he feels he could have/should have toned down his entrance.

Not familiar with the proper protocol in such situations, he belches a kind of reply with what he thinks can be interpreted as a masculine tone and resists a temptation to engage in any further communication with the person behind the stall door. Uncertain whether what he now has to do might prove even more disturbing, he chooses a stall a good distance from the one occupied.

Alas, there is no point in repressing what has to be done. Maybe, he can mask objectionable sounds by singing! A couple lines of potential mirth bubble up and he lets out a voice he was told (by someone some time ago) was pleasing to the ear...

From the folds of the rump
A pained and awful dump;
Not our favorite way to do-do...
Yet, it's got to be done
And though seldom fun,
For me as well as you...

Barry stops, suddenly aware that the unknown person in the other stall can perhaps feel more horrified and threatened than amused or entertained.

No laughter, no applause, no verses witty from her to add to his ditty? He waits a few moments hoping she might leave first. Or, perhaps, she rushed out during his song and he did not hear her do so. He counts slowly to ten, usually a good option in times of stress.

The automatic flush sweeps away all evidence of his presence with a deafening roar. He hopes that the audience for his near vulgar tune is long gone, and swings open the stall door at the very moment a lovely Black woman in a wheelchair emerges through the door of her stall.

The two of them stare at each other silently. As is his wont, Barry pronounces without filter what is foremost in his mind.

"Good Lord, you are ... disabled! And, and...gorgeous! And, Black!"

The woman, she with a radiant aura, is tastefully adorned in soft pastels of pink and purple patterns. A decade or three younger, she shakes her head sadly, as if breaking a trance. The stunning beauty of her face is not at all dimmed by the touch of dismay and disgust the sight of him seems to bring forth. Try as he might, however, it becomes clear that he is not as charming or well-liked as he thinks he meant to be. She rolls to the sink.

Barry, chastened sufficiently, moves to a basin beyond a customary polite social distance. "Sorry," he says.

His remorse is so palpable she breaks her own rule of silence when approached by strangers.

"I prefer not to converse with people in a public bathroom. It makes me uncomfortable."

"Of course. Yes. I understand completely. Please forgive me." He lets the water run over his hands.

"Also, do you know that a complete stranger's comments on a woman's appearance can make her feel uncomfortable?"

"I do know that! Had I been thinking clearly at the time I

might have kept my complete astonishment and awe to myself. But, in my own defense, my intentions toward you (or anyone really) are honorable. When I see something or someone beautiful or extraordinary, I just have to say so. I wasn't trying to seduce you."

"Uh huh..."

"I am sorry if you feel threatened, of course. I am also sorry if my singing and body noises annoyed you."

"You were singing? I wasn't listening." She points to earbuds hanging around her neck.

"Oh, thank God. What are you listening to?" he says in hope of continuing the conversation.

She dries her hands, places the buds back in her ears, flashes him a look that seems to say more than any words could, and rolls quickly out the room.

While the message is clear that he, Barry Strange, should and must back off, what floods his body is a surge of unexpected emotion that nearly knocks him off his feet. Who is this person? From here on in, there will be no power in heaven or earth that will be able to keep him from trying to make a stronger acquaintance.

Furthermore, it does not seem out of the realm of possibility that she somehow some way might be his to love with all his heart and with every ounce of his muscle and blood...'*How could this be?*'

The roar of another flush fills the room as the door of another stall in the room flings open with a BANG. A pasty man in a cheap suit emerges and stares at him with undisguised contempt. Muttering a curse, he storms out of the room.

Uh-oh. Had Barry been thinking out loud again?

Barry feels entirely exposed and vulnerable by the unexpected turn of events in the restroom. He walks past the main desk and notices Malcolm, the desk clerk, deliberately avoiding his gaze. His heart leaps as he sees the Black goddess roll into the workshop space. This delight, however, is dampened as he feels, and then sees, the man from the bathroom rush past him without a word. His mortification grows as he watches this bald, heavy-set man of white ethnic obscurity head straight into the ballroom where apparently both men will be sharing most of the next three days. '*Great.*'

Perhaps he should just turn around, get in his car, and go home. Yet, there were legal, social, and cultural ramifications should he back out of the commitment now.

He hates where this is all going inside his head. The legal resolution pursued and signed by several hundred people who he once considered to be his friends, his neighbors, his colleagues in business and other projects (*his* community for God sakes) would not result in any criminal proceedings or punishments should he now refuse to participate in this self-improvement seminar that the court order encouraged. If he, at this stage, does not go through what everyone expects, not much would happen except that just about everyone he knew would be royally pissed.

"It's not that we don't like you," his once so-called friend John explained. "We all just feel that you (and by extension all of us who know you) are affected by our association with you. All of us may benefit if you had a little more self-awareness and self-improvement. We know that you love to love everyone and that you love to share how you feel, but you just need to slow down a little and allow everyone else to catch up. Our research came up with this amazing seminar in DC. It is called, 'YOU BEING YOU!' Just go and get yourself improved! Knowing you, you'll probably have fun. But don't be *too* you, okay?"

'*No fun yet*', Barry thinks to himself. '*The first three people I meet don't think much of me at all.*' But to be fair, the seminar had not actually started. The desk clerk Malcolm stares at him. '*Can he hear my thoughts?*'

He guesses (from what little he knows about psychology) that his ego merely resents having to listen and now go over in his head everyone's tortured descriptions about how, despite all Barry's "fine qualities" and all the "good deeds" and numerous "kindnesses" to them, nearly everyone he knew had signed on to this petition for him to: "Get ye to a transformational seminar, Barry! To a transformational seminar, go!"

Lord knows, Barry tried to mellow and modify those facets and behaviors spelled out in the court "recommendation" that everyone seemed to agree were disagreeable, but everything he did (and did not do) in that period seemed to annoy all concerned even more.

He stands outside the door to the ballroom. He sees by his watch that he has a minute or two before the doors close. He hears the slow build-up of a familiar Edvard Grieg musical composition and enters the room. According to preliminary instructions, every participant is supposed to be in their seat at the conclusion of the piece.

The only empty seat he can see, among the 150 or so set up in the grand room, happens to be on the front row right next to the woman in the wheelchair he encountered in the rest room!

As the recording of an entire orchestra rushes towards frenetic conclusion, Barry walks to the front of the assembly and surveys each row, each chair in front of him. Each appear occupied. As the piece concludes its final dramatic note, he turns and collapses next to her.

Negative reactions behind him make him wince.

The first of many insights he will experience at the seminar assault him. *'This is one of those things John and other friends and neighbors don't like about me.'*

"I am not a performing seal," he says quietly to the man on his left. "People seem to think I'm trying to show off, but I'm not."

The man snorts derisively. Barry looks closely and discovers the very man who had inadvertently overheard everything in the toilet. A pair of blood-shot eyes stare at Barry in disgust. His lips appear frozen into a scowl while the ruddy complexion suggests a hobby of heavy drinking, an obviously aggressive person.

Barry looks in vain to his right for help. The goddess shakes her head in a decidedly negative manner. If there is a way to just disappear without drawing more attention to himself, he thinks he should do so.

The awkward moment fades when the lights go out and raucous, exuberant music floods the room. Spotlights follow a bouncing, dancing, enthusiastic and energetic young man as he prances up and down the ballroom gesturing and singing in a Czech accent to each person, "Hello! Hello! To you and you, and you and you...!" He is dressed in a loud pink shirt and shiny silver overalls covered with dozens of gold stars which glitter like the night sky. "Hello, everyone! I am so *thrilled* that you are here! My name is Anton and I am *delighted* to help facilitate our journey through the transformational experiences to come!" Raucous celebratory music sends the man on a prancing, dancing spree throughout every empty spot in the room.

"Oh, brother," mutters the man next to Barry. "Looks as if we are in for a *gay* old time."

"*Fantastic*!" Barry squeals with an effeminate flap of the wrist. He hears, or thinks he hears, a small giggle from the woman on the other side of him.

For the next two hours, Anton settles into a more professorial role and relays a condensed stream-lined version of the history of humanity with all the latest developments in psychology, philosophy, quantum mechanics, spirituality, sociology, gender and racial justice, economics, and environmental equilibrium to name just a few.

After the first hour of this intellectual tour de force, Barry cannot help turning towards the beautiful woman to his right and whisper, "I'm not getting any of this."

She shrugs with a kind of helpless expression as if to say, 'Too bad.' She couldn't and wouldn't be helping him out here.

Barry catches some of the principles and fragments of ideas. Anton stresses the 'universal imprinting from birth that we are separated and isolated from everyone' and that 'unconditional love for everyone especially ourselves is the key to liberation.'

Barry Strange is not a young man. At first glance, he appears to be decidedly older than every one of the other participants. Self-improvement, it would seem, is more an interest of the young. He thinks several times of stopping Anton's spirited presentation and ask for clarification, repetition, or to merely slow down a little bit, but the young facilitator cannot be stopped.

But then he remembers that this is one of those bullet points on the petition which so annoyed friends and neighbors. His former so-called friend, John, explained that many young people who attend town hall meetings, community forums, and social action task forces expressed frustration with that "old guy" always asking just about everyone to:

a) speak louder

b) repeat what was just said

c) rephrase what was just said

d) please speak s-l-o-w-e-r...

So, to avoid annoying everyone at the seminar, especially the two people who by a twist of fate sit on both sides of him, he will not at the moment try to satisfy his curiosity about what is being presented. His seatmates already have a history of being annoyed with him and he does not feel like piling on resentments.

He is not as concerned about the man on his left. What is his problem anyway? So what if Barry farted, sang, and tried to charm (*subtly* charm mind you) another person in the bathroom? If bald fat white guy (as Barry thinks of him) so much as gives him another disdainful sneer, he might certainly be moved to target a hard stare right back at him for sure. And there certainly could be a few choice words if any happened to come to mind.

But the woman on the right! That is another story. No wonder he cannot follow what is going on in the seminar. He keeps trying to come up with a few clever phrases that might allow her to forget all about the bathroom fiasco and concentrate on more attractive features of his personality, if he has any. Alas, no cleverness comes to mind. The thing to do is find some element in Anton's discourse that he can use as a starting point for a stimulating conversation.

Barry tries twisting his head down and to the right a couple times so he can at least see what is printed on her name tag. He gives up on that, however, when it feels as if he might be accused of trying to get a good look at her breasts. Which he is...

Anton, the enthusiastic facilitator, wraps up his two-hour synopsis of human experience with an apparent joke that has everyone in the room roaring. There is certainly an animated excited buzz as all in the room rise for a brief break.

"That was a joke?" Barry says, hoping to engage the woman with whom he is smitten. She ignores him and rolls herself away.

"Yeah, a joke, like you..." his bald nemesis says with withering scorn. Barry looks at him wondering for a moment if there is anything useful either of them could say.

'Hey, at least I have hair on my head!' he thinks to himself.

Out in the hotel lobby, Barry ambles near people he thinks might be open to small talk. A group of more mature looking, less youthful participants are going over things Anton must have said.

"That thing we call consciousness, our ability to maneuver in the physical world?" a wiry artistic Black woman is saying. Her name badge says that she is "Jane." "I liked his illustration— we are separate little islands poking our heads up through the surface of a wild ocean..."

"Yes!" the jittery, pot-bellied little white man named Ned interrupts. Barry recognizes a pants and shirt style popular among college students thirty years ago. He guesses Ned liked the fashion so well that he keeps buying it for three decades. "Like Freud's iceberg—the conscious 10% above water while underneath maybe 90% of the mind is unconscious..."

"Yeah," Jane says recognizing her husband's irritating habit of finishing the thought she is having. She glances at her friend, Mary, and pushes on. "In Freud's iceberg, the small part out of the water and the larger part beneath the water were both disconnected from everything else. Anton says that the part beneath the water, the unconscious, is connected to the unconscious of everyone else. We are all energetically connected whether we know it or not!"

"Fantastic!" Barry blurts out. "All that iceberg talk made me chilly." The four people in that group turn to him with surprise. They had not noticed someone lurking there on the periphery of their little conclave. He will soon learn that the two couples are church friends who decided to sign up for this experience together. For a moment, the loud interjection from a strange man feels like a violation. Who is he to intrude?

"Barry Strange," he says and adds with what for years he employs as a sure-fire ice breaker, "International celebrity!"

They laugh, of course. They almost always do. Only an idiot who is not a celebrity would make such a claim.

"I think I heard of you," jokes the man with the name tag of 'Fred.' "Weren't you on 'Ed Sullivan' doing some kind of plate-spinning thing?"

"Oh, yes! That was me," Barry plays along. "It did not go very well. I should have followed the stage advice—'Never follow Topo Gigio!'" Three of the friends get a good laugh. "Who is

Topo Gigio?" asks the woman with the nametag, Mary. Fifteen years younger than her husband Fred and the other couple she met at church, they were always having discussions that seemed to her ancient history. She makes a mental note to Google, 'The Ed Sullivan Show'.

After the laughter dies down, it seems to Barry as if he should say something since everyone is staring at him. There is a long pause. "I once dreamed I was in a lake, or maybe an ocean, and just my face breaks the surface. There didn't seem to be any struggle treading water, no fear of drowning. I could only look straight up at a clear night sky full of stars. I am familiar with the constellations of both the Northern and Southern hemispheres and kept wondering why I didn't recognize any of them. I was starting to suspect these were stars one might see from a world other than our own..."

"Interesting," says Mary in an uninterested tone of voice.

"The more interesting part came later when I wanted to feel something solid under my feet and, lo and behold, my feet felt a soft sandy sea bottom. I slowly walked out of the water and onto a clean white beach where the grains of sand looked like thousands of bright tiny diamonds each of which was the face of a human being smiling back at me..."

This little story is met with total silence—no chatter, no action, no music. It is a phenomenon that Barry always found oddly satisfying—a Zen moment where all human discourse and chatter cease.

The slow reed and string rhythms of the "Peer Gynt Suite" send clusters of seminar participants scurrying back into the ballroom toward their seats.

Jane follows her three friends toward the ballroom but politely looks back over her shoulder at Barry. "I'd like to hear more about that dream sometime. Is there more?"

"Oh, hell yeah!" Barry says although inwardly wondering if he made up the whole thing on the spot.

The ability to have a little moment with the four friends helps him feel a little better about being at the seminar. He enters the ballroom eagerly anticipating a chance to again sit near the beautiful person in a wheelchair. With plenty of time remaining to the end of the music, he leisurely strolls to the front row of seats only to be surprised to see every seat taken and the Black goddess nowhere in sight. Barry had not seen the memo or heard the announcement that participants were encouraged to find a new place to sit after every break.

As the intense conclusion of the piece draws near, he quickly scans every row and every filled chair. Ah, there she is at the end of a row about five rows back. Alas, someone had already taken the seat next to her. And there is the heavy bald guy a few rows behind her adjacent to an empty chair. He stares right at Barry, looks at the empty seat, shakes his head, and with some menace silently mouths the word, '*No.*'

As the recording is about to end, Barry spies another seat on the very back row. Despite being aware that nearly every eye is apparently entertained with what he might do next, he tears up the aisle as fast as his seventy-year-old legs can take him. For the second time that day, his rump hits the cushion at the very last note. The impact forces the last bit of air out of his lungs. Unfortunately, a combination of air pressure, physical exertion, and the position of his half-opened lips at that moment produce a very audible burping noise that very much sounds as if he had farted—loudly.

A spontaneous burst of embarrassed laughter from someone quickly subsides.

Barry shrugs his best pose of apologetic shyness and offers a slight smile to those near him. "Ah, the perks of fame..." he says to no one in particular.

The second session of the seminar moves beyond various theoretical descriptions about what reality might possibly be like and towards explanations of practical measures that may be of use to improve reality (whatever that is) and improve oneself and the world, whatever that is. *I'm never going to remember this,'* he thinks.

Barry notices several participants taking notes. Ah... He searches his own pockets hoping to discover one of those little notebooks he sometimes carries. But the search is futile. He considers asking a nearby woman if he might have a couple empty sheets out of her loose-leaf binder but hesitates when he realizes he would also have to borrow a pen and probably a book or some other stiff object to use as support.

Still, he doesn't wish to expend too much energy and attention scribbling notes that honestly might never be particularly useful or even read. *The truth of one moment can become a lie of the next.*

He recalls with a sigh an incident some, what? fifty years ago? In the throes of a dramatic and emotional mystical experience, he watched a sacred moment fade away as he wasted precious minutes trying to come up with just the right notebook and finding just the right fucking pen, for Christ sakes.

Still feeling relatively fantastic during this transcendental experience, he jotted down a few words to capture the same. After The Vision faded, he was compelled to deal with certain exigencies of consensus reality but looked forward to seeing what literary flair might have captured this quasi-spiritual, allegorical, and mythological experience.

After all, he had to go to work. Work!!! Good God! He had to make himself go to the library and work after a mystical experience? What was he thinking! After shuffling papers and files around for several hours, he rushed home to fish out the little red notebook that contained words he hoped might be for the Ages. Barry leafed through the few dozen or so pages which contained other snatches of inspired verse along with past cosmic comic philosophic socio-irrelevant gibberish...

The twenty-year old Barry resisted the impulse to indulge in past genius and flipped through several pages to the very end where he saw, in all its glory, the words from the previous night. He hoped they would reveal the essence of Life's Glory. In a barely legible, drunken-like scrawl were the words: *"there is an odd smell emanating from somewhere—is it the curtain?"*

If nothing else, that moment impressed upon him the importance of not taking his own thoughts, emotions, and experience seriously. Yet, thinking of this helpful fifty-year-old insight while planted firmly in a chair at the seminar, Barry is finding it ironic that Anton is describing a principle that seems to completely contradict it. Everything *is* important!

Some words of encouragement are projected on a screen that might help every person in the room get something useful out of the workshop...

PAY ATTENTION TO YOUR LIFE
EVERY MOMENT IS IMPORTANT

"Don't judge yourself," Anton is saying. The carefree, playful, flamboyant Anton has been replaced by his sober serious double. He is now also wearing a suit! His pace and gestures no longer dance and swing. "It is in your best interest to be aware of yourself. You can sit back in your chair and allow the cynic within to look at this workshop (or anything) as a bunch of crap. You can make fun of it. You can see everyone else as a loser. You can do nothing. And you will get what you put into it—nothing. Or you can try to participate. In a couple of minutes, we will do the first of many exercises to give each of you an opportunity to participate.

"There is no wrong way to do any of the things we will be suggesting. The first thing I suggest is that you merely look at what you are doing. In a way, it is all important. Whether you are holding back or letting loose, being completely honest and sincere or in a charade—just watch yourself!"

Some lively dance music begins softly but increases in tempo and volume.

"Ok, everybody who is able, get up and move!" Anton goes on. Elaine, Kevin, and two other workshop assistants quickly organize participants to help move every chair to create an open space. Anton continues with directions as if he is a robot. "Shake those arms!" He stiffly shakes his arms. "Move those legs!" Woodenly, he moves his legs. "Loosen up." No one has ever witnessed such tense mechanical movement. "Dance or just walk around. Keep your eyes open. Don't bump into anybody. Feel free to nod or smile at each other..." Anton assumes a rigid nod and smile. The music grows louder. "Now you do it. That's it, walk around but do it like a real human being, not like a scared robot. Yes... no talking or stopping...that's good. When the music stops in about two minutes, you stop."

Barry spends the time being one of the participants, looking lost and confused for a beat, then shy, then friendly, completely goofy, then genuine.

When the music stops, Anton resumes narration. "Stay where you are but just look around the room. When the music starts again, I want you to try to connect non-verbally with somebody else. Without saying a word or using hand signals walk, or if in a chair, roll. Make eye contact with everyone you see. Please, no touching." Music starts slowly. "As a group, you will need to figure out how to do this efficiently."

The group does as it is told. Some feel anxious at first, but all eventually seem to enjoy sharing a smile, a nod, or simply looking. Barry likes not having to talk, but after the first dozen or so solemn smiles and nods, he cannot resist trying out as many funny expressions as he can think of. He furrows his brow as if in deep thought, grins like a maniac, or opens his eyes as if in complete astonishment. Some smile in response. Some laugh. Some look very stern and annoyed. He makes mental notes to remember as many names as possible by associating some mannerism or physical feature of dress, hair, or body to what is written on their name tag.

'Beth with the blue blouse, Marvin moves like a mannequin, Kenneth keeps crying...' He sees one person stare back at him with unmistakable loathing and realizes it is the bald big man from

the bathroom, the one who was antsy and on edge when they sat next to one another, and the same who did not want Barry to sit near him again. *'Bart the bastard,'* Barry says to himself when he spies the name tag. The bald head jerks back in alarm as if Barry had loudly vocalized the epithet. Perhaps he had.

The next three or four people Barry acknowledges via smile or nod are a blur. Not much participation in the experience then. Whether said aloud or in his head, he feels embarrassed to have characterized Bart in such a fashion. After all, he does not know the man. Intellectually, he thinks the antipathy from both sides is an unfortunate misunderstanding. He feels a little queasy and frankly frightened. "Bart the bastard" twice already today somehow heard Barry say aloud thoughts Barry is sure were very personal and certainly private and best kept inside his mouth.

Such phenomena had popped up a few times back at home. In that list of grievances drawn up by his neighbors, colleagues, and former friends, two or three instances described "disparaging remarks" in situations when Barry recalled thinking such things but was certain he had not actually said them.

"It's may be a 'dementia thing,'" John explained trying to be helpful. "You believe you are just thinking something but, like someone with Tourette's, you blurt it out loud."

Apparently, according to the petition, he had, at many town halls and other meetings, delivered scathing rebukes on the character of various prominent citizens. While not necessarily untrue, such tirades made certain negotiations and dealings with these people problematic. As John pointed out, it may not be a crime to voice an opinion that Mayor Such-and-Such or Chairwoman So-and-So is an idiot, but it makes it difficult to get their cooperation on legislation or anything else.

As Barry presently wanders around the hotel ballroom pretending to be aware and smiling at all these strangers during the seminar exercise, he senses *something* tugging at his consciousness, pulling him to look at a doorway of some kind. What lies behind this door may destroy him completely or save him. Maybe he is losing it. And, if he thinks such a thing, is it not therefore likely he could at any moment say something scary out loud to the next person in sight?

As it so happened, the next person he comes upon is the Black woman who had earlier so sparked a longing for connection, communication, and love. He thought such things for him were long gone. Just the sight of her, ten feet away and staring right at him, has the effect of melting every vestige of psychological armor and existential terror. *'Here is life, here be love...'*

She is seeing him in such a raw state of vulnerability, it stuns them both. She looks at him without judgment or fear. On the verge of tears, he drops his eyes to her name tag. He makes a deliberate effort to just think and not say aloud what he is thinking.

'Handicapped Hope in a chair. Thank you, Hope!' Barry thinks with all the kindness and goodwill he can muster. She acts as if she hears him.

Barry begins to close the ten feet gap between them. To be nearer seems akin to a sacred purpose. She rolls away to smile or nod at someone else.

The music stops. Anton stands before them once again in a change of clothes. His suit has been exchanged for a pure white shirt and pants. No words are said for the next several minutes.

When anyone begins to stir or whisper, Anton raises a single finger to his lips to quiet them. He slowly moves through the crowd to stand in silence before each person. By gesture alone, he is able to sustain the silent meditation.

Once every person has been seen, Anton bows and sits cross-legged on the floor. It is clear that all are invited to follow suit. Elaine and Kevin quickly supply a chair for those who appear to need one. Hope remains still and attentive in her wheelchair.

In the meditation exercise that follows, Anton asks every-one to imagine and visualize as much as they can a peaceful beautiful "sanctuary." The DJ, Kevin, plays ethereal music to accompany the journey.

Barry finds himself descending to an underground lake, rowing out to an island, following a path through a virgin forest then along a flowered garden path to a tiny shelter he imagines out of rocks and branches, a safe place in which to dream and totally relax.

The sound of a drum sends him deeper into reverie. He fol-lows the rhythm to a setting that feels to him like Home. Around him are family and beloved members of a community that love each other, take care of each other. He is lying on a mat woven by his own hands out of reeds from a nearby river. He opens his eyes to a mural painted upon the ceiling of a mammoth cave where he and his people have lived for generations. The spirit of the man now known as Barry recognizes himself among the many figures depicted. The scene fades.

Despite Anton's explicit direction to stay alert and not fall asleep, Barry, flat on his back, is soon visualizing such deep rest-fulness that steady grumbles inform everyone within earshot that snoring is taking place. Elaine gently tries to wake him, but the roll of snoring turns into discordant wheezes and snorts which have the effect of driving everyone out of their quiet imaginary sanctuaries to see who is actively dying.

Elaine lifts him to a sitting position, but the snoring continues with more intense somnolent sputters. When at last she is able to rouse him, participants surrender up a few chuckles and attempt a return to their peaceful spot.

"Thanks, Elaine!" Barry says. "I needed a nap."

Anton continues to guide the meditation, but his voice betrays annoyance as he tries recapturing the atmosphere of serenity. Irked at his own impatience mostly, he rushes to wrap up the exercise and move on to the next scheduled item.

The tranquil soundtrack signals its end. Anton takes a breath. "It is time to leave your sanctuary. Stow away in drawers and closets any of the creative tools you may have been using. Close the door of your spiritual workshop, walk back through the garden and the forest trail. Back to the water's edge and into your boat. Row across the calm blue water. Climb the stairs at the beach and slowly return to your place in this safe room. Check in with the sensations in and around your body...When you are ready, slowly open your eyes."

The room buzzes with the sounds of people rustling, yawning, murmuring. Anton gestures to Elaine. "Who snored?"

Elaine bends close to his ear. "Barry," she says. "You know who he is?"

"Yes, of course. I spotted him as a problem child the moment he walked in the room."

Elaine laughs. "Kind of cute, though."

Anton waves her off and rises from his seat to address all the participants.

"Is that fun?" Not much response. "Huh? Can't hear you. Yes? No?" Mostly positive shouts. "How about you, Barry? Get a good rest?"

"Could have been longer," he says playfully. "Sorry about that. Great dreams, though."

"No worries. I know a good snoring remedy, however. Come talk to me about it later."

"I was snoring?"

Barry has a moment to think about all that has so far transpired. All in all, he is having a pretty good time. A rather interesting dream, but no startling transformations and self-improvements as far as he can tell. But he does feel so very fond of the woman, Hope. He hopes he won't go "too far." He has been told he can often care "too much" and scare away potential friends. As far as the workshop is concerned, he feels as if he is learning useful things, especially about himself. He should write down some of them.

Once again, on impulse, he checks his pockets in vain for a notepad. Whatever had been the thought he wanted to take note of vanishes by the time he pulls an empty hand from his pockets.

There is much in life he had learned. There is much in life he could learn. He enjoys the feeling but feels a twinge of regret. There are just too many things to forget. He thinks how he might respond should St. Peter at the Pearly Gates ask him what he thinks about Life. *'Oh, I think I understood some of it'* might be the best he could do.

CHAPTER TWO

As many people here in the workshop and in the wider world are quick to point out, Barry is, after all, a "Senior Citizen." When a young, well-meaning person at the workshop uses that term, Barry informs him with a straight face that he prefers to be called a "Senor Citizen."

He can tell that the kid, in his early twenties, struggles to make amends and frame what he hoped to say in political, ethnically correct ways.

Barry wonders what he might be able to personally contribute to the growing accumulation of collective goodwill, out and out caring, and awareness. He had grown to like having something of value to add to whatever positive things human beings were trying to do. But as happened many times, he is not sure what those things might be.

He tunes in to what Anton, now dressed totally in drag, is saying.

"By this time, you might be wondering what we are all doing here. Anyone wondering that?" Not a few silently raise their hands or wave fingers in affirmation.

"We are trying to be free. Sometimes we throw out a few exercises and suggestions that might help someone bust through the restraints." He takes a deep breath. "I can't pretend to be any kind of expert on anything, but I sometimes get lucky and see how an effective nudge in one direction or another might help someone get on the path they would like to be going!" He takes a huge, upper-cut swing as if punching someone in the jaw.

"So! I need a volunteer! Someone willing to be my first guinea pig, someone to stand up here all alone with me and allow us to demonstrate one way to look at issues, bust a few barriers, and find lifelines to move forward. We will do this a couple times today, a few more tomorrow, and maybe work in a demonstration or two on Sunday. Who wants to be first? Ha! You don't know what you'll be getting yourself into, do you?

"Anyone still wondering why you are here, what's in it for you, maybe just a little bit hopeless? If so, you're the perfect candidate as our first volunteer! C'mon! Who is ready to let everyone know that you are the brave one?" He/she swishes his/her dress and brushes back her/his flamboyant orange wig.

Barry jumps out of his seat and jauntily marches forward. Everyone claps. He flexes his biceps like a boxing champion and offers an upper-cut jab to an imaginary jaw of his own.

"Yes, Barry! I think you've been dying to get everyone's attention. Here, let me clip on this mic. Let's hear what you have to say."

"I must be out of my mind." Laughter. Anton gestures an admonishment to the throng.

"True. Sometimes that is a good thing—maybe get the person or ego out of the way of what you *think* you are so that who you really are can come through..."

"Huh?" Barry mugs, playing dumb.

"Let's get real. Who are you?" Barry looks as if he is thinking awfully hard on how to answer this. "Don't dive for the deep stuff yet. I just mean, what's your name?"

"Barry..." he says. He starts to add his last name and go into the bit he is starting to think is not as amusing as it used to be, his usual '...*brave or famous celebrity.*'

God knows, he has played that role so many times he could successfully pull it off here with Anton and 152 of his newest friends.

Fortunately, Barry is astute enough to know that there is just not enough time for any act. '*Is that a piano over there in the far corner?*' He tries to re-focus on what he is supposed to be doing. Another kind of doorway appears to beckon, inviting him to go somewhere else. Where will he go now? The sound of a distant drum lures him toward a dream. With some effort, he resists and opens his eyes.

A young man dressed as a woman is staring at him. A crowd of complete strangers are watching him with great intensity. For a second, he has no idea where he is or what he is doing.

The man dressed as a woman places a hand on him. "Barry. Still with us, my friend? Welcome back! You kind of checked out there for a few seconds."

'*Oh, yes! I remember now!*' Barry thinks.

"You okay, really?" the man called Anton says. "Whew. Glad to give you time to think, meditate, pray—whatever. But you were so still! Another half minute, though, and I'm calling the stroke unit."

"I'm okay. I was thinking about going somewhere…maybe tell you about it later. Is that piano in tune?"

"You can check it out sometime when we're not in session. Maybe sing us a song when we have our talent show."

"Talent show! Oh, goody! I wasn't singing just now, was I? Or, talking?"

"No. Quiet as a mouse. You seemed to go into a little trance. Is there anything we should know about your medical history? We'll look at what you shared in your registration." Anton looks at the workshop assistant, Kevin, who nods. He is already looking into Barry's file.

"I'm good. Really, Anton."

"Great. Super. What we all would like to know is…. why did you come to this workshop?"

"I am reluctant to say…"

"Do you know *why* you came? What you hope to get out of it?"

"Those are two different questions."

"Are they?" Anton can see Barry is holding back, as if the reason he is here is shameful. People were so weird and shy about the oddest things.

"Ok, I'll tell you. Unlike everyone here, maybe, I am not doing this of my own volition."

"You're not? Someone forcing you to do the seminar? Wife? Husband? Court order?"

Everyone laughs.

"Court order."

"Ok. Tell us about it."

"It is a bit embarrassing. I've lived in my little city, Charlottesville, for over fifty years. I have family there, a lot of friends. Since retiring from the library, I got involved in several projects and organizations—some cultural, like theater and museums; volunteering to help people read; political meetings; and meetings for matters that are useful like the food bank, affordable housing, health care... At any rate, a few of these acquaintances and friends, and some family members too, organized a petition that they got some judge to present to me as a non-compulsory 'suggestion.' The gist of it is that although they say they like me and appreciate what I might contribute to them personally and to the community, I apparently annoy them all and have for years. They hoped I would work on it." He looks out at the 150-plus faces staring at him with what may have been concern or, perhaps, an expectation of a punch line. "For the longest time, I just saw it as an unfunny joke or sophisticated prank. It even got a little story in the paper. But then, people would keep bugging me everywhere I went—'Are you taking the workshop? When are 'You Being You'? Getting any self-improvement, Barry?'"

"Why are you telling us all this little story? It's not true, is it?"

"It's true! Friends and neighbors, associates and colleagues, all want me to *improve*, so improve me, dammit! Or show me how to do it."

Kevin, at the command console, holds up a digital clock for Anton.

"We don't have a lot of time to fool around. Why don't you tell us what you really need? What improvement or transformation do you want for yourself? If the people in your community are weary of your behavior..."

"Maybe that's it..."

"Or, maybe they just don't like you...Do you try too hard? Change and improve if you want to! We're here to help. But do it for you, not to get other people to like you. I'm talking about the people here and the people back home in Charlottesville. We all act as mirrors for each other. We reflect to you how we see you. You can participate as we help each other. But don't come here because someone forced you."

"Okay. Sure."

"Very good. We still have a minute or two to get into specifics. You don't have to tell everyone right now what it is, but I want you to think about some secret you hold. A secret fear. Something you think we would really dislike about you. Are you thinking of it, yet?" He nods. "Is it something I would dislike about you?"

"Oh, I don't know. You might like it."

"It is not a universally disliked quality?"

"Hmm, no. Some people think it a great quality or maybe more like a condition than a quality."

"Well, now I'm intrigued. Is it something like being very handsome, a quality or condition some like and some do not? Is that what it is—you are just too damn sexy?"

This elicits huge guffaws.

"All this laughter, Barry, how does it make you feel?"

"Oh, it's okay. I like hearing people laugh."

"Even if you feel they are laughing *at* you?"

"Mmm, it feels like they're laughing *through* me. It doesn't bother me too much. I usually can see the humor in anything."

"Even if people think it funny that someone might think you're sexy?"

"Oh, I know I'm sexy." Some more laughs and a few snorts from those trying hard to suppress a laugh.

"Hey, I'm not saying you're not. So, your secret shame, if I can call it that, is not about sexiness. You can tell us all now or save it for when we do a one-on-one session. That is what we will be doing for our next exercise. One other person will listen to you, then you trade positions and listen to them. It is one thing to admit your deepest darkest sin or desire, mistake or misgiving, to 150 people, another thing altogether to trust just one other person.

"What is at risk? What's the worst thing that can happen if you tell everyone? And the worst if you just told one person?"

Barry thinks for a second. "If I tell one person, only one person might dislike me. If I tell everyone now, 150 people might hate me."

"You may not believe me, Barry, but aside from some awful violent behavior, there is virtually no quality or condition you could tell me to get me to dislike you. We are all flawed beings. That you may have a flaw or two will not, I predict, make me dislike you. I like you a lot. As a matter of fact, I will go so far as to let you know that I love you."

"Aw, come on..."

"You have given me no reason not to. I love you, Barry. Anybody else feel this way?"

"We love you, Barry. I love you, Barry..." Versions of this statement circle through the room with various levels of sincerity and tone.

Barry knows it is manipulative and corny but, for the heck of it, he allows himself to let it in and just cry in response. When he recovers a bit, Anton congratulates him on being able to cry but pushes him a little more. "I do not know if this is true, but if I were to say, 'Hey, Barry, telling us your secret means you can at last be your true self! By doing so, you may not only know what you want to do for the rest of your life, you may have in your hands and heart all the tools you need to do it. But, if there's a chance everyone in this room will positively hate you for a short or maybe even a long period of time, would you do it?"

"Oh, I don't know, maybe. This is all so hypothetical. But, if the revelation of the secret poisons any chance of trust or genuine friendship, what good is it?"

"It is that bad?"

"I know this thing about me has already spoiled a number of friendships and relationships."

"But it is a true thing? If you keep it secret, there's a chance of friendship, a chance for love maybe. If you tell anyone the truth, no chance of friendship. Is that an accurate assessment?"

"Yes," Barry admits. "No chance of friendship at all."

"The friendship, the relationship, may be an important thing for you. But do we have a choice in this decision? What if we were to tell you that although we could be deprived of being your friend, we are willing to sacrifice that fine thing in order for you to become truly liberated, enlightened, or transformed? It would be nice if we could be both things to each other, you transformed and all of us friends. But, if in fact, it is just a struggle between Truth and Niceness, which side are you on?"

Kevin, at the command console, airs a second or two of a

labor union ballad, "Which Side Are You On?"

"Do you want us to like you, Barry, or do you want to break through your chains?"

"It's not that big a deal, I guess. If I don't tell everyone now, people will probably be bugging me all weekend. Okay, here goes—a lot of people in Charlottesville know about this already. I think that's what is behind the petition and court order. It is the reason my former friends, neighbors, my church, the food bank, the library, City Hall, Black Matters Alliance, Scientific Council, Live Arts Theater, Poor Folks Forum, Botanical Gardens, Environmental Climate Consortium, and others just don't like me anymore and sent me here to improve my personality. I try to tell myself it is the condition or circumstances I find myself in that is the problem—not me, myself, my heart and soul, my personality."

A short pause. "And the circumstances are?"

"The truth is—damn, why is this so hard? The truth is I have become a—rich man! Extraordinarily, obscenely rich!"

"Oh, no!" someone cries out sarcastically. Others ham it up with fake pity.

"That's your terrible secret? You're wealthy?" Anton says.

"It's not entirely terrible. When I won a billion dollars in the Powerball Lottery, I thought, *'Oh, yeah! Daddy gets a new pair of shoes!'* At first, I had a ball buying stuff, donating a shitload everywhere and to everyone. I went everywhere, did everything I wanted, lived like a king. Then the chickens came home to roost. Except for some privileged rich assholes like myself, I no longer seemed to have any real friends. When I try to make new friends or do anything worthwhile, all goes well until people discover the truth. I'm either resented or envied, despised or totally conned. Any chance for love and happiness disappears." Barry's voice quavers, he feels perfectly miserable. He cannot help himself and cries. "No one and I mean no one need pity me. I'll pity myself."

His ears conditioned to pick up on such remarks, he detects a few snide mutterings in the crowd.

Anton places a hand on Barry's shoulder. "I can't speak for everyone, but I will have no trouble liking you, being your friend, or even loving you no matter how much money you have. Some of my best friends are rich." Anton speaks to everyone. "We will be spending some of our Sunday session looking at financial issues. It will be interesting to see if some of Barry's misery on the subject has shifted by then. Okay with you, Barry, if we put a check on this and take another break?"

"More than okay." Anton hugs him and the room erupts in applause and begins to disperse while Kevin, the sound and light man, plays a lively show tune, "If I Were a Rich Man," for their exit.

Seemingly oblivious to any sensitivity Barry might have on the topic, many of the departing participants sing merrily along with growing exuberance.

Jane, the wiry artist attending with her husband and church friends, turns her head in time to see Barry step happily away from Anton and the staging area. His buoyancy, however, is short-lived. Jane can see the song lyrics suddenly come upon him as mockery. He staggers backward and appears burdened as he trudges across the room towards the door.

As luck would have it, the music and the clamor of song and

chatter stops just as Anton exhales mightily and expels a couple of thoughtless and somewhat disparaging words that he later insists were not more than a whisper to himself. His mic still live, the words, "What a moron!" are projected loudly throughout the ballroom.

Barry does not look back. He quickly strides onward in great fury and shame. Jane has to grab him to slow his stormy exit.

"You okay, Barry?"

"Apparently not. Apparently, I'm a fucking moron.".

"He didn't say, 'fucking' moron," her husband Ned offers.

"He might as well have. Probably fits."

"He wasn't talking about you!" she says uncertain.

"I think I've had enough of this. If people wonder where I am, tell them I said 'Good-bye.'" Barry looks at the two couples as if for the first time and shakes Jane's hand. "Good-bye..."

"Barry!" Anton approaches, a little out of breath. "You are *not* leaving."

"Oh, yes, I am. Only a complete moron would stick around after this treatment. And I," he says proudly, "am not a complete moron,"

"Oh, Barry. I'm sorry the mic was still on, but I wasn't talking about you..."

Jane pokes Barry in the ribs. "See. I told you."

"Who were you talking about—Donald Trump?"

"Kevin, the sound and light man, is a professional DJ. He is usually surprisingly good at selecting background music. I can't believe he chose that song. A bit insensitive."

Fred jumps in. "I thought it was cool how everyone sang

along. Don't think it was meant to be mean."

"Maybe didn't feel great to Barry..." his wife, Mary, says.

"It doesn't matter," Barry says. "I don't really care, even if folks are singing and having a great time making fun of me. Anton, I don't know if I believe you about the smart-aleck moron thing, but it doesn't make a difference either way. I am out of here." Barry Strange, Quantum Celebrity, turns and walks out of the ballroom, across the lobby, through the vestibule, and out into the street.

Not ready to give up, Anton rushes after him.

CHAPTER THREE

On the sidewalk outside the hotel, Anton begs Barry to see that it matters little whether his neighbors in Charlottesville, or the people working or attending the seminar, *like* him. What is vital, he argues, is whether Barry can like himself.

Anton can tell that this line of reasoning is not, at first glance, all that persuasive. Yet, Barry listens carefully to Anton's description of some of the exercises to come and seems a little intrigued.

"I'll think about it," he says and walks down the street alone. There are a lot of other things he could do besides attending a stupid transformational seminar. When he reaches the end of the block, a few lines of poetry by Whitman float to the surface. He once memorized many verses. He crosses the busy street and stops for a minute to recite out loud.

I am of old and young, of the foolish as much as the wise,
Regardless of others, ever regardful of others,
Maternal as well as paternal, a child as well as a man,

Stuff'd with the stuff that is coarse and stuff'd with the stuff that is fine...

A weary Black man sitting on a plastic tarp surrounded by what could well be his entire worldly possessions stares as Barry struggles to retrieve the next line. For the benefit of this homeless citizen, he repeats what he had just spouted and jumps ahead several stanzas.

I exist as I am, that is enough,
If no other in the world be aware I sit content,
And if each and all be aware I sit content.

The man, unshaven and beaten in spirit, breaks into a huge smile, heartily laughs, and applauds. Always glad to have an audience, Barry laughs with him and bends down to look straight into his rheumatic eyes.

"Do I contradict myself? Very well, then I contradict myself, I am large, I contain multitudes..." he recites.

The traffic on New Jersey Ave. suddenly becomes frenetic, the smell of diesel from a passing truck nauseating. The August humidity makes it hard to breathe.

Barry looks at the man's sign on which is scrawled a single word, "HUNGRY!" He reaches into a pocket and places a folded wad of cash into the hands of the hungry, homeless human. He is not sure how much is there, at least a couple hundred, certainly enough to make this guy's day.

He places both hands over the man's very cold hands. "Barry

Strange," he says. "Famous rich celebrity. Who are you?"

"Joe," he says trembling. The hands of this crazy white man are very warm. He cannot remember the last time anyone touched him in any type of a kind way. A painful memory of a cop throwing him into a wagon makes him wince.

"Hey, Joe. How would you like to have a nice hot shower and a soft bed in a hotel to sleep in for a few days? C'mon. That money is yours to use however you want. Put it in your pocket. Let's go!" He helps a dazed Joe pack a couple bags and the tarp into a grocery cart. Barry tries not to go too fast as he pushes the squeaky, wobbly cart back toward the hotel. "You want me to see if I can get you into the seminar I'm taking?"

"Seminar? What's that?"

"Mostly privileged white folks but a few good, kind Black people as well. We sit around looking at what's gone wrong in our lives and what we can do to make it better."

"I don't think so."

"Yeah, I wonder myself. Listen, is there anyone you'd like me to call? A relative or friend, maybe, to let them know where you'll be?"

Joe stops. "I ain't doing no sex things…"

"Me neither, Joe." Barry keeps pushing the cart. "You'll have the room to yourself. What do you think? You want to do it? This is the place I have in mind." They stop at the front door but don't go in.

"Looks awful fancy."

"Let me do something nice for you, okay?" They stare at each other in silence. "It will be okay, you'll see." Joe nods. The rattle of the cart draws more than a little attention as they go inside. Barry parks it near a snow-white sofa and suggests Joe take a seat. He approaches the front desk clerk who watches with some concern.

"It's Malcolm, isn't it? Barry Strange, Famous Old Man…"

"I remember you."

"I would like to book a room for my friend Joe here," Barry says as he pulls out a card.

"I am afraid there are no vacancies," the clerk says pretending to look at a screen.

"I am afraid that is not the truth. I already looked online," he lies. "Be a decent human being, won't you? It is at my expense and won't reflect badly on this establishment at all. A person down on his luck can have a bath and sleep in safety and comfort for a change. Whatever he wants in the way of room service or other amenities will be paid for." Barry places his card in the payment device. "And a healthy gratuity may be bestowed on any staff member who can help make him feel welcome." He slaps a 50-dollar bill on the counter.

Malcolm taps the screen. "A room just became free. What is his name?"

"Joe…" The clerk tilts his head and waits. Barry shouts to the man about to fall asleep on the white couch. "Joe! What's your last name?"

Joe thinks about this for a second. "Smith," he lies.

"Joe Smith…" Malcolm types. "Address?"

"Joe, you got a mailing address? Maybe they want to send you promotional materials. Where do you live and sleep?"

Joe turns his head towards them. Why are they doing this? The pain and stress from just trying to stay alive feels as if it is pulling him into the sofa. His entire face starts to shudder. If he starts crying, he will stand up and leave. The poet man, Barry, has a look of kindness and nods. "Sometimes I sleeps at the Shelter on New York Avenue. Other times, I just find a spot in an alley behind the General Dollar store off Independence Avenue."

"I need an actual postal address," Malcolm says.

"Use mine." Barry and Malcolm conclude the registration process.

"That will just about do it," Malcolm says. "Just a moment. I need to check on something." He enters a nearby office.

Barry steps closer to Joe and notices, for the first time, a strong disagreeable odor. "Just a little while longer, Joe. I am paying for three nights but you do not have to stay that long if you don't want to. You can order whatever you want from room service. There will be a menu in the room and a list of other things they can get for you like a razor, toothbrush, and even a new shirt and pants! There will be a robe in the room so you can relax and watch as much TV as you like while they have someone do all your laundry…"

"Jesus H. Christ."

"You can use some of the cash I gave you to tip the staff who help you out, if you want."

"Damn. Can I use the minibar?"

"Why the hell not? Enjoy yourself. But do not OD on me, okay? I don't want that on my conscience."

Out of the corner of his eye, Barry notices Malcolm come out of the back office looking their way with a well-dressed woman, a manager perhaps. She seems to brush off whatever concern he is sharing with her and returns to her office.

Malcolm walks from behind the counter and hands one key card to Joe and the other to Barry. "You are in Room 417, Mr. Smith. Take the elevator to the 4th floor and follow the signs to your room number."

"I been in a hotel before."

"Excellent! Please do enjoy your stay, sir. Do not hesitate to call down to the front desk if you desire anything at all. Checkout is 11am, Monday morning. Thank you both for choosing the Regency!"

On automatic congeniality now, Malcolm shakes Barry's hand but recoils slightly when his hand touches Joe's. He is not sure what type of substance he feels from it.

Barry notices Elaine of the seminar staff staring at him and Joe as they work their way towards the elevator. The wheels of the shopping cart alert everyone to their presence. Barry gives her a smile and a little wave, then pushes the button to go up.

The ride alone up four floors in the stainless-steel box seems made for the sharing of significant words. But none are said. Joe's legs are shaking. The doors open.

"Room 417 to the right," Barry says.

After several tries, Joe can make the key card work but stops halfway through the door.

Barry gives him time to take it all in and waits patiently behind him with the cart. "Everything okay?"

"Man, this is *nice*!" They check out every feature. Joe is impressed by the shiny and spotless bath fixtures. Barry explains what the bidet does, helps Joe with the TV remote and thermostat, and points out the room service menu and other amenities. "I can't get over how clean everything is!" Joe repeats every ten seconds or so. "I feel like I done died and gone to heaven."

"When is the last time you stayed in a hotel?"

"Probably when my brother died 30 years ago. I stayed in a Motel 8 in Louisville for a couple days before and after the funeral. Made the mistake of engaging a hooker, though, and caught a bad case of the clap."

"I hope you have a better time here."

"I know I will, Mr. Barry, thanks to you. I can't wait to get into the hot tub."

"It's all yours. Listen, I'll be in and out of this hotel all weekend doing that seminar I mentioned? If you run into any trouble or need something, the staff can find me."

Joe nods his head. "All I got to give you is my thanks."

"That is more than enough for me, Joe. Have fun." He closes the door behind him and hears a cry of sheer joy erupt from within.

On the voyage down the elevator and across the lobby, Barry holds a debate with himself on whether to return to the seminar. Would he likely receive anything worthwhile by further participation and, more germane perhaps to what he personally finds more important, would he be able to offer anyone there anything more valuable than a few dollars? He takes a deep breath and enters.

CHAPTER FOUR

Anton, this time dressed totally in black, is finishing up a presentation. He notices the door at the back of the room open and slightly smiles to see Barry walk and take a seat in the back row.

"And that, my friends, is the most important idea you will ever hear anyone ever say at any time in the history of the human race..."

The seminar participants laugh and clap enthusiastically. *'Whatever was just said must have been a doozy,'* Barry thinks. The man in the seat next to him bobs his head up and down and from side to side in what seems apparent agreement. Had Barry once again voiced aloud some silent thoughts? *'Not again!'*

If there is an "Enthusiasm Regulator," Anton then seems to turn his up a notch. "Everybody, stand up!" Barry stands up with just about everyone else. He looks for and sees Hope on the end of a row to his right. She is, of course, not able to stand up. "Put your hands over your head and wiggle your fingers!" Barry, like everyone else including Hope, wiggles his hands. "Now, find someone, anyone, to say 'Hi!' to." Barry, like everyone else, turns to a nearby person and exchanges greetings. "Now, look at each other's nametag. If you are able, take turns and look each other in the eye and then say their name out loud. Go on, do it!" The sound of 150 names being said out loud shakes the room. "Now, take turns to say your partner's name followed by these words— even if you do not really feel this way, say out loud to him or her..." And, at this point, Barry sees Anton looking directly at him across the room. "Say, 'Barry (or whoever), I am glad you are here'!"

The man, Bill, standing next to Barry, is able to say those very same words, "Barry, I am glad you are here!" Barry turns to Bill and, instead of completing the task, says. "Barry (or whoever), I am glad you are here!" Bill laughs then Barry repeats the exercise using Bill's name.

Anton recovers everyone's attention. "I get the feeling everyone is glad that everyone is here. This is progress, indeed. Moving on...Our next exercise will be one we will repeat several times this weekend. In a moment, the screen will display over 152 numbers. Ah, there they are—one through one hundred and fifty-two. Your name tag, as you no doubt notice, shows your number." Nearly everyone checks their badge. "Kevin, there on the console, will push a button to randomly match your number to the number of another person. Once you see your number paired with another, we will give you a little time to find each other. Sound like fun? No? Too bad. Ladies and gentlemen, find your partners!"

The screen shows 10-12 pairs of numbers at a time while a digital clock counts down a few seconds before another display of paired numbers appears. People scurry to check out each other's badges.

Once everyone finds a partner, Anton is still and silent as all quietly look at him for direction.

"Everyone is looking at *me*. How very nice to receive attention! The next thing we all will do is look at each other. For the next few moments (I won't tell you how long) I invite you to look at the person we have randomly chosen to be your partner. Just look at each other. Go ahead, start! You can smile but I encourage you to merely look at each other, without nervousness, without judgment or any agenda beyond paying each other simple attention."

Barry does his best to take the assignment seriously but feels compelled to offer his 20-something partner, Rainbow, the goofiest expressions he can to make her/him smile, then laugh. When other couples also begin to crack up, Anton announces a re-shuffling of the numbers. New partners repeat the exercise until another contagious string of laughter ensues.

"Believe it or not," Anton says, "This is meant to be one of our most serious exercises." (Laughter) "I'm not kidding." (laughter) "Okay, we will do this one more time."

On the third display of numbers, Barry sees his number "37" matched with number "123." Like everyone else, he wanders through the crowd muttering the number he seeks, "1-2-3, on the lookout for number 123, 123, 123." He decides to sing it, "123, where are you? 1-2-3, you and me…"

Barry sees the woman, Hope, staring at him from her wheelchair. "You are number 37?" she says. He walks up to her, takes off his badge, and holds it so she can see.

"Nice to meet you, number 123. I am number three-seven,"

he states in a robotic voice. "What are the odds?"

She starts to roll away but stops and looks back when she realizes Barry is not following. She jerks her head. "Let's get away from the crowd."

"What do you think we will have to do together?" he says while the rest of the group find their partners. "Some kind of sex thing—I'm hoping..."

"That's the last thing I'm hoping, old white man." Barry is grateful she smiles while saying this.

He laughs. "I shouldn't have said that. I'm sorry. You are very pretty, though. Oh, dammit. I forgot. I am not supposed to say what I think. Let me introduce myself." He holds out a hand. "I am number thirty-seven. You seem like a beautiful person to me, number 123."

Hope takes his hand but neither of them shake or exert any pressure. She is surprised to feel a palpable warm energy travel up her arm and flood throughout her body. Her eyes well with tears. *What is going on?* She has not felt anything in her lower extremities in years.

Barry loves holding her hand but withdraws his. He sees her tears and hopes he is not inadvertently distressing her.

"Are you okay?" he says kindly.

She nods and takes his hand again. The electrical-like current is still there, running through her. She will not let go until this very pleasant warmth subsides. Elaine, carrying a chair, appears behind Barry who is bending his head to stay near eye level with Hope. The caring soft way Elaine touches his shoulder and directs his attention to the seat behind him seems beautiful to Hope. It feels to her like a ballet, a series of caring and graceful gestures, an art form like some Oriental theater she had seen. Elaine says not a word and exchanges a questioning glance at Hope '*Are you ok*ay?

Hope smiles back. She is glad that she had a little edible pick-me-up snack during the last bathroom break. She tried to tell herself that she could get something out of this workshop without medication of any kind. But sitting in a chair for hours on end is, as always, painful and exhausting—*HELLO! Perfectly legal to take something for any medical and spiritual reason,* she tells herself. *In fact, it's the right thing to do!*

Yet what sometimes happens with this remedy, Hope gets a little too high and she starts believing in miracles. She had been down this track on this train of thought before. Believing this healer, this meditation, this drug, this surgery, this way, that way, this won't work, this never will...

She liked to say that 'Peaceful Putty,' her favorite brand, is 'a fabulous font of fantasy!' She even wrote an email offering their marketing department this little beauty of a slogan—*gratis*.

The thought that this enlivening of her lower limbs is not real, but a momentary fancy, an imagined ecstasy induced illusion, no doubt contributes to the disappearance of the sensation that her legs were not only paralyzed but alive, ALIVE! She withdraws her hand and smiles a little shyly at this man now sitting in front of her.

"I have probably held the hands of hundreds of people but, I have to say, this was the absolute best," Barry says.

"It was good for me too," she says laughing. "I forget—is this the first or second time you were able to make me laugh?"

"Who's counting? Could be dozens—if you were laughing

on the inside."

She laughs again. He holds up four fingers with a questioning look on his face, then changes it to three. Hope smiles but holds back a laugh. That damn Putty! If she weren't careful, she would be volunteering to be the next public spectacle. "Peaceful Putty" helps one of her personalities, "*The Showgirl*" come out to play. Would not take much to push her over the edge and get everyone singing and dancing along. Only she could no longer do any of the dancing. Well, except for chair dancing, of course.

Hope is glad this old guy is so patient. She will calm down and come down off the ledge in another minute or two.

Anton waits until all are quiet. "Everyone got a partner?" A brief look around. "We're going to do it differently this time. Anyone know what an *allemande* is? It's a folk-dance move. We are going to have some fun tomorrow after dinner. Hope you all like square dancing!"

Barry jokes, "I'm more partial to round dancing."

"There is such a thing, doofus. Oh, I love to dance!" Hope says enthusiastically. Barry starts to smile and resonate with her joyful tone but stops as if noticing her disability for the first time. There seems no sarcasm or bitterness in her demeanor. She looks at him evenly, almost daring him to say something stupid, but lets him off the hook. "It's not as much fun as it used to be. But I still love it."

"I like it, too. I'm very partial to contra dancing, as well. You ever do that?"

"Omigod, yes! I went to school in Cambridge..."

"England?"

"No, Massachusetts. Harvard..." She pauses for the usual

dumb white guy awe and is glad there is none. "Lots of contra dancing up there."

"No official dancing during this next exercise but you are free to do so, if the spirit moves you," Anton is saying.

"Oh, goody!" Hope says with a laugh. She can be a little snitty if she wants to.

"Look at your partner. Decide which of you is A and which is B."

"I'll be A," Hope says decisively.

"Makes me B." He starts to sing just to her very softly. "*Makes me be happy/Makes me be sad/Sometimes we're sappy/ Often we're mad...*"

"You are the weirdest white man I've ever seen. And I've seen an awful lot of weird ones."

"I bet you have. I'll try to look upon that as a compliment." Barry says.

Anton moves more forcefully towards conclusion. "You will be taking turns. Whoever is "A" goes first. For 15 minutes, B gets to talk without interruption. No advice from all the A's, no judgments. Then, we switch roles—the B's talk, the A's listen for 15 minutes. Everybody ready?" He looks at his watch. "Ready, set..." There is an uproar of voices asking questions.

Anton raises his hand for quiet, his tone more reassuring now. "Don't worry, there are no right or wrong answers here. This is just an exercise in listening and sharing, so take your time. The goal is to be present, not perfect." The room buzzes with nervous energy, but a few people nod, seemingly comforted by his words.

"What do you talk about? How are you supposed to listen?

Okay, okay. A few suggestions—talk about what is important to you, why are you here, where you want to go, what's standing in the way, what is your life story, what you fear, what makes you happy...

"To listen effectively, just listen. For your partner's sake, look as if you care even if you don't. If you feel comfortable doing so, you can encourage your partner to say more...get to what's really important! Partner A, begin talking!"

"Are you okay with this?" Barry asks Hope.

"Rule One: whoever's turn it is to speak must not concern themselves what their listener may be feeling or thinking..." Anton advises.

"Oops," Barry says. "Hope, I feel like you should take all of the time. I feel like I got my time in front of everyone already. I'm good."

"Whoa, buster. You're not getting off that easy. Tell me your little privileged white boy life story or anything you want. Start off by telling me how great you are and then you can go on with how pissed you are that Liberals or maybe Donald Trump and the Republicans ruined the world. And I would bet money you'll be dying to either tell me what I need to know about racism and my own people or, if you are the other kind of racist, you would let me know you don't see differences in skin color and wholeheartedly support equal rights and even reparations for Black people."

"That's more like me..."

"Shit. I am sorry. I'm supposed to go first..."

"Be my guest."

"No, you go," she says. "Maybe I'll get beyond my resentment and trust you enough to feel safe enough to be honest when it is my turn."

"Okay, I'll go."

"Before you get going, I have to ask you—are you really that rich or was that just a bunch of bullshit?"

"Complete crap," Barry lies.

"I knew it! I knew it! Everybody was talking about it during the break when we all thought you were bailing out on us. I told Jane (the only other Black woman here) I was sure you were just playing with everyone."

"I sure was."

"Hmm. Well, I don't care either way. You are just another person to me. Another insane white person, but a person."

"Uh, just checking, but is this my session, or yours?"

She looks at her watch. "It is yours. I'll give you a few minutes of my time."

"No worries. This is where I am right now. I just want to help somebody. Back in my hometown..."

"Charlottesville."

"Yes."

"You there during that Nazi white supremacy thing a few years ago?"

"Well, yes. I tried to stop it. When people started throwing things and punching each other, I stepped in between the two sides and hollered, 'Hey! Can't we all get along?' But nobody could hear me—it was so loud! Then someone punched me in the face."

"Bullshit. But I'd like to hear what really went down sometime from your perspective."

"Of course. As I started to say, it is true what I said in front of everyone. Many of the friends in my hometown drew up a petition to ask please would I do something to make myself a better person. 'Go get some counseling!' they said. 'Take a workshop and get transformed in some way that is more acceptable to us,' is how I saw it. I cannot describe how that made me feel…"

"Sad?" she says without a trace of sympathy.

"Yes, s-a-d…" Barry says slowly. "I felt fortunate to have both time and resources to contribute to community causes I thought were important…"

"You retired and wanted to 'give back' to the community…" Hope is not happy to hear the snarky tone in her own voice.

"I tried hiding my pretentious bullshit. I just wanted to help, like you heard me say earlier. People, both black and white seemed to like my help—my ideas, my energy, and yes, my money. But apparently, they didn't like me. The message I eventually got is, 'You are just too irritating, Barry. We wouldn't mind if you found another town to live in and do your thing.' "

"They actually said that?"

"No one person seemed to have the nerve to say that to my face. My friend, John, heard that anti-Barry factions arose in almost every organization I was involved in. Somehow the factions got together and compared notes on how annoying I was. For a joke, a joke mind you, they worded a petition to ask the mayor to strongly suggest I go into exile or at least take a year-long sabbatical."

"You're that annoying?" Hope has an expression that seems to say she has no trouble at all believing that.

"Apparently. I did not find out about the exile/sabbatical

petition until after the second, more strongly worded petition was delivered."

"The one that urged you to come to this workshop and improve yourself?"

"Yes."

"So, here you are. Do you want to improve yourself?"

"Yeah, sure. Why not?"

"Well, get to work, brother!"

"Honestly, I'm terrified!"

"Of what?"

'*Of you,*' he thinks. '*Of dying, of living, of everything.*' "Looking in the mirror, I guess..." he says out loud. He feels a cold lump of fear gather at the base of his spine that causes him to tremble fiercely. "I'm scared. I'M SCARED!!!" his voice booming. Hope looks around and is relieved to see other participants in the throes of their own distress. Elaine is a few steps away observing their session.

Hope remains unworried and serene. He is not her problem. "I think I heard someone say it is okay for men to have feelings. Go ahead and feel what you're feeling. Shake out that motherfucking fear! Shake it!" She shakes her own torso mightily while crying out in a little girl's voice, "'I'm scared. I'm scared.' C'mon, Barry. Shake the devil right out of your body and soul! Do it! 'I'm scared'...Like a little boy, 'I'm scared.'"

Barry does as directed. He shakes that lump of fear until it rises up his spine and seems to shoot out the top of his head. The shaking, the whimpering of a lost little boy from 65 years ago, roars through him. Without any conscious effort on his part, the terror is transformed into grief. He sobs completely out of control for several minutes.

Hope watches more than a little amazed. Some of the strongest men in her family would let themselves cry at funerals, maybe, but she had never seen anything like this. She thinks about how she might record this in her journal. "Saw a white man cry today, sobbing like a baby..."

Elaine places a box of tissues on her lap. Hope pulls one out and hands it to Barry. His weeping subsides. Huge belly laughs suddenly take over. He laughs so hard he falls off his chair and rolls helplessly to the floor. The laughs die down but then he looks at Hope and resumes the rather embarrassing spectacle of guffaws, hoots, howls, and snorts.

Hope hands him a few more tissues to catch the small streams of mucous. She starts to get a little concerned. Is he having a psychotic break, a heart attack?

Anton's voice comes out of the amplifier soft and slow. "Client A should begin to wrap up her session now. Take a deep breath. Find an image of what you just experienced. Is it a storm? A calm sea? An explosion? A small bird or a mighty lion? Imagine a picture, a photo or a painting with all the emotion and creative energy that just transpired. You can put that picture in a little box, close the lid, then place the box on a shelf in a room of your sanctuary. You can come back to it sometime and take another look. For now, look at the person who was there with you for the last 15 minutes, and thank them for their attention..."

"Thank you, Hope!" Barry says calmly, peacefully. He takes her hands into his. Hope feels warmth pour through her arms, into her head and torso and light up nerves and tissues of her dead legs and feet. Legs!!! Feet!!!

The ecstasy of what she earlier thought of as a drug-induced illusion now seems terrifyingly real. The edible most certainly should have worn off by now. Rocking back and forth in her chair, Hope holds onto this strange man, determined to not let this welling up of hope and healing fade away.

"Client B!" Anton calls out. "If you are ready, your time is now. Client A, listen well!"

As the Listener, Barry inches closer to Hope and holds onto her hands while she trembles with eyes closed for the next 15 minutes. Something is going on, he can tell. She moans, she cries and curses, she appears to be in horrible pain but stops him every time he attempts to say or do anything but hold on...

It feels as if a fire is burning every cell and muscle of her thighs and calves. Her feet impossibly hot. She looks to see if flames are shooting out from her toes. One thought obsesses her—if she could restore her lower body to numbness, would she? Something seems to be telling her to just let go, surrender. Perhaps, it is her resistance to these sensations that is so painful. Perhaps it is death. If she lets go now, will she die?

'Okay, die if I must,' she thinks. Something happens then which she will never be able to understand or explain. No longer feeling inflamed, a slow wave of energy washes through her. The lower part of her body is neither numb nor in severe pain. She feels it pulsate and can sense the circulation of blood and neural energy while the lower body connects with the upper.

Somehow, some way, her body feels whole, feels connected to her spirit, united with this man and with everyone in this room—a sense of Oneness with Everything.

Anton's voice comes through an amplifier soft and slow. "Client B should begin to wrap up their session now. Take a deep breath. Find an image of what you just experienced. Is it a storm? A calm sea? An explosion? A small bird or a mighty lion? Imagine a picture, a photo or a painting with all the emotion and creative energy that just transpired. You can put that picture in a little box, close the lid, then place the box on a shelf in a room of your sanctuary."

"I don't want to put it in a box," she whispers.

"You can come back to it sometime and take another look. For now, look at the person who is there with you for the last 15 minutes, and thank them for their attention..."

"Thank you, Barry," Hope says while tears flow down her cheeks. Barry releases her hands and gives her a tissue.

"My pleasure," he says. "Was that good for you?"

"Oh, yeah," she says laughing. "Damn good! I feel like I can walk again." She says this but does not believe it for a second. Just another imaginary fantasy trip.

"Yeah?" Barry says. "Let me see."

She laughs happily almost certain she would fall if she tried—'almost certain,' she thinks. 'But, what if...'

"I'll catch you if you fall," Barry says. He gently lifts her feet and folds back the pads. He looks her steady in the eye and stands. "Maybe you can, maybe you can't."

"Maybe you can," someone watching repeats. Hope sees that others now surround her watching, waiting, hoping...almost willing her to become whole. Maybe... she feels her legs, but can she stand on them, move them?

She places her hands on the arm rests and presses down.

Ten years of propelling the big wheels of chairs, of pulling herself up and down, sometimes crawling across a room, have made her arms strong. She has lifted herself from chairs hundreds, thousands of times. But now, her arms wobble like rubber bands from the effort.

She watches her feet rest on the floor and wonders where these red and black shoes came from. Her hope rises as she lets go of the chair and becomes fully erect. She feels the floor beneath her and takes one tentative step towards the man in front of her.

His face eager, radiant with joy, watches her take two more steps. He steps back to give her room to move even further forward. His happiness, his tears of joy, the broad smile on his face, no longer is that of a strange white man. He suddenly looks just like her own father, gone from this earth for at least twelve years now.

Hope becomes delirious and, for a moment, feels herself transported forty-eight years into the past. She is in the living room of her parents' home in Arlington, Virginia where at 12 months of age she takes her first tentative steps toward the wide-open arms of the smiling, joyful man that is her father. He takes her in his big strong arms and directs her toward the waiting hands of her mother.

At this moment, Hope both in her memory and on the floor of the hotel ballroom, begins to stumble. In this time, a tall, strong and old white man catches her.

"Gotcha," he says.

CHAPTER FIVE

After her brief, short walk, Hope returns to present time and apparently returns to full use of her limbs. She laughs and cries with joy. Barry and what seems the full contingent of workshop staff and participants rejoice with her. Barry points her towards the waiting arms of Elaine. Hope walks to her and then to several other people before Anton feels moved to return everyone's attention back to the program.

"Good time for another break! Let's meet back here in about 10 minutes when we'll see if we can drum up another miracle." Elaine sticks close to Hope while she walks out of the ballroom on her own steam. The room vibrates with excited chatter. No one has seen anything like it.

Anton walks up to Barry. "What the hell just happened?" He is upset, discombobulated.

"I have no idea." As sometimes happens with Barry, one of his favorite characters from his theatrical days, Bubba the Country Boy, comes out to color his response. "I thu-ink," he drawls as his face assumes an appropriate expression, "...it is a *MER-ACUL!*"

Anton is not amused but Barry gets a laugh and a shot of

that audience love-vibe from someone else listening nearby. He snaps back to his usual personality, as worn and pedestrian as it may be.

"I really don't know. She didn't say much at all during her time. I could tell she was going through something. When her time was up, she said she thought she could walk. I have no idea why she was in a wheelchair in the first place. Far as I know, it was nothing more than a little unsteadiness or fatigue. I hope I am not betraying confidentiality when I say that she did not share anything of her history or current condition. I told her sure, go ahead and walk. Seems a pretty big deal to her. Hope she is okay. This kind of thing happen much during these workshops?"

"Oh, sure. All the time. Healings are my specialty." A kind of mask appears to fall away. Something uncontrollable has happened and he does not know how to handle it. "No, it is not part of the program! We have a detailed set of things we like to see happen, but this is not one of them. You didn't know her before today?"

"No, I did not. Are you okay? You seem a little pissed. Are you thinking she's faking it?"

"I don't know. Something is not right. You're not some kind of fake faith healer, are you?"

"Not that I know of. I'll keep my eye on her, though. If I see any suspicious behavior, I'll let you know."

Although Barry thinks his mock conspiratorial tone a deft light-hearted touch certain to ease Anton's anxiety, the seminar facilitator seems to experience it as pure mockery. He turns on his heels and is about to rush away when a commotion at the rear of the room makes everyone turn their heads.

Elaine rushes through the door, her aura flashing Code Red. "Anton!" she shouts. "Come here, we need you right away!"

"What is it?" he says dashing her way.

"It's Hope. Barry! You come too!"

Elaine points to where the wheelchair sits and someone grabs it.

"She just collapsed. Perhaps too many steps too fast."

"Conscious?" Anton asks. Before Elaine can answer, they are close enough to see for themselves. She is sitting up against a wall having a drink of water. A group of five women and one man hover nearby. Other participants gather in several clusters in the hallway and lobby. Hotel staff and guests walk dully along going about their business. '*Like in Brueghel's Icarus,*' Barry thinks. '*Someone has fallen far but everyone on the scene has somewhere to get to and sails calmly on.*'

Anton and Elaine stop and stare at him. Hope and others are also looking at him funny. "Uh-oh," he says in a voice loud enough so he can hear himself this time. "Am I thinking out loud again?"

"You sure were!" Hope replies with an energy that surprises everyone. "What's that Icarus stuff you talking about? Is he that Greek kid who flew too close to the sun and got his wings melted?"

"That's him! You know what his dad Daedalus said after his son fell in the sea?" No one responds. "'I should have had Aristotle teach him more science!'"

Hope chuckles and the caring folks around her laugh along, relieved.

"Are you hurt, Hope? Did you fall?" Anton bends down, takes her pulse, and does a quick test for concussion.

"I'm okay," she insists. Her chair appears. She gives it a hard stare. *Friend or foe?* It scoots an inch or so away from her when she reaches for it. Someone holds it steady. Other hands help her into the seat. "That was fun while it lasted. I never heard of a paralytic obtaining the ability to walk for only a couple of minutes."

Hope appreciated all the attention immediately after her legs gave out from under her. But now, feeling disheartened but more like her usual self, the caring words and multiple offers of help seem a bit too precious and claustrophobic.

She tries to roll away, but Elaine is not ready to let her go. Her voice is soft and loving, each syllable a kind of caress. "If you haven't used your legs for a while, they would tire pretty quickly. Maybe they just need to rest up some."

"No, I can tell," she says. She slams her fist down into the meat of her thigh. "Nothing. Not even a sense of pressure. Thank you, all! Really..."

Barry, the famous melodramatic star of hundreds of spontaneous ad-lib melodramas, drops to one knee and takes the hand she had used to strike herself. She is surprised to sense the brief hand pain caused by her test immediately vanish.

"We are with you, Hope. I think I speak for everyone when I say that we would be glad indeed to help you any way we can. I think I can say, without fear of any contradiction, Black Lives Matter! And a lot more than white lives, really."

All the white people gathered, good liberals all, gasp at what had apparently been offered in fun. The very few people of color close enough to hear, Hope included, let out a sharp snort that sound a bit like a laugh but also have hints of disgust. Who is this guy?

Hope looks at Jane. "Weirdest white man—ever."

"Do you need anything, Hope?" Anton says. "Elaine can sit out here with you if you'd like a little time away from the workshop. Or, if you're up to it, join us inside the ballroom for the next rip-roaring session."

"I'm good!" Hope says with some force. "Let's go!"

Anton directs the seminar staff, Elaine and Kevin, to prepare for the next session, now hopelessly behind schedule. The musical summons urge all participants to once again take a seat. Barry tries to push Hope's chair for her, but she will not let him. He walks behind for a step or two then boldly walks alongside her. She can tell he has something to say.

"Would you mind if I sit next to you?" He places a hand gently on her shoulder. She stops and looks up into a kind and gentle face, his touch renewing a warm and steady electrical vibration.

"I would like that. I need someone to hold my hand." Hope parks her chair at the end of the front row while Barry takes the chair next to her. The music ends and Anton assumes his usual position facing everyone.

"Believe it or not, there are more exciting things to come! Let's see if we can all completely relax for a moment. Take a few deep breaths. Close your eyes…"

Hope grabs Barry's hand. Gentle, meditative music fills the air.

"Breathe in…breathe out. Imagine, if you will, the molecules of oxygen inside this room charged with golden healing energy. Some of it flows into your lungs and throughout every cell of your body. Take it in, hold it for three seconds—one, two, three. Let it out. In—hold one, two, three. Out...in.

"As you inhale, imagine that golden healing energy coming in through the top of your head at the same time. Everything in the world is surrounded by this healing energy—all you have to do is let it in..." Anton says.

"Yeah, right..." Hope whispers derisively. Barry gives her hand a little squeeze.

"Let that light in through your nose and through the crown chakra, through the third eye and through the throat and heart, down through the solar plexus, the sacral chakra, all the way down to the root at the base of the spine.

"Now, take that energy back up through all those energy centers, all the way back up to the crown and let it shoot out the top of your head..."

"Ka-pow!" Barry says softly. "Good-bye, Energy!"

Hope laughs. '*That's four*,' she whispers to herself.

As Kevin's meditative music ceases, all open their eyes to a dark room lit by a kaleidoscope of multi-colored stars. Spears of light shoot out from the sleeves and leggings of Anton's newest costume, a paisley jumpsuit complete with cape and a wizard's hat. He climbs three stairs to make majestic pronouncements from a small stage.

"I AM HERE TO INFORM YOU OF THE GREATEST AND ONLY BIT OF TRUTH YOU NEED TO KNOW! (sound effect of thunder along with spectacular show of lightning and shooting stars) **YOU ARE HERE NOW!!!** (more thunder and lightning)"

Barry turns to Hope with his mouth open wide in mock wonder, "Wow!!!"

Anton turns toward them, his eyes somehow full of sparks and fire. "**YOU ONLY <u>THINK</u> YOU ARE HERE NOW!** But like nearly every person on this planet, you are trapped by time. Mentally and emotionally, spiritually and physically, we all inhabit an imaginary universe sometimes called the past and sometimes called the future." He removes the wizard's hat and drops the dramatic persona and tone. "Who here has seen the movie, 'The Matrix'? Nearly everyone! Fantastic. For those not familiar with the premise, the world the characters perceive as reality is actually a simulation, the Matrix, created by machines. The bodies of most humans are wrapped in a kind of cocoon to be a source of energy for the machines. Conflict and battles ensue. Creepy Sci-Fi, right?

"Like the characters in the film, we here in a non-cinematic simulation are not actually in our bodies. We are in a mental construct passed on by our parents and others when we were babies and reinforced by our cultures as we develop. This construct, our version of reality, our Matrix if you will, is the result of leaving our bodies behind and suppressing and sedating emotional response. We become mentally fixated on both the past and the future, ricochet back and forth, up and down, with stories and dramas about grief, and fear, and anger." Anton gazes upon the people before him, returns the wizard hat, and once again climbs the steps of the small stage. "I am here to tell you that the way to rid yourself of anger, fear, and grief is not to suppress, sedate, and distract yourself from them. It is okay to feel these things, allow them to become part of your emotional perception."

Soft pastel light bathes the room. Meditative music returns. "I invite you to close your eyes and take deep circular breaths with no gaps between inhale and exhale. Your mind may drift and that's okay. You may catch yourself thinking about the past or the future but just return to your circular breathing. Let this be your mantra, your gateway to the present moment—'I (inhale) Am (exhale) Here (inhale) Now (exhale)'. Repeat..."

After several minutes, Anton brings the meditation to a close and allows everyone to experience the silent peacefulness that comes over the room without any more commentary from him. Although the warmth of the elderly white man next to her is calm and reassuring, Hope is more than a little disappointed that she is not feeling it through her legs and down to her toes. She withdraws her hand from his and tries to find a place of peace on her own. It had taken years for her to accept the reality of her paralysis, years to try to enjoy life and find something good in life without ever walking again. For a few blissful moments she not only actually walked but was also joyfully pain-free.

How could all of this have happened! She is suddenly furious. How could he be so cruel as to awaken such desire and hope in her? Without warning she brings her fist down hard on Barry's leg.

She feels him flinch and exhale a soft, "Ouch."

Horrified by her own behavior, Hope turns to him stricken with fear.

If he is angry or in pain, Barry does not show it. It is the last thing she expects to see but on his face is a look of complete neutral attention, as if he had not felt a thing. She mouths the words, *I'm sorry.*

He smiles and allows his spirit to project, through his mouth and eyes and his whole being, an emotional-cognitive state of awareness he had learned to think of as '*Unconditional Love.*' He is glad to see she does not turn away.

Hope does not see his lips move but very clearly hears the words, "*You can hit me a hundred times and I would still love you.*"

Perhaps, he is a ventriloquist and maybe a hypnotist who is able to put her in a trance! By his own force of will he somehow compelled her useless legs to move like an automaton. Who else but a seducer could be so manipulative? Now she is scaring herself.

She almost has to force herself to turn away from his magnetic stare.

Anton is talking and she tries to pay attention to that.

"As mentioned earlier, boys and girls, from time to time we attempt to allow a few lucky individuals to come up here and accept my expert investigative efforts to knock out of the way any blocks to the emergence of their true selves and fuller potential.

"Any of that happen when you were up here, Barry?"

"Gee, I don't know..." he answers with genuine ingenuousness.

"Well, sometimes the magic works and sometimes it doesn't...At any rate, it is time for another lucky person to be the beneficiary of our collective attention. Anyone feeling the call to be next?"

"Me!" shouts Hope.

Her chair shoots forward as if motorized.

"Ah, I was hoping there would be Hope!" Anton guides her

to an optimal position for everyone to see and has her attach a mic.

"Hello, Hope!"

"Hi, Anton."

"Love your name." He grabs a chair to put himself at her level. "Hope. Gives me a lift whenever I see or hear the word."

She laughs. "That's about five times for you."

"Five?"

"Yes. You have made me laugh about five times. Could be six. I haven't been keeping strict count since you weren't directing your humorous comments to me alone."

"Okay..." Anton says uncertainly.

Hope begins to laugh a bit out of control. "It is just a silly thing I told myself mostly when I was younger. The women here may know what I mean. When I was in high school, and college, and working at some job? I told myself I would not ever let a man have sex with me until he could make me laugh 10 times."

"Whoa!" Anton cries. "Don't have to worry about me, sister! I only look for sexual intimacy with the brothers."

"Guess that's six," she says. She happens to look over at Barry who is comically counting on his fingers. "That didn't mean I had to sleep with him. It just told me this joker *might* have a chance." The Showgirl in her wags a single finger gaily.

When the laughter dies down, Anton tries to steer the discussion in a more meaningful direction. "Hope. What are you hoping? What do you hope to get out of this seminar? What would you hope to get out of life, Hope?"

This, for a moment, stops her. Anton, the 143 or so white people in front of her, along with the very few black and brown faces all share an appearance of caring.

"What is your big issue, Hope? What do you need to do here?"

"I was just fooling myself that I was all over this."

"This?"

"Being crippled. That I accepted it, could live with it, had moved on—all that jazz. Wrong."

"Still a problem then?"

"Anton, you say 'hope' gives you a lift? To me, it is the cruelest thing I know. Sometimes, praise Jesus, I get a feeling I just might walk again..."

"Like today..."

"No nothing like what seemed to happen today. Usually, it is just a feeling that with some new drug or regimen or spiritual practice *maybe* I can walk. Today I walked, I walked. Didn't I?"

"Sure looked like it."

"But now I can't." Despite a huge effort to stop it, she begins to cry. "It is like dying all over again." Anton holds her hand until the sobbing seems to subside.

When she looks up at him, Anton repeats the words, "Like dying all over again..." Her discharge of grief resumes.

This counseling technique is repeated two more times until Hope puts a stop to it. "Enough already!" she cries out then begins laughing long and hard. She recalls how relieved her counseling partner, Barry, had seemed from all the laughing and shaking he did in his session and she decides to do the same.

Hope vigorously shakes the huge knot of fear lodged in her back until she feels it work its way up and down her spine. She stops when it feels as if her legs are tingling.

She moves not a muscle, says not a word, for what seems to all an awfully long time. Such fierceness she has in those moments halts Anton's every gesture to intervene or impulse to speak.

When, at last, Hope releases a huge sigh and visibly sags in her chair, she looks at everyone and mutters, "It is gone."

All of Anton's subsequent entreaties to discover what it is she means, what else she would like to say or do or get help in addressing, are fruitless. There seems nothing he or anyone can do to reach or pull her out of this total sense of despair.

"What's going on, Hope?" he asks her three times.

At last, she says, "Thank you, Anton. Thank you all. I'm done." She rolls back to her spot at the end of the first row.

A bit annoyed, mostly at himself, that they have apparently wasted too much time, Anton announces another break. The dispirited assemblage gets a little more bounce to their steps on the way out when Kevin fills the room with the energetic sounds of a popular rock song from the Stones—"You Can't Always Get What You Want."

"Are you okay?" Barry says putting a hand on her shoulder. She roughly slaps it away.

"No, I am not okay, you stupid goddam motherfucker!" Her voice rises in volume and fury with each word. "I have probably never been okay and never will be okay for the rest of my stupid fucking life! Don't you ever, EVER, touch me again, you manipulative ASSHOLE! I don't know what your game is, what you're trying to sell—but I am not buying. I do not need me some White Savior, thank you. Stay away from me! Go to fucking hell!"

When Elaine and Anton, Jane and Mary, and one or two others approach her, she aims the next series of invectives toward them. "Stay away from me! All of you! Back off, dammit! STOP LOOKING AT ME!!!" A blood-curdling scream bounces off the walls. "Stay away from me. Leave me alone. Please...no, no more, please!"

Her voice is now that of a little girl reliving some childhood horror.

Elaine's voice, calm and strong, tries to bring her back with each word a caress. "We love you, Hope. You're safe here."

"You're safe, we love you, Hope," many repeat from the growing circle surrounding her.

She puts her hands over her face and rocks back and forth while repeating the word, "No. No. No. I can't do this anymore. Someone please—just kill me!"

"No one is going to kill you, Hope," Anton whispers as if to a jumpy horse. The EMT training from his other life takes over. "No one is going to hurt you. You are safe here among people who care about you and want to help you. But you must come out from wherever you are and meet us halfway. Open your eyes, Hope. Let us in."

Hope drops her hands and looks around. Sweat and tears had turned her make-up into blue and gray streams.

'My God, you look terrible!' she thinks she hears Barry utter with his thrown, ventriloquist voice. That he would say such a thing in this situation is outrageous enough to get a small laugh out of her.

"That should be about eight laughs, if you're still keeping score," he says out loud.

"You are such a goofball!" Hope smiles feeling a little lighter. Someone hands her a tissue. She wipes her face and seeing the make-up smears cries, "Omigod! I am such a mess. Sorry."

"No need to be sorry about anything. You want some help getting to a washroom?" says Anton.

A cup of water is put in her hands.

"I'm exhausted. Barry, can you push me? I'd like to talk to you."

"Of course. I am at your service."

Barry pushes the chair forward as Hope waves to all offering their heartiest best wishes. Once in the lobby, she has Barry stop before reaching the restroom.

"Let's talk," she says.

"Okay." He places her near a chair where he can sit and look at her. "You're looking better."

"I'm sorry I dumped on you."

"Hey, you were upset! I get it. It can be hard to hear someone you like a lot tell you that they think you're an asshole, but I always keep in mind something Eleanor Roosevelt said—'what other people think of me is none of my business.'"

"That can be true, but not always. If I think you're a racist, that is more your problem and your business than mine."

"You think I'm racist? Is it because of something I said or did? Or do you think I'm a racist because you believe all white people, and especially white men, and more particularly all older white men are racist?"

"I didn't say I thought you were racist. I am just using that as an example of an objectionable trait that you, or anyone, might not take responsibility for because of what some old white First

Lady said a hundred years ago. Damn! If you are not racist, you might want to do something about your white fragility!"

"Okay. Is this what you wanted to talk about?"

"No. I wanted to apologize for attacking you like that. You've been nice to me. You listened to me very well during our one-on-one session. You seem a kind, loving, and attentive person but all this voodoo stuff you been doing suddenly got to me when a lot of heavy emotional stuff was going on with that thing with Anton."

"Voodoo? Do I remind you of a man?"

"What man?"

"The man with the power."

"What power?"

"The power of hoodoo."

"Hoodoo?"

"You do."

"I do what?"

"Remind me of a man..."

"What man...?"

"The man with the power..."

"Oh, for God sakes! Who the hell are you? Is it because you know you can't fuck me that you keep fucking with me with crazy assed shit like this?"

"Cool down, Sister! I'm just trying to have fun. I take it you never saw 'The Bachelor and the Bobby-Soxer' with Cary Grant."

"A movie?"

"Yes. From 1947, I think. Came out a little before I was born but they used to show it on TV all the time. That 'Hoodoo' exchange is a famous comic bit a lot of us kids used to say. You can Google it. Too silly, maybe."

"You wear me out, Mr. Barry."

"To get back to your original concern—I don't know what you mean by 'voodoo stuff.' Here's the truth, if you want it. I do not know why I felt immediately fond of you. Not sure myself what is behind what to me seems a strong urge to just be here for you—whatever you need. You need someone to care for you? I am telling you straight up, this is real. You need me to back off? Fine, I'll do so. To go fuck myself? Okay. But if you need a friend, someone who has got your back, someone to be your champion, someone to amuse, challenge, and simply love you, God help me, I want to do my best to be that person. Another thing comes to mind—I was not completely honest with you about being wealthy. I am obscenely rich."

"Oh, God. Who cares..."

"I care. It's a huge burden..."

"Please...Have someone else forgive you."

"I don't want forgiveness. I want to give away my money, many millions of dollars, maybe all of it. I have an idea you can point me to some good causes."

"Oh, for crying out loud. You are just too much. I can see why everybody wanted you to get out of town. I'm sorry, Barry. Maybe we can talk about this later. Right now—the only thing I want to do is lie down. My back is killing me from sitting and I must get horizontal. I don't care about any of this crazy love and transformational stuff. I have to go to sleep. I should just drive home but I'm afraid I'll doze off at the wheel."

Her head falls to her chest and rests for several seconds but then jerks up. "Oh, Barry. I've got to lie down. Help me."

"Let's get you a room so you can rest for a while."

"I can't afford this place."

"No worries, Hope. I'll take care of it."

"I don't want you to do that. Call a taxi to take me home."

"I can do that but would you want to wait another half-hour or so or do you want to go to sleep now?"

"I don't know, I don't know what to do."

"Let's find a bed here, right now. They got a lot of them. Trust me."

She surrenders and nods. Barry heads to the front desk where Malcolm has been quietly watching.

"Hello, Mr. Strange. How nice to see you again. How may we be of service?"

"I would like another room, please. My friend Hope, from the seminar here, is in some distress and needs a place to rest."

Malcolm taps the screen. "I am sorry to say we are totally booked up."

"Nothing? Are you sure?"

"Positive. Many seminar people have rented a room here. Perhaps one of them would allow her to rest in one of their beds?"

"Good idea!" Barry scans the lobby but sees that the break is over. The lobby is near empty and the door to the ballroom has closed. "Oh, I don't want to disturb them. Besides, it would maybe take a while to get it arranged. I know! I already have a room with two beds. Maybe Joe wouldn't mind if Hope rested in one of them."

Malcolm does not look as if he thinks this is a good

solution. "I could find a roll-away and maybe a quiet office or storeroom..."

"No, that's okay. I'll call Joe and see if he'd be all right with someone taking a nap in the extra bed. Can I use this phone?"

Barry calls Room 417. Although nervous about the prospect, Joe doesn't feel he can say no. Barry tries to reassure Hope that Joe seems a gentle, peaceful soul but he will stay in the room with her while she rests, just in case.

Hope is too tired to argue and allows herself to be wheeled into the elevator and down the hall to the room where Joe, in a white terrycloth bathrobe, waits with the door open. He bows and invites them inside.

"Nice to meet you, Joe," Hope says politely. "Are you sure this is okay?"

"Is okay with me. Sorry the place is such a mess." Joe has to raise his voice to be heard over the roar of a wrestling match from the TV. Instead of trusting the hotel laundry, Joe hand washed every clothing item he owns and draped them over the bathroom curtain rod, the closet hangers, and every available piece of furniture. He pats the extra queen-sized bed that is still made up. "I had put some of the clothes on it to dry. The top is still a little damp."

Barry checks it out. "It's not too bad. I realize this is a terrible imposition, Joe, but like I said on the phone, she's in a lot of pain and needs to nap for a while. Can we turn down the TV?"

Joe turns off the screaming voices. "You just make yourself at home, Miss Hope. There's some leftover pizza in that box. And some chips and cookies. Sorry to say, I drunk all the beer and liquor but there's still wine and lots of soda and water."

She tests the duvet and throws it to the other side of the bed. She twists behind her in search of something in the chair pouch there.

"Need some help?" Barry asks.

"There's a red flat board back there. Can you get it out for me? I usually get it myself, but my back is killing me." He pulls out the board. Hope wheels the chair into position, so she faces the foot of the bed, lowers the arm rest, and takes the board. "I am really good at this. Special Olympics didn't think much of my suggestion that bed slides be a competitive event."

She slid one end of the board under part of her rear and the other on the edge of the bed. In three short bursts, she hoists herself up the slight incline, shoves the chair out of the way, and lies down with both legs still dangling over the side. She shouts "No!" when Barry moves to help her. She grabs first one pants leg and then the other onto the bed. She pulls the duvet back over her.

The two men express astonishment.

"I have polled other crips and no one has ever done it faster," Hope states with just a touch of bitterness.

"You must have strong arms," Joe says.

"I do. Strong arms and hands, strong back and neck. Nerves of steel. You don't want to mess with me."

"No, you don't!" Barry tells him. "Okay to pull the curtains?"

"That's fine," Joe says. "I'll get dressed and get out of here for a while." He examines some of the clothes.

"You don't need to do that, Joe." She finds a couple earplugs. "I'll probably be able to sleep if you all don't watch TV or do a lot of yelling."

"Your things dry enough?" Barry asks Joe.

"I've wore them wetter." He grabs a shirt and goes into the bathroom.

"Sweet guy," Hope says.

"I can go also. Or, stay here with you, whichever you prefer."

"Go. Please. I shouldn't sleep too long. Maybe check back in an hour?"

Barry moves closer and gently places his hand on her forehead. "You might have a fever. Want me to find a thermometer?"

"God no. I should take something for pain, however. Would you mind getting a small metal box out of my bag?"

He hands her the box and her water bottle. She gives him a little smile when she opens the box. She removes two gummy bears, one red and one blue, and offers one to Barry.

"Would you like one?"

"Thanks, but I don't care much for candy."

"It is sweet, but it is not candy." She pops the blue one into her mouth and keeps the red one hovering over the open tin box. "Last offer. It is medicine, good for what ails you, believe me. You have any ailments? Aches? Pains? Anxieties?"

"Is this something legal?"

"Absolutely. Take it with you and do some research if you want. 'Peaceful Putty,' a fabulous fantasy for what ails you."

"Oh, I get it now. Drugs." He takes the edible and examines the happy little red bear in which it is shaped. "Been a long time for me. Maybe save it for a glum, rainy day."

"Suit yourself. I just think you might like it. Thanks for helping me."

Barry thinks this is a hint for him to step away and let her rest, but he has something else on his mind.

"Do you live alone, Hope?"

"Yep."

Barry takes a deep breath and dives in. "I live in a pretty big house in the country with a lot of rooms. It is nice. You'd love it. Why don't you think about living with me? It's beautiful. I have wi-fi. You can work remote maybe. If we get on the internet, I can show you some pictures...You'll have your own room, of course."

"Just when I am starting to like you, you start in with stupid shit like that."

"We haven't thought it through yet, sure. I'm just asking you to keep it in mind."

Joe emerges from the bathroom. "I'll be going now. Can I get either of you anything while I'm out?"

"I'll be fine," Hope says.

"I'm going too. We can let her sleep for about an hour, then see what she wants to do."

The two men, one black and one white, one poor and one rich, stare down at her both eager to please and help her do whatever she wishes. Would she like to live in a white palace?

Hope feels, for just a second, a bit like a princess or wise queen. Her wish their command. She had not been in that role since a little girl. For just two seconds, she is back in someone's barn playing "pretend." The other kids soon tired of being obedient servants to her royal will, but she'd had a ball while it lasted.

"You have my permission to leave," she tells her current servants with a regal wave. "Bye-bye, boys!"

As the door closes behind them, Hope lets loose a huge sigh of relief. *'Men! Even when as nice and good as they can be—completely insufferable.'* She keeps thinking about this kind but weird white man. His invitation about a "pretty big house" sounded serious. Maybe he really did have a lot of money. She cannot help wondering what she might do if she had some of it. She thinks about checking her list of the dozen or so deserving organizations she knows can benefit from the generosity of a mysterious philanthropist. But her eyes are too heavy to go to work now.

As she drifts to sleep, her partially dreaming mind takes her back to "Barn Theater" where once the ten-year old version of herself held court. She rules, among other edicts, that the neighborhood boys in the role of "Black Knights" wage a holy war for the liberation of all the people in the kingdom. The boys, all too eager to maim and kill white bankers and landlords, had to be guided toward more peaceful revolutionary means.

Hope wonders what she would do if she had a billion dollars. She can think of twenty non-profits that could transform a community with just a million dollars each. When she realizes her reverie is fantasizing about city, county, state, and federal reparations that at least try to heal the racial wounds of her culture, Hope allows herself to ease into a type of narcotic balm and molecular peace.

She feels as if this near oblivion might be what death could very well be like for her. In a way, she could see how she might welcome it. When her Time came, she imagines liking it. But *'Not today,'* she thinks. *'Not today.'*

Hope sleeps.

CHAPTER SIX

Barry and Joe, two quite different men, begin their elevator descent in silence. Before coming to a stop, Joe feels bold enough to say what is on his mind.

"You know that gal is too young for you, don't you?"

"Is she?" Barry says after a beat or two. "I know there are many years between us, but in some strange way she seems way older, or at least wiser than I am. Not too young for me, but I may be too old for her."

"I can't tell you what to do but you got three strikes already. One, you're too old. Two, you're white. Three—shit, I forget what three is."

The elevator stops and the doors open waiting for them to step out. "I know what three is: she just doesn't like me that much."

"I don't know about that," Joe says. "Three has to do with her disability. She can tell you feel sorry for her and she don't like that."

They step through the doorway before it closes on them.

"I'm not too sure about that," Barry says. "What I feel for her is compassion, not pity. Is it so bad to want to help somebody?"

"I appreciate you helping me. Getting clean, resting on a nice bed, staying cool on a hot day—those are things I like and need. But there is something about do-gooders that can stick in your craw. Seeing you be—oh, I don't know, just so nice to Hope, so nice to me—it is as if someone is standing over me with a big mirror. I keep looking at myself through what seems like your eyes and the message I keep getting is—*'I ain't sufficient. I'm hopeless, dirty, worthless, so pitiful someone has to be taking care of me like this.'*"

Barry finds this observation quite impressive. "Yes. I see how you and Hope might see things like that. For what it is worth, I make a deliberate effort not to be judgmental about you or your circumstances. I often find myself in a position of either doing nothing or doing something that might help. From what you are saying, I might be resented either way. Guess I prefer to do too much than too little." He notices Elaine by the ballroom door staring at him. "I should have a word with that woman. Everyone will be wondering what happened to Hope and me. You can wait for me if you want the company or just go on your way."

Joe decides to just stand still while he thinks about it. Barry nods and approaches Elaine.

"Where have you have been? Where's Hope? You just disappeared."

"Hope is fine. She's exhausted. I got her a room, Number 417, if you'd like to check on her in an hour or so. It's actually my friend Joe's room." He waves at Joe still waiting across the room.

"You should have told someone. Anton is in quite the state. You and Hope have thrown him off his game plan."

"Oh?"

"I'm just here to help the workshop go smoothly. I'm not supposed to comment on any participant's issues or material."

"Fine with me, but you're the one brought it up."

"The success of the seminar depends upon everyone's commitment to participate. You just cannot come in late or attend only some of the sessions. It is a serious disruption."

"I understand. Barring another psychological or physical emergency, I will do my best to be a better attendee."

"Anton will probably be talking to you some more about this." She starts to open the door. "Go on in. There are a couple empty seats on the back row."

Barry looks back to see Joe standing in the same spot. "Um, sorry Elaine. I should probably finish up with Joe there."

"Oh, for God sakes. I don't really care. I just work here. However, Anton may very well kick you out if there is another incident."

"I'm still on strike two, then. One more and I'm out, maybe." He turns to go. "You are really exceptionally good at this stuff, Elaine. If a rating system is in place, I will give you five stars!"

His ebullience in delivering this message makes her smile and laugh slightly. '*What a nut,*' she thinks.

"You been a bad boy?" Joe says when Barry gets nearby.

"Could you hear that from here? You must have rather good hearing."

"I couldn't hear the words, but I know a good tongue-lashing when I see it. I also know how to read lips."

"Besides worrying that I may have kidnapped Hope, they don't like me skipping class so much. I probably should get back in there."

"I'm going to walk around and maybe spend a little more of your money. You want me to find you before I go up to the room?"

"Probably a good idea. Thanks!"

Barry disappears into the ballroom.

Joe throws a cheerful wave to Malcolm as he leaves the hotel. He looks up and down New Jersey Avenue as if seeing the street for the first time. He spent his entire life in DC. Yet, for too many years now, the only places he goes to are homeless shelters, soup kitchens, and places to panhandle.

With more money in his pocket than he'd seen all year, what can he do? He tries remembering the last time he had gone to a movie but has no idea in which direction to go. Standing frozen in one spot, his legs begin to shake. He investigates the faces of the people walking back and forth for hints about whether this person or that person would be willing to help him.

This kind of surveillance is what Joe does every day, but today it is not about the money. As he often finds himself doing while sitting at his spot hoping for change, Joe imagines what this white lady in a pink dress might be doing today, where this group of high school students have been on their school field trip, or what business anybody has strolling past the hotel.

But he does not feel the need to be so selective. He spots a dashing young white guy in an expensive suit and red power tie walk fast toward him. Such a person usually projects the message, '*Don't bother me! I'm on an important mission.*'

"Excuse me, sir," Joe says politely. He steps directly into the man's path. The well-dressed pedestrian makes a step to his left but Joe again moves in front of him. "Can I ask you a question?"

"No, you can't!" the suit says rudely and cruelly. With unintended malice, he knocks Joe to the ground and rushes onward. Joe rests on the sidewalk.

The nearby hotel doorman takes a step and helps Joe stand. "You okay?"

"Yeah, nothing hurt but my pride. I don't have much use for that anyway."

"I see that guy go by almost every day. You want to press charges? I'll testify it looked like assault to me. There's also a surveillance video." He points to the camera mounted near the door.

"That's okay, brother." The two Black men, one maybe thirty or forty years older than the other, exchange a friendly fist bump. "I ain't hurt too bad." He rubs his shoulder to make sure. "Thanks, though."

"This is not a good place for soliciting. Part of my job is to make sure there's no panhandling in front of the hotel. I need to ask you to find another spot. Sorry." He points down the street toward where Joe usually sets up.

"I'm not begging. I just wanted to ask that guy if he knew where a movie theater was. I'm actually a guest at this hotel."

"You're a guest?" The doorman takes another look at Joe's shabby attire still wet from the hand wash. Joe shows him the key card. "My apologies, sir. What room are you in?"

"417."

The doorman taps a small tablet. "May I have your name, please?"

"Joe Smith."

"Very good, sir. Aside from being knocked to the ground and asked by a staff member to move along to a less nice part of town, I hope you are enjoying your stay. Anything else I can help you with? My name is Elliott, by the way. You can usually find me here or somewhere in the hotel. Other staff won't mind helping you look for me."

"Hey, Elliott! Fantastic. Any movie theaters within walking distance? Also, a place to get some new duds. These about wore out."

"There are a bunch of places you can spend a lot of money for clothing, but where I'd go is the Goodwill on South Dakota Avenue."

"I know where that is. Kind of far. Guess I could take a bus..."

"Sure can. There's a stop down the street. Take D6 for about ten minutes, at D and 15th Street. It's about a minute down 15th to a stop at Isherwood..."

"Wait a minute, wait a minute..."

"Don't worry! You got this—the B2 takes you to South Dakota."

"Uh, okay, okay."

"The drivers will help you, man. Don't worry. Take D6 to B2. Unless they are a real jerk, they won't mind if you just ask where the Goodwill is. If you get in a jam, just tell them you know Elliott, the doorman at The Regency on Capitol Hill."

Elliott back peddles through the front doors. "I got a lot of friends in town. You'd be surprised!"

Joe watches Elliott disappear through the door, a huge grin on his face.

The reaction a little slow, he mutters, "Wait. Where's a movie theater?"

He thinks about asking another passerby but then remembers something and laughs to himself. Joe strolls into the lobby with a bit of a bounce to his step. He spots the doorman talking to the desk clerk. Had he once known his name? Malcolm! He gives himself a virtual pat on the back for remembering.

Elliott says to Malcolm. "Look who's coming, Malcolm! I believe it is our old friend, Joe! Joe Smith. Welcome back to the Regency, Joe."

"Everything satisfactory, Mr. Smith?" Malcolm asks.

"Indeed, it is, Malcolm! Elliott has been most helpful. I meant to thank you for coming to my rescue out there, Elliott."

"Glad to be of service, Mr. Smith!" he says smartly clicking his heels.

"Maybe you gentlemen could direct me to the nearest movie theater? Plenty of good movies on the big TV up in my room, but I feel like sitting in a cool theater with a bunch of other people all laughing or crying at the same time."

"Oh, I am sorry, Joe. I plumb forgot to tell you!"

"Be prepared, Joe! At this time of day, you may well be the only person watching the movie—if they're even open."

"Good point," Elliott adds. "Malcolm, why don't you see what the Miracle is showing today?"

Malcolm scrolls his phone. "Yes, the Miracle is the theater

I'd recommend. It shows older and more interesting movies than a lot of the other places."

"And closer too!" Elliott says with a smile. "Malcolm told me some white man is paying for your room?"

"Don't ask me why. I came into his life at the very moment he needed to do something nice for somebody. Lucky me!"

"I'll say. I'd like to meet someone like that."

"Oh, that reminds me of the other reason I wanted to see you. I'd like to share some of the luck."

Joe places a folded five-spot into Elliott's coat pocket.

"No, Joe. You don't have to do that. Thank you, but I'm doing fine."

He tries to give it back, but Joe won't let him.

Malcolm shares the news that a Cary Grant movie begins in about thirty minutes. The two staff members agree it is probably a ten-minute walk. Tickets are five dollars. No other movie watchers now but there are usually around 15-20 regulars.

Joe, uncertain, stares at them. Elliott fetches the $5 out of his own pocket and hands it back to him. "Go! Watch it on me! Seriously. We need to keep passing the money around. Giving it when we can, taking it when we have to."

Joe likes the astonishment on Malcolm's face to see the doorman be so generous and decides to take it.

"Thank you, Elliott. Thank you both. You inspire me to be a better person."

CHAPTER SEVEN

Back at the seminar Barry tries to focus on the demonstration of counseling techniques. His attention, however, is drawn to his new and maybe only friends today, Hope and Joe.

He knows, absolutely *knows*, that reality is not all about him, Barry Strange, Interstellar Celebrity indeed. It is not his job to try to fix every problem. Not every person needs to be a fan, he often reminds himself. He does not feel as if he were capable of "saving" either one of them, even if he wanted to.

Maybe the workshop is partly responsible for opening him up in a way that had him stop and talk to a homeless man and care disproportionately about a disabled Black woman. Barry is enjoying himself and grateful for an opportunity to extend a helping hand, especially to Hope. Despite some words to the contrary, she likes his attention. There definitely is something going on between the two of them—a molecular spirituality and vibrational chemistry well worth exploration.

Barry does not know why but he knows he tends to go overboard and obsess about another person's personal issues and material. That was at the top of the list passed around social media that went on to become part of the non-compulsory court order. The "50 Things We Don't Like About Barry Strange" petition became a viral sensation.

His former friend, John, explained this thread as a type of "ironic joke" because everybody *liked* him. *Sure*. Since there was nothing in him anyone could dislike (John said), people began to just make up stuff. True, some of it was disgusting! But it really got out of hand when Barry inserted himself into the thread and tried to charm his way into being '*Liked*.'

The usual crazy shit, certainly.

But this thing with Hope is unusual, very much so. Okay, he can accept that she might never get excited about running her hands over his old, wrinkly, white skin. Of course, he had been infatuated and in love many times during the fifty-plus years of his adulthood. But nothing like this, nothing close to this palpable supercharged electric current that seems like love, seems like healing, seems like awareness, seems so real and near the very edge of enlightenment, if not enlightenment itself!

Barry is having a hard time concentrating on what is now happening at the workshop. Can he even care about the little anxieties of yet another privileged white person receiving Anton and the seminar's group attention. He worries more whether Hope and Joe will be okay. Are they lucky that he happens to care about them, or will it prove a huge mistake? It is true that both will almost certainly tire and then surely resent what Barry thinks of as Love and what they may experience as neurotic weirdness.

Such anxiety and the tell-tale signals of hunger and

light-headedness alert Barry to the need for a snack. When the time comes, he would be sure to suggest to the organizers that future seminars provide donuts or something for those with blood sugar issues. At the moment, he does not want to bolt out of the room and deal with another lecture from Elaine. He goes into a pocket and pulls out the gummy bear Hope gave him. Maybe that will do the trick. Barry figures he can handle any psychoactive reaction. Hmm, good! Raspberry!

Much as he had probed Barry, Anton up front continues to tackle the fears and concerns of a white suburban widow, mother, and grandmother by the name of Janice. From the vantage point of spectator this time, Barry can see Anton chip away at her defenses, her walls, to get at something underneath.

It seems a brave thing to go for. Whatever is holding Janice back, she is going to be strong and look at the clog in the stream of her spirit.

"Of course, we care," Anton says on behalf of all. He takes her hands into his and watches her face surrender all resistance. A dam bursts, the tears flow.

Unlike the emotional discharge of Barry and Hope, Janice's session before the attention of the entire group comes with a story. A bright little girl terrified by a mother, ignored by a father, abused by a brother, and left to flounder on her own in a school seemingly indifferent to students such as herself who were neither brilliant nor disruptive. Did she know what to do with her life when the nightmare sentence of childhood tension and educational torture was over? Of course not! Dear Janice becomes engaged to the first man who seems to want her—the first to want to have sex with her, the first to want her be on his support team, cook and clean for him, be the mother of his legacy...

Although certainly grateful at times, her two children from this union mostly grow up taking for granted all her sacrifices, all her time and energy—all her emotional, physical, and spiritual energy. And, in what seems no time at all, Janice then morphed into the role of doting grandmother to her children's children.

"You are one hell of a nurturer!" Anton manages to toss in.

"I sure as hell am!" Janice confesses with vehemence. Indeed, it had taken a bit of work to peel away decades of self-doubt for her to assert such self-appreciation. For a solid ten minutes, Anton insists that Janice "go over the top" and proclaim to everyone present a lengthy string of validations that she is "beautiful," "smart," "creative," "funny," "strong," "capable," (etc., etc.).

Janice resists each one of these suggestions, but Anton, God bless him, persists. He insists that she frame each of these declarations with a posture, facial expression, words, tone of voice and confidence that obviously contradicts her completely useless patterns of distress.

To counter sixty years or more of her telling herself she is not "worthy of love", Anton has her try out a few phrases until one arrangement or another hits pay dirt.

The tears wash away buried layers of grief, fear, and rage. Partitions, which hid and divided so many parts of herself, collapse.

And, yes, to her utter astonishment there is something very real down there; beneath all the muck, something quite powerful indeed, a quality of awareness and love that Anton suggests

Janice can label (if labels are needed).

"Inside you, inside every person in this room, and inside every damaged or blessed person on the planet is what, in the end, can be called... (wait for it) *a human being*." There follows a significant pause allowing everyone to take that in.

"And that's a good thing?" the familiar voice of Barry Strange, Famous Disturber of Pretense, pipes up. Although not meant to be humorous, the spontaneous questioning and questionable outburst from the back of the room gets a few laughs.

"Yes, it is a very good thing," Anton says with great seriousness. "It is no joke that too many of us do not see the goodness of our being, the power of our own mind, the potential within our very soul. If we can do anything to help each other get rid of the distress that blocks our vision and realization of who we really are, then we have taken one small step towards being a fulfilled evolved human being."

Anton, in a serene tone of voice, closes out the session with Janice and pronounces everyone free to spend the next ninety minutes as they please.

The church pals appear beside Barry as they leave the ballroom.

"That was amazing!" Jane says.

"Indeed," Barry agrees. "I don't know what the heck it was, but it was amazing." Ned and Fred, the two men, get a good laugh from this, but Barry is not sure why. If it were to encourage him to say more cutting remarks that might disparage the evolutionary work going on here, he is not taking the bait.

"You could have been a stand-up comedian," says the man, Fred.

"Oh, really..." Barry pauses in a way that has Fred thinking he is seriously considering a career in comedy.

"Of course, to make it you should have started hitting the comedy clubs about 35 years ago!" His pal Ned gets a big kick out of this remark. Barry exchanges looks with their wives, Jane and Mary. They seem to share Barry's momentary bewilderment. Barry is not being a comedian here. He is not on stage. Life is not a joke.

Although he should just shut up and ignore them, Barry thinks he can say this... "If what I say is *funny* and if people actually laugh at what I say or do, what difference would it make how old I am?"

Ned and Fred exchange a look of bewilderment themselves, then burst out laughing.

Between sputtering spurts of laughs and giggles, Ned manages to convey what he deeply feels to be hilarious. "Depends... on the...material...hee, hee, hee."

Suddenly, Barry feels as if the floor beneath his feet is rocking back and forth. The earth is tilting on its axis. The walls of the building become transparent. The electrons, the waves of energy, or whatever they are, swirl into and out of everyone and pass through every object in the room until there is no division to anything. Everything is flowing in and everything is flowing out.

Hope's little edible gummy is kicking in—big time.

"If you'll excuse me, I need to get something to eat," Barry manages to say. "My blood sugar is running low."

"Come eat with us!" Ned bellows. "I could use some more laughs." Barry looks a little more closely at *Overfed Ned*. Yes, this is something new! Barry can somehow *see* vibrating threads of energy flow in and out of the formation of Ned's own vibrating accumulation of energy, *i.e.,* Ned's body! And there, in the lower right part of his abdomen, is what seems a tangled skein of slow-flowing energy rolled into a brown ball. Shit! Is that a tumor? A nearly round ball of fear? The way this bundle of nerves loosens a little each time Ned laughs reminds Barry of the heavy, gut-wrenching laughter and tremors during his recent sessions with Anton and Hope. Is a huge lump of fear seemingly dissolved by such discharge? If Ned and Fred or anyone else, can laugh their way to liberation, why wouldn't he want to help them?

"Some other time," Barry says barely managing to stay on his feet. "I want to check on our friend, Hope. She was exhausted earlier and needed to rest." He also wants to find out what was in that gummy.

"Poor dear," Jane says kindly. "Such a hard life! But she has really accomplished so much despite it all."

"Is that so?" Barry perks up. "She didn't have much to say during our session."

"We had quite the good chat. I should probably keep to myself the more personal stuff, but she may not mind me bragging on her behalf. Did you know she is a lawyer high up on the chain of the Civil Rights Commission? She helps with disability issues, especially those of minorities. An incredible career. You can Google her."

"I will!" Barry says with enthusiasm. "Soon as I find out her last name."

"I know what it is, but I'll let her tell you yourself. Just in case you intend to stalk her."

"I would never do that," he says.

Jane puts a reassuring hand to his arm. "I know that, Sugar."

Ned gives Barry a comical stare. "Don't be so sure, Jane. You never know about these old white men!"

"You're quite right, Ned. We don't." Barry tries to smile at everyone. Without thinking, however, he gives Ned a playful poke at the precise spot of the tangled energy in the lower right abdomen. It does not hurt but sure surprises him. A hot shot of something catches a *Shakti* spear of energy that shoots up his spine and out the crown of Ned's head.

"What the..." Ned's first inclination is to panic. Is he having a stroke? Had Barry stabbed him? But a strong, reassuring feeling of peace suddenly stops all worry. It is a feeling that sometime comes over him in church during a meditation or hymn. He feels wonderful.

Under the influence of Hope's magical gummy, Ned, jolly rotund white Ned, husband of the Black artist Jane and friend to Fred and Mary; dear Ned, with such an urgency to jettison the lump of fear deep within, becomes a ball of energetic threads. In just one inexplicable instant, Barry suddenly *sees* the flow of energy which is Ned and the blockage of energy which needed but a slight push to get moving again.

"I will see you all later," Barry says. "Have a good dinner."

He walks away grateful at last not to hear someone laughing at what he says or does.

By the time Barry reaches the door to the street, he is in full emotional panic. He has to get away. This medicine is way too much. The confidence learned from others, what courage and will he was able to gather; the power of love to ease pain—these had inexplicably vanished. What the hell happened? Had the edible triggered a full-fledged acid flashback? And did he really punch someone in the stomach?

"When the vibes start vibrating, man? Just sit back and watch...". Thus, sayeth his college friend, Hosa, AKA "The Legend." He, the wise bearded mentor on all matters psychedelic, guided Barry and others on trips to Fantasia where one experienced colorful "hullabullutions," very much like what he just experienced with Ned.

He remembers tripping in a UVA dorm watching the grain of wood on a chest of drawers shimmer and flow into a 3"x 8" image that incredibly turns into an animated cartoon of the word *LOVE* while listening to a song by the band, "Spirit." On this occasion, the twenty-year-old version of Barry stared at his roommate's girlfriend and saw streams of purple flow into and out of her purple sweater. When she shook her head, blond streams of light sailed across the room far beyond where the tips ended.

No one had a body. Multi-color threads of light went into and flowed out of slower moving accumulations of the same energy that did not stop at the end of a hair, the tips of fingers, or the cluster of hues which everyone thinks of as clothes. People were not things! Things were not things! Everything was energy that flowed into and out of everything.

Despite several additional trips, Barry never again had one that was quite as intense. Until today.

Outside on the street, the hallucinations continue. He watches the stream of vibrational energy flow up and down New Jersey Avenue. The too-too solid edifice of the Regency Hotel sways backward and forward and from side to side as if blowing in the wind. He follows a stream of yellow light fly off the roof of a cab and melt into the gray façade of a bank. Barry drops to his knees and prays.

'Dear Mother of God and all that is holy, be with us now and at the hour of our deaths...'

"Are you alright, sir?" a hand sits lightly on his shoulder. Barry looks up into the face of a kind Black man in the costume of a hotel doorman. A badge on his lapel displays the word, "ELLIOTT."

"I am just saying a little prayer." Barry lets the young man help him stand. "I wasn't praying out loud was I?"

"More like shouting..." Elliott informs him.

"Jesus..."

"Yes, praise be to Jesus and the Mother of God. I don't mind you praying, sir. But you look a bit in distress." A few people almost crash into them. "Let's stand over here. Folks in such a hurry on this sidewalk. They may not notice someone has stopped to talk to the Lord and could run right over you."

"Thank you. Everything..." Barry pauses to look up into the sky and sees huge thunderheads about to collide and bring on the end of the world. "Everything is just so overwhelming. Do those clouds look like Armageddon to you?"

"Uh, no. Looks like we might get a thunderstorm though. Can I look at your eyes for a second? You on medication?"

"My girlfriend gave me a little red gummy bear called something—'Peace Putty', I think it was."

"Jesus! What milligram?" Barry shrugs helplessly. "You ever take edibles before?"

"Oh, I take edibles every day," Barry says brightly. "Breakfast, lunch, and dinner. Snack time also."

"I mean edible cannabis or psilocybin, dude! It can hit you hard if you're not used to it. I saw you come out of the hotel. Are you a guest?"

"Yes, I am! Well, sort of. I'm renting room 417 until Monday."

"417? You the one paying the room for Joe, that homeless guy?" He pulls out and taps on his little tablet. "Your name?"

Barry grabs his hand. "Barry Strange, a famous and fabulous person in my own mind. Yes, I offered Joe a posh sanctuary for a couple days. Not much help in the long run, but maybe something."

"And there is another person also staying in the room, someone named Hope?"

"Yes, that's right! She's just taking a nap. She's my girlfriend, only she doesn't know it yet. I'm totally in love with her, Elliott. She's confined to a wheelchair and maybe thirty or forty years younger than me—hard to tell with some people. But God help me, she is so smart and a beautiful, beautiful Black woman to boot."

"Uh-huh. Man, this is some messed up shit. This is what you should do—go up to Room 417 and have a little talk with this Black girl. You need to find out why she gave you an edible like that, you an old fucker! She trying to knock you off by bringing on a heart attack or stroke?"

"Oh, I don't think so."

"It's not my business but you seem too high and crazy to be on the street right now. Head up to your room, now! Go on!

You might need to lie down and just chill 'til you come off the ledge."

"Ledge?"

"You know what I mean. You want me to go with you?"

"No, I can handle it. I probably should get something to eat though." Barry looks up and down the street as if in search of a restaurant.

"You with those seminar people? I heard they got some food set out for you in the ballroom."

"Good idea, Elliott! Thank you so much. You have been a great help. Who knows? You may have saved a man's life today." He put a hundred-dollar bill in Elliott's hand while shaking it. "Barry Strange, Famous Crazy Man."

Barry turns and heads back inside singing a little song...

Too high and crazy
Too old and lazy
The path forward hazy
When all hope is gone

Feeling a little less wrecked, Barry surveys the lobby. The quantum field between objects and humans still shimmer with both high and low frequency waves but he no longer feels as if his body and all the bodies around him were about to dissolve and merge with the cosmos. There were a few familiar faces from the seminar chatting with each other, but he is not eager to engage. God knows what nonsense he would feel obliged to share.

He marches up to his old friend, Malcolm, behind the front desk.

"Malcolm!" he says brightly in a tone he hopes is not too cheery. "Barry Strange, Famous Pain in the Ass."

"Yes, Mr. Strange. Your fame precedes you. How may I be of service?"

"Any word from our friend, Hope, resting in Room 417?"

"Not a peep, sir. Have also not seen or heard from your other friend, Mr. Smith, since the two of you came out the elevator a while ago."

"Been an hour, maybe ten, has it? Can I ask your opinion about something?"

"Certainly."

"I'd like to check on Hope but am undecided how to proceed. Should I jar her awake with a phone call from here or better to startle her by going to the room? And, if I go to her room, should I use the key I have or perhaps knock?"

Malcolm stares at the strange man in front of him. Little sparks seem to shoot out from his eyes like pinwheel pyrotechnics. Is this old guy stoned?

"Not knowing either of you very well," he says calmly, "I am not sure I can say. She may be momentarily surprised no matter which course you take but, if you feel it is time for her to be aroused, I am inclined to suggest you call first."

"Excellent advice. May I use your phone?"

"You certainly may. But there are plenty of little nooks and crannies around here for more privacy, if you want to use your phone."

"I don't own a cellphone," Barry says picking up the desk receiver.

If one had been watching from a distance at that very

moment, they might have thought from the way Malcolm stands there, with his mouth wide open, that the sky had fallen. Suddenly, it occurs to him that he had never actually seen someone in this country without a personal phone. He certainly knows that millions of people all over the world do not have their own phone, but Malcolm had not, until that moment, met any white American over the age of 12 (much less someone this old and well off) who did not carry one.

"Just hit the room number?"

"Yes. You did this once already to call Joe." For a second Malcolm wonders what century this guy is from. He points to the small sign next to the phone:

TO REACH A GUEST: PRESS * then Room Number

As the phone rings for Room 417, Barry shoots Malcolm a jaunty '*thumbs up!*' Keeping one ear cocked towards the strange Mr. Strange, Malcolm taps something on the screen in front of him and a soothing game of solitaire beckons. Juanita, the new attractive young "*la doncella,*" as he likes to call her, gives him the eye along with a big smile as she walks by the desk.

"*Ole*, Juanita! *Como estas*?"

"*Tres bien, merci*, Monsieur Malcolm," Juanita teases.

"*Parlez-vous Francais, mademoiselle?*"

"*Oui, oui. Si, yes, Senor.*"

"Juanita!" he gestures for her to come near. "Have you ever seen anyone in America who did not have a phone? *Esta ahi, el Viejo no posee un telefono.*"

Juanita does not understand what Malcolm is trying to tell

her. It is obvious the old man, *el Viejo,* is holding a telephone. She mimes holding a phone to her ear. "Yes, he has phone," she says in English.

"*Si.* He has the hotel phone, but he does not own a *telefono movil!*" He smiles and laughs to let her know that this is funny, but she does not get it.

"No telephone mobile? *Por que?*"

"I don't know why he doesn't own a phone," he replies with rising irritation. "He just does. *Muy insolito,* very unusual."

"*O si, si. Hasta luego,* Malcolm!" She walks away confused what that is all about. Perhaps he makes fun of her? This is sad, especially since she is just starting to like him a little bit after he stopped teasing her about perhaps being undocumented.

"Thank you for the phone, Malcolm! And, for the advice!" Barry says hanging up.

"What advice?" he says sharply. He is feeling a bit thrown off by the brief exchange with Juanita. Unlike his previous impression of her, it seems she does not really like him at all. But then, such a conclusion is consistent with a depressingly persistent thread in his life since high school—no one really likes him anyhow, anywhere, anytime...

"You were quite right about calling first. It gives her time to get ready to rejoin the living without some old white guy hanging around in the room waiting for her."

"I am pleased it worked out," Malcolm says without an ounce of pleasure.

"Are you okay? You don't seem your usual chipper self." Thanks to Hope's medicine, Barry is still in a state of elation that leaves some room for empathy to others.

"Maybe you have some good advice for *me*. What do I do when it is obvious that everyone, especially girls I am interested in, just don't like me, that no one likes me?"

This question and the look of total sorrow on the young man's face nearly breaks Barry's heart but he manages to summon a few coherent words without breaking into tears.

"Oh, I have had that problem. And have that problem now, frankly. This has been my experience—often the feeling that no one likes you is just that, a *feeling*. You must face the possibility that what you are feeling is not the reality."

"And, if it is the reality, what do I do about that, *dickwad?*" Malcolm regrets the insult as soon as it is uttered. "Sorry about that. Saying what is on my mind is one of the reasons people do not like me."

"Oh, I have that problem, too," Barry says pleasantly. "But this is the real thing you need to keep in mind: no one, and I mean no one, is going to like you or love you until you learn to love yourself."

"Oh, brother. Go on up to 417 and annoy someone else for a while."

"That cute Mexican girl, she the one you're sweet on?" Malcolm pretends to ignore him. "My opinion, for what it's worth…" Barry went on.

'*Probably little…*' Malcolm thinks.

"You are going to have to take it slow. She must be cautious, for three reasons. One, you are co-workers. Two, you're white and probably a neurotic Americano. Three, you are male. Women need to trust a man before she can love him."

"Very good advice, Mr. Strange. I shall take it to heart," he says in that ultra-polite, fake solicitous tone of voice that the manager, Madame Kohl, had decided would make him the perfect front desk clerk. "And, for your information, she comes from Honduras, not Mexico."

"You sure? Her accent sounded more Mexican than Central American."

"There's a difference? Were you listening to our conversation? I was just joking with her, but I don't think she got it."

"There is usually something lost in either language or cultural differences. I would not worry about it, if I were you. I could tell by the tone of her voice that, for some reason, she thinks you are very cool. *Adios!*"

Barry turns and heads straight for the elevator. Malcolm turns to see someone at the other end of the desk impatiently waiting for his help. At the moment, it does not matter what grievance, if any, this person might hold. He likes believing in Mr. Strange's observation that Juanita thinks that he, Malcolm Strickland, is '*cool*.'

If possible to have a more thrilling elevator ride than the one he takes to the 4th floor, Barry cannot imagine it. Freed from the strain of trying to not sound insane in the short phone call to Hope and managing (he hoped) not to appear a blithering idiot while aiding Malcolm maneuver his dream of romance, Barry's drug-induced consciousness expands big-time as soon as the metal doors of the cab close.

The initial jolt of the lift literally shoots his awareness through the roof. The earth and all thoughts of everything vanish with a roar that becomes a yellowish vibrating band of energy hovering horizontally in front of him. Of ineluctable and utterly terrifying power, the vibration totally consumes him.

Barry Strange, Famous Nobody, is a goner about to be obliterated by the ultimate force of the universe which eventually takes all things living. Death. Here it is. *Oh, well. Omigod! So, this is what has happened to the billions of people before me and will happen to the billions after me...*

He can still feel his face, but it is as if it were coated by a thin veneer of clay that had hardened into a mask. As he "dies," the mask cracks open and falls away.

Although he is near certain that he must have died, he becomes aware that he continues to breathe deep, invigorating breaths. Breathing had never been so wonderful—in and out with such increasing strength and depth that he is breathing along with the planet, along with the sun and all the stars.

All restrictive bands break apart. Nothing of his little life, his little dreams and plans, thoughts and fears, desires and attachments, nothing which he thinks is his, remains. Yet, he still breathes and feels himself make profound connections that tie him into a type of web where appear the faces of every person he ever knew along with millions of faces he never knew personally, but now know and can see. All are connected.

This is good! All is good! All is God! All is Love and Joy!

A bell dings and stainless-steel doors open. A well-dressed couple in their 30s seem frozen in place looking at an old white man writhing on the floor of an elevator staring at the ceiling. The doors close. The bell rings again and the doors re-open. The couple see him sitting on the floor this time.

"You okay, mister?" the man asks.

Barry springs to his feet a little too quickly and they rush inside the car and grab him before he collapses. The doors close behind them.

"Never better actually!" Barry says. "Is this still the 21st Century? Planet Earth? This the 4th floor?"

He quickly pushes the 'Door Open' button and with a jaunty thumbs up, exits.

Barry walks slowly down the hall to catch his breath. So far, he has to admit, he is having fun! It is not every day that a person can become One with the universe.

CHAPTER EIGHT

Barry Strange walks down a corridor suddenly forgetting where he is going or why. Every ten feet or so is an unmarked door. Maybe he should be going in the opposite direction? More unmarked doors—no sound, no whirr of machinery or indication of activity from within. He stops before one of the doors and contemplates knocking or just entering.

What would he say if someone was there? No one could advise him of his purpose for being in this hallway, his purpose for being aware and alive. To ask some complete stranger—"Do you know what I am doing here?"—seems preposterous. Yet perhaps someone on the other side of the door can inform him of the nature of these premises, where he is or how he belongs in the grand scheme of things.

He knocks three times at one of the non-descript doors. There's no answer. He pulls down the handle and enters the unlocked space. There is another corridor that stretches before him an enormous distance. On both sides of this passage are hundreds of doors identical to the one he opened. A little scared now, he opens a dozen or more doors each one an entrance to hallways with hundreds, maybe thousands, maybe an infinite number of doors...

Barry sits on the floor wondering what could have happened. Has he died? A memory surfaces of himself writhing on the floor of an elevator. He was on his way to see someone—someone he liked very much. Hope is her name! The number 417 seems important!

He runs along a hallway keeping the number 417 in the forefront of consciousness. He checks out one door after another, some madness or his own imagination telling him he might see the number appear. Some smudges on the passing doors try to assume the shapes of numbers. After hundreds if not thousands of indecipherable markings, real numbers appear—some now in the 400s!

He stands in front of a doorway marked 'Room 417.' Barry counts to 10, and knocks.

"Come in!" he hears a woman yell. He recognizes the voice.

He feels lucky indeed to discover a hotel key card in one of his pockets. He feels very lucky indeed to happen to know exactly what that is. He inserts the card and opens the door.

A woman he knows is called Hope looks calm and content sitting up in bed reading Gideon's Bible. She smiles as he walks quietly closer and does not resist when he holds her hand.

"How are you feeling? Were you able to rest peacefully?" He himself feels as if what flows from his voice is a peace that passes all understanding.

"Yes! Fell right to sleep after you and Joe left. I was dead to the world until you called. Where's Joe?"

"I don't know." It all comes back to him. "I sat in on a seminar session. I think he said he was going shopping. Oh, shit! I was going to bring you a sandwich but got to talking and forgot. Let me go back down or call room service to get something."

She grabs his hand. "That's okay. You don't have to. I always keep some food in my bag. Are you hungry? Want a power bar?" He nods and quietly wolves down his bar while she nibbles hers. "You seem different. Not so crazy."

"That's weird. Don't think I ever felt as crazy as I'm feeling right now." He crosses his hands in front of his chest and spreads them out as far as they will go in what he hopes conveys the oneness and immensity of the universe.

"Oh, you had your little gummy bear, didn't you? How was it?"

"How is it, you mean. Tis with me still. You didn't warn me it would take me to the edge of the cosmos and back. Almost didn't come back. Quite the trip."

"The medicine affects everyone differently. It can be especially powerful if you're not used to it. Not sure why I gave it to you in the first place. I would not have thought I liked you that much. Hey, I didn't give you the red one, did I?" She looks into her tin box of meds "Oh, shit, shit, SHIT! I been saving that one for when I'm ready to permanently check myself out." Hope furiously pounds the bed with her fist.

Barry grabs her hand. "It's okay, Hope. I felt as if I died alright but, hooray! I came back. That's not *why* you're mad, is it?"

Hope laughs at this but is still upset. "They say it is a good way to die. But you didn't die so I guess it doesn't work as well as they say."

Wondering about the best way to handle this, Barry sits

quietly holding her hand. "Maybe I did die, for real. Kind of hard to tell though. It would be a relatively good way to go, if that's any consolation. I sort of met God and, in a way, saw All That Is! If indeed the Afterlife is anything like the Oneness, the Beauty, and the Love I experienced during my ride up on the elevator we got nothing to worry about when our time comes. I saw pathways that went in a million directions but had no idea why. I guess, in my case, my time had not yet come. Or maybe it did." He gives her hand a squeeze. "We still got more to do."

"What you mean, '*we*,' white man!" Hope yanks her hand out of his.

"Sorry. Tell me, is me being white a deal-breaker for you?" Barry asks in a serious tone.

"You never heard that joke about the Lone Ranger and Tonto?"

"Huh?"

"Lone Ranger and Tonto are riding along when they become surrounded by hundreds of Indians on the warpath. Lone Ranger says, 'We heap big trouble, Tonto!' Tonto says, 'What's this *we* shit, white man?" The pidgin language and con-descending tone of voice Hope assumes for the white man and the urban black tone for the Indian is especially amusing. They both enjoy a good laugh, the hilarity no doubt enhanced by the residual effects of substances they had separately ingested.

"I'm surprised you even know who Tonto and the Lone Ranger are," Barry says when the laughter subsides. "I used to watch it. You weren't even born when they were on TV."

"Someone did have to explain it the first time I heard the joke." She taps away on her smartphone. "The last show was in

1957! That was 70 years ago. You must be really old!"

"Let's change the subject, please. They are taking a break now. You want to re-join the workshop when they resume at seven? Anton says there is going to be a variety show, starring us. You got a song or maybe a short stand-up routine?"

"Stand-up? That's very not-funny. But I do want to dance!" she says.

Barry pauses. "Okay. Sure..."

"You helped me walk earlier, Barry!" She grabs both his hands, her eyes ablaze from the medicine and a fervor overtaking her. "I know you can do it again. Help me, Barry, please!"

"Oh, Hope. Dear, dear Hope. I wish I could." She begins to cry, slowly at first, then building to a deluge of tears. "I have no idea what in heaven's name happened earlier. You were crying and shaking, we were holding hands. Then, suddenly, you walked."

Hope grabs Barry's hands and desperately holds on like a person about to go under and drown. Too worked up to notice anything beyond her own panic and despair, there is no hint of the powerful vibrations that earlier fired up her nerves and animated her legs and feet. For Barry's part, he feels unable to summon the calm, peaceful sense of attention and presence which mysteriously appeared and passed between them both during the seminar session.

There seems an awkwardness to the way his arms must cross his body while he holds her hands and sits in the chair. Although only room enough for half his butt, he moves onto the bed beside her and their upper bodies embrace. What patterns each of them project to maintain separateness and distance dissolves.

Resistance becomes futile. His seventy-plus years of unre-quited love and emotional baggage finds a way to merge with her tangled forty-plus years of grief and fear, hope and desire. It is not so much a physical attraction as an exchange of electri-cal energy. He flows into her; she flows into him. It is beyond description, beyond what either of them have ever previously experienced.

So intense and involved they both are with this embrace, neither hear a soft knocking at the door. They do not hear the click of a lock being released and a door opening. But they do hear a person entering.

"Oops! Sorry!" the person says. They disengage and turn surprised to see Joe with his mouth open in astonishment. He turns quickly and leaves the room. Barry and Hope exchange a look in silence.

"Go get him!" Hope shouts. Barry rushes and opens the door. Joe, shaken, is leaning against a wall.

"Sorry, Barry! I knocked! I didn't think anyone was here. I am so sorry..." Barry puts his arm around him.

"It is okay! You aren't interrupting anything. Come on in." A bit sheepish and reluctant, Joe must be pushed inside.

"Joe!" Hope cries. "You look fantastic. Nice haircut! And a shave? You get new clothes too?"

"Sure did. Got some others in the bag. Maybe put them in the closet?" Barry shrugs. Joe throws the bag beneath a row of hangers.

"Make yourself at home, if you're still wanting to stay here a couple days," Barry says.

"You might want to use the hangers and the drawers to keep them from getting wrinkled," Hope suggests.

"I ain't worried about wrinkled clothes since, well, never. But might as well." A bit self-conscious, Joe hangs a couple shirts that suddenly feel way too flashy for him. He stores a folded pair of pants, a sweater, socks, and underwear.

"You got some nice-looking clothes there, Joe," Barry says.

"Yeah, thanks to you and your money."

"Not my money. Never was. It is yours and millions of other people who played the lottery."

"You got rich playing the lottery?" Barry nods. "Well, I'll be..."

No further words from Joe are forthcoming and Barry takes the opportunity to reassure him that he can do whatever he wants with the money.

Joe opens another smaller bag he has with him. "I picked up a couple sandwiches while I was out. Got a meatball for me and thought you might like a veggie, Hope." He pauses with a stricken look on his face. "Not sure why I didn't get one for you, Barry. Crossed my mind for a second. Sorry. Guess I thought you'd be busy with the seminar. But you can have half of mine." He pulls out two foot-long submarines.

"Good God, those things are huge!" Hope says laughing. "Take half of mine, Barry. I could never eat all that."

Hope, still sitting up in bed, lets these two men get drinks from the mini-bar and lay out the sandwiches and other snacks. She sees their ministrations and attention to her every whim or need not as pity but kindness. While they munch away, she is thoroughly entertained by jokes, anecdotes, and quirky tales from their lives.

Joe, somewhere in age between she and Barry, never lived outside D.C. city limits. He seldom stepped or rode out of his childhood neighborhood, Anacostia, and claimed to have never seen more than one or two white people until the age of ten when his father took him and his older brother, Frank, on a bus to see one of the last baseball games played by the Washington Senators before they moved to Texas.

"I never knew there were that many white people!" Joe tells them. "I heard about them, of course. Kids in school were always talking about them, sharing the terrifying things they would say or do. My Mama wouldn't let anybody mention them in the house. They upset her too much. We were probably the only people on our block who didn't have a TV for the same reason. I never found out if it was something horrible some white man did to her or what.

"I had never seen anything but neighborhood baseball games. To see and hear thousands of people watching that game against the Tigers was the most thrilling thing that ever happened to me. I was interested in the game itself, of course. But I also couldn't help staring at all the white people sitting all around me. One little white girl about my age in a pink dress seemed so pretty I couldn't stand it. My eyes were so glued to her, her dad, I guess it was, had enough and told me and my father that if I didn't stop looking at her, he was going to smash my 'black face' and called all three of us what we now think of as 'the N-word.'"

"Jesus, Joe," Barry says with true sorrow. "I am so sorry that happened to you. What did your father do?"

Joe struggles to answer. "I now understand why, but I'm sad

to say he didn't say or do anything until the white man left us alone. But then, he did something I never forgot. He grabbed me by my shoulders and yelled and shook me like I was a rag doll, as if it was all my fault. It hurt so much, I cried, which made him even angrier.

"I was in terrible pain for the rest of the game but never said a word during the bus ride home. I told Mama I didn't want dinner and tried sleeping but my shoulder hurt too bad. After several days, she noticed, and I ended up in the ER where they tried fixing a fractured collarbone."

"They *tried* fixing it?" Hope says.

After Joe describes, in excruciating detail, how an orthopedic intern seemed to take a kind of sadistic pleasure in re-breaking and setting the bone without anesthetic, he pulls down his shirt to show them the malformed handiwork and finishes up with a few light-hearted accounts about how his clavicle predicts rain.

"Good story, Joe," Barry says. Hope has a more compassionate response. To lighten the mood, she relates a couple humorous stories from her childhood.

Barry listens, smiles, and nods at what she has to say but is feeling somewhat disturbed by Joe's childhood experience. He struggles with a slight pull of resentment that feels a bit ancient in origin, a childhood grievance of his own, perhaps? '*Yes, there it is,*' he thinks and finds himself, at a young age standing alone beside a creek in the park!

He sees it all very clearly now. His father, his whole family, had inexplicably abandoned him after a picnic. While Dad, Mom, brother, and sister pack up the food, the drinks, the toys and books and games, young seven-year-old Barry ducks behind some bushes to pee. He hears the car doors slam, the engine start. His father, as always, would be impatient to go, but the youngest member of the family cannot loosen the zipper on his shorts. He doesn't think to cry out, even as he hears the station wagon spray gravel as it tears away.

An overwhelming sadness hit him as he returned to the picnic table by the creek. Was he being punished by irate parents? No, he was merely overlooked and forgotten and assumed to be lying down in his usual spot among all the supplies in the cargo area, if he was thought about at all.

Later, when they realized Barry was not in the car, and after thirty awfully long minutes rushing back to the picnic area, they resumed the journey homeward. All but Barry seemed to enjoy the hilarity in replaying the incident and particularly that moment when they realized he was not in the car.

Brother and sister had sung a song and repeated a few riddles when Mom noticed the youngest was neither singing nor laughing. "You are awful quiet back there, Barry. Barry? Barry!!!"

For the rest of the ride home, Barry humored his family by smiling and trying out the role he would perfect in the many years to come. What would he be when he grew up? Why, be the person he imagined everyone wanted him to be, of course! The joker, the pleaser, the one who agreed, the one who could play the part of a lover, who could put on the mask of total enchantment and engagement, the one who could give and give and give, and who appeared to totally be there, but was nowhere in sight.

This event was a good sixty-five years in the past, but Barry still feels the terror of being abandoned forever. While his two new friends, Hope and Joe, are now chatting amiably about some of their favorite foods, Barry is presented with a stark image of a past he had not thought of in decades. He relives the relief of seeing his family return for him that quickly vanished when he recalled the shame and horror of his father verbally attacking him for not getting in the car in time. How dare he cause them so much worry! Dad's fury ceased the moment his wife yanked his arm and the little kid in front of him burst into tears, but some serious damage had already been done. He and Joe shared a remarkably similar traumatic experience.

Hope notices Barry's attention strays from a debate she and Joe are having on the best way to prepare collard greens.

"You don't have an opinion on collard greens, Whitey?"

"I like them okay. Is that an opinion?" he snaps. "I know you're just teasing, but I prefer not to be called 'Whitey.' You wouldn't like to be called, 'Blackey,' would you?"

"You'd find out how much I would not like it, if you did!" she says, her wrath quickly ignited.

Joe could see it is up to him to break the silence which follows. "You two lovebirds stop your bickering, now," he says. "We are having such a good time, why don't we play some cards?"

Barry stares at the clock near the bed. By force of will, he abandons his peevishness. "Cards would be fun, but I think the seminar will be starting up again soon. You up for that, Hope?"

"Sure, let's go. Been fun hanging out, Joe. Hope we can do it some more."

"More fun I've had since I don't know when. Don't know what I can do with myself now. Watch TV, maybe. Whenever I'd get free time seems like only thing I'd think to do is drink, if I could get hold of something. Somehow, I just don't feel like it now even if there were something in the minibar 'sides wine. Shoulda picked up some booze while I was out."

The three of them look at each other not quite knowing where to go from here.

"Come with us, Joe. I'll see if we can get you in the seminar," Barry says.

"Uh, I don't know..." Hope says almost to herself. "They probably don't want folks joining in the middle like that."

"That's okay," Joe tells them. "Don't know exactly what you all are up to with these meetings, but I'm almost sure it is not for me."

"You never know until you try," Barry says warming up to the idea. "We'll see if you can maybe just sit in as an observer. Might be more interesting than TV. There are some nice people there. Something good just might happen to you."

"Wouldn't hurt to ask..." Hope adds.

Sinking in that two strangers might give two shits about him, Joe's eyes fill with tears.

"I am feeling like it would kinda be weird being in this room alone, like something terrible will happen to me. If half of these people might be half as nice as you two, it could be good to be around other folks for a little while. If it starts feeling too strange, I guess I can always leave and come back to the room."

Barry gave him a friendly hug around the shoulders. "That's the spirit, Joe! We'll check it out. I don't think there will be as much of the heavy stuff as we did earlier. People sharing songs and dances and such. Will there be a little dance from you, Hope?"

Joe frowns and shakes his head in disapproval at Barry's poor choice of wit.

"I think there might, Mr. Strange," she laughs as she slides from the bed to her chair.

When Joe disappears into the bathroom, Barry watches Hope take the tin pill box out of her bag and pull out a blue edible.

"You don't need another one, do you?" she asks him.

"No. I'm still flying way out of control from the red one. You in pain?"

She tosses the gummy into her mouth. "A little. You probably think I'm a drug addict..."

"That had not crossed my mind at all until you mentioned it. Are you?"

"I gotta do what I gotta do to stay functioning. You can think what you want about me all you want."

"I don't think you can handle the truth about what I think and feel about you."

"Lay it on me, old man. I can take almost any negative vibe except maybe the N-word. That's a deal-breaker."

"I got nothing if you're expecting the negatude." He pulls up a chair to look her straight in the eye. "I don't know why. I don't know how. Don't know if it's real or total delusion." She lets him hold her hand. "But what I feel for you is so badass positive and chill—it has got to be love, baby."

Hope pulls her hand away. "Let me stop you right there. You ain't going nowhere wit dat urban slang shit. If you got something to say, say it from your own mind and heart not from where you imagine I'm coming from. I done went to Harvard, boy! I understand educated grammar and BS."

"Ok, sure. Sorry. I can't seem to ever say anything straight from the heart. I always feel as if I must joke around, approach every angle from the side. Why is that? Because I'm scared shit-less, Girl! I should say, 'Hope', not Girl. Hope, I'm frightened to be feeling it so strong. You had me when I sees you rolling out of that bathroom stall this morning."

"Oh, boy..."

"I don't need you to be my girlfriend if that's your worry. I just need you to let me love you, care for you, be there for you in whatever way is helpful to you. I can be your roommate, friend, or just stay the fuck away."

"Can you write me a check for like ten thousand dollars?"

Barry sits back in his chair and sighs. "Sure, if that's what you really want or need." He checks his pockets. "Don't have my checkbook, though. I can give you a card that has maybe a billion dollar limit." He pulls a card out of his pocket. "Passcode is 1020." Hope waves him off, not believing him for a second. "I should probably ask you a bunch of questions first. Like, is it to support your drug habit?"

This pushes her button. She is about to let him have it both barrels, but Joe emerges from the bathroom tucking in his shirt tail. They stare at him in silence.

"What? My zipper down again?" he jokes and feels his crotch. "Oh, shit. It really is." He zips up while Barry and Hope let out a laugh.

"You know, Joe, they say it pays to advertise. But, when you get to my age, not so much," Barry says smiling. "You ready?"

"It is nice of you to invite me, but I'm not sure I ought to join you down there." Joe turns on the TV and scrolls through one calamitous news story after another. He stops and stares at a scene depicting the fires and mayhem of a city street.

Hope rolls to him, takes the remote out of his hands, and turns off the television. "Come with us for just a little while, Joe. You never know, you might run into something good."

Joe tears up. "I just don't get why you two are so nice to me. I don't deserve it."

"Sure, you do!" Barry says moving nearer. "Well, we're both a little stoned, if that helps you understand it better."

Startled, Joe stares into his face and then into Hope's. "Well, I'll be damned."

Without another word, they go down the hall and wait for the elevator.

Barry sings.

>Sooner or later
>Will come the elevator
>Hope there's not an alligator
>On the elevator.

The doors open. After entering, the doors close, and Barry continues the song.

>What takes us down
>Won't make us frown
>Things will be greater
>When off the elevator.

He stops—hoping another verse comes to him.

"Yeah, I see it now—he wasted," Joe says.

CHAPTER NINE

By the time the elevator from the 4th floor reaches the lobby, Barry is able to persuade Hope and Joe to sing two short songs they all know, "My Girl" and "What a Wonderful World." The bell chimes and the door opens.

"Hey, it's the 'Church Squad'!" Barry cries as they step and roll out the elevator.

Jane, overjoyed to see Hope, happily hugs her while Barry offers Mary a wave and a ridiculous handshake. He notices Ned and Fred projecting a serious and cautious demeanor and acknowledges them with a stiff robotic, "Ned. Fred."

After gushing over Hope, Jane warmly greets Barry and grants a friendly smile to the bashful Black man a step or two to the side. Barry puts his arm around Joe and pulls him into the circle.

"Jane and Mary. Ned and Fred. This is our good new friend, Joe. Joe, this lovely woman is Jane. And this is Mary. And these fun-loving guys are Ned and Fred."

"How do you do?" Joe says politely.

Jane answers for everybody. "Doing very well, thank you. And you?" Jane offers her hand that Joe, with awkwardness, takes as if to shake, but then semi-gallantly air kisses. "How did you meet up with these two characters? You're not one of the seminar people who know how to make themselves invisible in a crowd are you?"

Uncertain how to even understand what Jane says, Joe remains silent.

"We just met Joe today. We're going to see if we can get him inside to at least watch what is going on tonight," Barry answers for him.

Joe feels as if he needs to explain what has gone down with people who appear somewhat normal. He jerks a thumb towards Barry. "This guy sees me on the street begging for change. He bought me a room here, some new clothes, a haircut, and a great meatball sub for dinner. He brought this woman up to the room so's she could have a nap."

Jane at each person in turn. "Is this true?"

"Absolutely!" Hope answers. "We had a great time up in the room trading stories of misspent youth, but we thought Joe might enjoy seeing some of the talent at the variety show tonight."

"That seems to be the plan. Everyone is supposed to come up with a song, a dance, a joke, a prayer, a speech, a magic trick—something to show off for everybody," Jane says.

"You probably got a trick or two up your sleeve, don't you Barry?" Ned says with a bit of an edge to his voice.

"Magic was never my thing, Ned."

"No? That was a pretty slick trick you pulled on me a little while ago."

"Did I? I'm afraid I don't remember."

This makes Ned tremble. He has not stopped talking with his wife and friends about the transformative little poke in the gut. How could Barry forget that?

"Joe, did you know your new friend here is a goddam miracle worker?"

"Ned, stop!" Jane hisses.

"No, it's true. I have had IBS, ulcers, and other troubles in my innards for years that recently took an ugly turn when a cancerous tumor was discovered. I am scheduled for surgery next month. Our friend, Barry here, a little while ago punched me." He points to his right side. "I don't know how or why but I could feel all intestinal pain, pressure, and discomfort shoot up my spine and totally disappear. I am more than anxious to get tested and find out if it is for real. Is it real, Barry? Is it?"

"I have no idea, Ned."

"No idea..." Ned snorts. "And something similar happened with your other friend, Joe. After a little of his voodoo work on Hope here, she was able to walk for the first time in more than ten years. Isn't that right, Hope?"

"Voodoo?" Barry says.

"You do," Hope plays along.

"I do what?"

"Remind me of a man."

"What man?"

"The man with the power..."

Mary laughs recognizing the movie bit. "Yeah, he has the power of voodoo alright."

"All that true, Mr. Barry?" Joe asks.

"I don't know, Joe. If Ned says all that stuff is true, I got to believe him. I kind of remember touching him but not awfully hard. I think I was in a type of trance."

"He did say his blood sugar was low," Fred says.

Ned grows more agitated. "I got to know what's real..."

"Don't we all..." Barry says.

"Could my cancer possibly be gone or is it some kind of perverse parlor trick or elaborate con?"

"I don't know what it is, Ned. I really don't."

Ned seems more disturbed. Joe is moved to put a friendly hand on his shoulders, "Why you so upset? If the cancer is gone, that's a good thing, right? And, if you find out it's still there when you see your doctor? You are no worse off than you were before, are you? Enjoy being pain-free while you can, for crying out loud."

"Damn, Joe!" Hope says. "You may not always have a lot to say but when you do, it's great."

"I know," Barry heartily agrees. "That's one of the things I really like about him." Barry embraces Joe with a manly side-to-side hug. He has never been hugged by a man before.

For a moment, no one has anything to say. Joe scans everyone's face on the lookout for any familiar signs of sarcasm, mockery, or scorn. There is an unfamiliar warm feeling in the depths of his belly glowing like an ember of a campfire. He has not felt anything like this in what seems centuries. It seems impossible to believe, but this small group of people may like him, care about him, and even in a new untraveled way, love him.

"I hope you can join us at the seminar, Joe," the woman named Jane says. Ned and Fred, the quiet younger woman Mary, and, of course, Barry and Hope all agree.

"We should see about that," Barry says taking charge again. "You still willing, Joe? These folks are super nice but wait until you meet Inez and Frederico, Janice and Elaine, Tyco and Mohammed, and about a hundred other superhuman beings."

"I guess so. But I been thinking—I should've told you this earlier. My name isn't really Joe."

"No!" Barry exclaims as if he knew this all along.

"It's William. I also got a street name, but I'm keeping that to myself for the time being."

Hope grabs his hand. "Nice to meet you, William. I get it. Why should you trust some crazy white man who takes you off the street and puts you up in a nice hotel with a bunch of other half-crazy people you don't know?"

Fred and Ned perk up with this news and insist on being apprised of more details about this person, William, aka Joe, also known by some street name. That these men, their wives, his benefactor Barry, as well as Hope, are all inexplicably eager to know *who he is* overwhelms him completely. No one, absolutely no one, has ever shown any interest at all in him in what can only be described as an exceedingly long time.

In a terse, unemotional testimony, William/Joe manages to tell his life story without blame or judgment and, to his own astonishment, without pity and loathing toward himself.

Ned is relieved to notice his own lack of criticism and judgment toward "Joe Willy," as Barry now calls him. He never much cared for this tendency of his to "nitpick," as Jane called it. He could try extremely hard to not close his heart and mind when someone had a story like "Willy Joe," as Hope calls him.

Without much education and less opportunity, this man who becomes homeless and pretty much forgotten made things worse for himself by 1) smoking 2) drinking 3) not giving a flying fuck 4) drugs 5) despair 6) isolation... *'Well, don't do those things!'* Ned would think. *'Got an addiction problem, bro? Do something about it.'*

Such are the thoughts Ned might usually have. But not today, a day that had him put aside annoying silent or verbal lectures on things another person should or should not do; a day that had a stranger punch him in the stomach and send an ancient, tangled ball of fear out through his head and perhaps out of his life forever.

'Here is a moment to remember,' Ned thinks. While the homeless man in front of him describes in a quavering voice how it feels to feel hopeful for the first time in many, many years; how he thinks maybe he can climb out of a dark and desperate abyss; how the pain in his heart and head may not go on forever—Ned watches his wife, Jane, listen with such tender attention and love.

He has seen this look before, of course. It is the compassionate way she could sometimes look at him throughout their 30 years of marriage. But now, on this day, at this moment, it is as if he sees her for the first time as the strong, loving, and wise soul she happens to be. This picture is quite apart from how she could be available to fulfill his needs, pump up his confidence and self-esteem, and do everything in her power to help, nurture, and please *him*.

Ned feels yet another wall break inside him. He touches her on the arm and softly kisses her on the cheek. She turns and smiles at him.

"Having fun?"

"I am, indeed, my love. Thank you for making me do this. You are such a beautiful, marvelous human being. What an honor to know and share a life with you."

This moment is not lost on the others of this group. William stops the most powerful speech of his life to join the others in staring and listening. A tearful Mary feels as if her husband Fred is about to make what might well be a hurtful joke and jabs him in the ribs. Hope stares in disbelief and shakes her head sadly when Barry puts on sunglasses and begins to sing a song from his favorite album, "Songs in the Key of Life."

Although Hope and Jane generally dislike seeing white men mimic the voice and personality of Black people, they very much enjoy how Barry throws his heart and soul into the performance. Mary and the other men may feel a little embarrassed at the public display, but they also like it—for a little while.

Later, when they have a chance to discuss it among themselves, they all agree it would have been a better experience had Barry seen fit to limit his full-throated rendition of the song to the first few bars. Would it not have been better for him to stop and not try to sing the choral sections all on his own when he is unable to get the six of them to do so?

Yes, it is mildly amusing to watch him get on one knee and profess, via this song, his love for Hope. And, yes, she did laugh heartily as he deftly spun her chair as if a spirited pirouette. But, when it becomes clear that this *tour de farce* engages the attention of dozens of seminar people as well as others in the lobby, everyone except Barry Strange share an opinion *en masse* that the act should come to an end.

He persists and is determined to get to the bridge where he can belt it out:

> *We all know sometimes life's hates and troubles*
> *Can make you wish you were born in another time and space*
> *But you can bet your life times that and twice its double*
> *That God knew exactly where he wanted you to be placed*
> *So make sure when you say you're in it but not of it*
> *You're not helping to make this earth a place*
> *sometimes called Hell*
> *Change your words into truths and then change*
> *that truth into love*
> *And maybe our children's grandchildren*
> *And their great-great grandchildren will tell...*

Barry rushes to reach the end when he notices Ned and Fred are no longer present and Joe Willy stands off to the side pretending not to know him. He had sung this song in this manner a couple times before but feels pretty darn good how well he pulls it off here. There is a small smattering of applause from somewhere but not the tumultuous ovation he feels it deserves.

"Well. That is something," Hope says with a noticeable lack of enthusiasm. Jane seems about to offer a more positive review, but Anton appears on the scene under a full head of steam. Why, oh why, is he dressed like a clown—red rubber nose, huge shoes, and all?

"Come folks, come. The seminar variety show will be happening inside the ballroom, not out here in the lobby, Barry.

Come, come all ye workshop people come..." He starts to run off.

"Anton! Just a second...I'd like you to meet someone." He gestures for William to come closer. "This is my friend, William."

"My friend, too," Hope says.

"And ours!" Mary says looking at Jane who nods in agreement.

"How do you do, William?"

"Okay, I reckon," he says retreating to bashful mode.

Barry presses ahead. "We have all become very fond of him. He has no good place to go this evening and I wonder if he could join us for tonight's gathering. Perhaps more as a spectator than a participant? You wouldn't be any trouble, would you, William?"

"I doubt it. Barry says it is talent show but you don't have to worry, I don't have any."

"He's way too modest," Barry says. He can tell Anton is working out in his head how to tactfully turn down the request. "I can understand you may not want to set a precedent. If you let us invite a guest, maybe everyone will want to. I am more than willing to pay the full enrollment fee and even pledge to donate to the Foundation I heard about."

"No! We can't be bribed to change protocol. I'm sorry, William, but this is just not the way we do things."

"That's okay. I weren't sure I wanted to do it anyway."

"Sure, you did!" Hope cries.

Jane takes charge. It is what she does. "This seminar has transformed and helped a lot of people already. What is one more? I even heard a couple people dropped out. Why can't

William take one of those places? This whole thing supposed to be about caring!" Her tone rises with indignation. "If someone shows up at your house starving—do you tell him to go away 'cause that's not the way you do things? Well, William could be starving!"

"I ain't starving..."

"Hush, William. I'm trying to make a point...You could be starving for some spiritual substance. I mean, this could be an important moment for him to be near some decent caring people! It can't be any skin off your nose if he sat quietly in the back maybe so he can hear someone like Barry here sing a sappy song about love, or redemption, or, for the love of God, maybe even a song or dance about the love of God!"

Anton is about to make another point, but Grieg's entrance music puts a stop to it.

"Okay, okay." He looks around the lobby. "Sounds like it is time to go in. Tell you what—let's do it democratically. I'll bring it up to the whole group. If everyone is okay with him being an observer, it is alright with me. How does that sound, William?"

"I don't know. I don't know about any of this."

"Barry, we can talk about the Foundation, later."

"Let's just do it, for crying out loud!" Mary shouts as if on the verge of going mad.

Without a word, they all file into the ballroom. Ned and Fred have saved four seats at the end of a row where Hope can park her chair. Anton takes his position up front to face everybody as the music stops.

"Everyone have a great dinner? Are you hungry for a different kind of sustenance? Before we get started, we're going to veer off script—again! To promote continuity and a sense of community, we discourage anyone from part-time participation in the workshop. We cannot prevent you from leaving whenever you want, however. Two people have decided this is not for them and have departed. We wish Larry and Elizabeth well.

"We now have a request from a handful of participants to allow a local resident to sit in for some or all of tonight's session. I could be a tyrant and insist upon adherence to the seminar's guiding principles but I have been persuaded to leave it up to you all. I think it only fair that if there be anyone at all who, for any reason, objects to opening our collegial workshop community to an outside observer, we should respect that.

"In order to better judge whether to accept this visitor, or not, I would like to invite him to join me up here so we all can meet him. William?" Anton looks at where William sits and urges him forward.

"Uh, no. No, nope, no. Never. No way." William crosses his arms adamantly and shakes his head from side to side. "No. Thank you anyway."

The entire room stares at him in silence and waits. Some stand up for a better look. He wants to get up and walk out of the room but cannot move a muscle.

Jane whispers. "It will be okay, William. You can do it." She can feel him tremble and places a hand on his arm.

Always one to speak up when no one else will, Barry rises to his feet. "Ladies and gentlemen, allow me to introduce you to this kind and gentle man. Like all of us, he was born into a family who loved him the best that they could. He has faced heartache, prejudice, indifference, and a hundred different challenges that could break even the strongest and bravest. Yet, despite deprivation and loss, isolation and the ravages of despair, this man can still project, given half the chance, the best qualities that make a human being—intelligence, love, and a quiet yet powerful sense of dignity. He also has a heck of a sense of humor.

"Dear ones, one and all—although I've yet had the honor and privilege of getting to know everyone at this workshop as well as I'd like to, I feel quite confident saying that I am sure there is room in our hearts to welcome another soul among us. I can assure you that this shy and unassuming man can neither harm nor disappoint you.

"It is with great joy that I present to you a very fine human being, Joe Willy!"

Barry claps loudly. To his great relief, the church squad and Hope enthusiastically join in. Except for Hope, they stand and clap. She moves her chair so Willy can get out, but he remains seated shaking and sobbing, unsure what is going on.

The sound of dozens and scores of people clapping make him lift his head and open his eyes to the sight of everyone on their feet cheering and urging him on.

"Stand up, man!" Barry cries over the din of the crowd. "When is the last time you took a bow before an adoring crowd?"

"Like never," he says standing. He bows his head in acknowledgement and sits back down.

Anton's voice booms through the microphone. "Guess that is your answer! Welcome, William, to the seminar!" The crowd roars. "Who says we can't be a little flexible?" Anton says regaining control. "William, do join me up here so we can all get to know you a little better."

"Didn't you hear me, man?" William says, a little pissed. "It's still no."

"Alright, alright. I think we all should feel free to participate as much, or as little, as we like. The rest of you have the advantage of knowing what you might be getting into when stepping up to the plate, so to speak. As usual, we'll start with a little meditation..."

Once again, Anton guides everyone down the stairs to a boat at the water's edge, across the moonlit lake, onto a pristine beach, along a floral path through a luxuriant forest, and to the sanctuary of their own creation. Once inside, all are invited to open a closet door, don an "ability suit" that would contribute to the creative activity of their choice, and then visualize themselves doing the activity.

Some visual artists, like Jane, imagine wearing a painter's frock complete with a French beret to better see themselves creating an oil painting or sculpture. Her husband Ned, an aspiring writer of adventure and suspense novels, chooses to visualize himself in a colorful Hawaiian shirt and gaudy boxers typing out stories on his computer. His friend, Fred, sees himself in a new outfit swinging a golf club and making a hole-in-one. Mary, perpetually afraid to speak aloud, visualizes herself in strong, professional attire making an impassioned speech. Hope, in a flowing skirt of many colors, liberates herself from the wheelchair and dances, and dances. William, aka Joe or Joe Willy or Willy Joe, is new to this type of exercise. He is still trying to decide what kind or color of rowboat to take him across the lake when Anton informs everyone it is time to get back in the boat, row back across the lake, go back up the stairs, and open their eyes.

And Barry? He chooses the blue tights and red cape of Superman and spends his visualization time flying around the world. Later, he would swear that he not only imagined faraway places. He is actually looking down into the streets of Berlin, Iquitos, and Bledington, England. Were they actually Morris dancing there?

When the meditation ends, it is time for the evening's main event—"The Variety Show of Talent!" Kevin, on PowerPoint, projects everyone's number on the screen and randomly arranges all 152 of them into 15 groups. While chairs are cleared from the center of the room, Elaine holds up a card for each group. All the numbers under the letter A are to congregate in one spot, all the B numbers in another, and so on.

As everyone with a number gathers in their groups, it becomes clear there is one person without a number. Elaine quickly goes to where William stands dazed and confused.

"You can be number 121, William. It is the number of one of the guests no longer here." He stares at her wondering why in the hell he is not up in his room watching TV. She points to the screen. "See your number puts you in Group J."

"Why?"

"Why what?"

"Why am I in Group J?"

She puts a gentle hand on his arm. "This may all be going a little fast for you. Your friends want you to be a part of this, William. Anton, the man leading this workshop, will explain what we will be doing in a minute. You don't have to participate, if you don't want to, but I think you will like it. Most people just sing a song. Can be one you make up on the spot, or just something you like. It is one of the exercises we do which everyone seems to really enjoy. C'mon."

Elaine leads him to where someone is holding the card with the letter J and speaks to the nine people standing there. "You okay if William joins this group? He's a little nervous about what is going to happen."

"Aren't we all?" jokes a man with the name tag, George.

All but one person offers William some form of reassurance. A bald, heavy-set white man, with the name tag, Bart, stares at him with a look of derision and disapproval that seems all too familiar.

"I don't know who you are, William, but I would not have been one of those who would have voted to bend the rules so you could join us, if there had actually been a vote."

The others hiss and jump on what they perceive as a rude, even cruel remark. Although unusually kind to his wife, his own children, and to cats and dogs and other animals, Bart discovered many years ago that he could get an almost drug-like shot of adrenalin when something he'd say or do could elicit emotional venom directed at him or at some opinion or statement of his.

In truth, he is one of those who would admit to missing those all too brief Trump years. Suddenly, it seemed Bart no longer had to pretend to be nice. Here, at last, was someone on the big stage calling out the phony BS of Jeb Bush, Mark Rubio, Ted Cruz, the Clintons, and Obama! Throughout both terms, Bart took an almost masochistic joy defending everything Trump said and did, even when he had never supported a lot of those things in principle or practice.

It was not exactly a pleasure to keep at it throughout the two Trump presidencies. In some ways it was no fun at all to have friends, co-workers, and family despise him. Sometimes he could repair the damage his own words would do to relationships. A lot of times, he would not bother.

Bart stoically absorbs the rebukes from the apparent liberals of Group J. He thinks about saying something "nice" to William but the look of shame and the demeanor of weakness infuriates Bart even more. He thinks a few choice words to provoke him even more could be a kindness, but it seems time to move on to whatever bullshit Anton and the seminar team have in store.

"Take a look at everyone in your group, make eye contact but remain silent," Anton tells everyone. Bart plays the game. He pretends to smile as he looks straight into each person's face. The pitiful William, most likely a drug addict and certainly alcoholic, avoids Bart's eyes altogether. Although not proper seminar behavior, Bart would have liked to shake the hell out of him!

Anton continues. "You each have up to three minutes to do whatever you wish for the other people in your group. Make a speech. Cry like a baby. Rage like a madman. Dance up a storm. Sing your heart out! Whatever is inside you, let it out! You can turn it into a full expression of your creativity and talent or a silent prayer for peace. It can be your favorite song or poem. You can say what needs to be said. IT IS UP TO YOU for you to be you!

"As an observer of these acts and actions, your job is to watch and listen. Make sure the singer, dancer, or madwoman stays within your circle and stays safe. One more thing—when everyone has had their time the group will vote on one person to perform their song or whatever for the benefit of the entire group. Sound like fun?"

"Sounds dreadful," Bart pronounces for the benefit of his little group of ten. "Who'd like to be humiliated first?"

"You spoke up first, Bart," George says in a kind voice. "Show us what you got!"

Bart agrees. He chants, he sings. Bart screams at the top of his lungs. He is remembering something his ex-wife Sarah had told him when she walked out on him.

"If you ever find yourself in a space where you can feel safe enough to just let loose of that anger, do it!

Bart rages. Bart lets it all out. Fortunately, or unfortunately depending on your point of view, no one can understand a word he says. No one, except William that is. He once had a deaf uncle, Uncle Virgil, who showed him how to lip-read. And, boy, does William get a lip-full from Bart! He wants to do something terrible to someone named Sarah! For some reason, he is still angry at Hillary Clinton! This is disturbing enough. William is about to look away from these lips expelling a good deal of froth when Bart begins venting even more objectionable material. No one can hear the N-word, but William recognizes all too well how the lips pull back on the first syllable and return to a rest position on the second.

The sound of the first performers of each group simultaneously singing, howling, and striving to make themselves heard above the wailing of everyone else ensures that no one can be heard at all. Bart's face turns red, swollen, and contorted as he rails and discharges every demon within. With all the other singing and screaming going on, no one in Group J (except

William) has any idea what he says.

After three minutes of such cacophony, a blast from a bull-horn announces that time is up. The physical and psychological release of so much built-up tension feels good to Bart. He also feels relief that no one could have been offended and collapses into the arms of Lois, a pretty college student from Georgetown. She doesn't hold onto him for very long and he slides to the floor.

"Let's hear it for all the brave ones who went first!" Anton shouts. "My apologies to everyone about the sound. Everyone had difficulty being heard. The acoustics of this room make it difficult to sing or orate as loudly as we may like. Partly my fault for suggesting screaming. But maybe it was blessing some of those screams could *not* be heard."

"You right about that!" William shouts in obvious recognition of Bart's outburst. William is no longer afraid of Bart, or anybody. At that moment, he looks around the room wondering what became of his improbable new friends. He sees Barry staring at him from a couple groups away. *'You okay?'* his raised thumb and lips seem to say. William smiles and returns a thumbs up.

What is the chance William could remember enough high school math to figure out what is the probability that at least one from the group outside the elevator—Barry, Hope, Ned, Fred, Mary, or Jane—would have been randomly assigned to the same group as William?

Not much chance of coming up with an actual number, but he feels intuitively that the odds are good. He feels strangely calm, almost relieved not to have a familiar friendly face upon which to rely among these mostly friendly white people.

Notwithstanding the apparent racist, mean-spirited pill, Bart, the people in his group are remarkably open-hearted and welcoming. He feels safe. Something stirs deep within.

"I'd like to go next," he tells them. William is not sure exactly what to say or do, but he feels strongly it is his turn. He can hear two or three soft songs coming from other groups and a plaintive prayer from another. He sings in a hip hop manner to Group J...

At an early age
I learned to count
(poof poof)
Numbers and things
In huge amounts.
(poof poof)
Learned to add
And multiply,
Subtract, divide,
And wonder why...
(poof poof)
Why the numbers
Went this way;
What they did,
And what they say...
(poof poof)
Father told me
That they pay
To play with numbers
Every day...

There seems more to come but William's eye happens to catch the unmistakable look of contempt in the face of one of his onlookers, the contrarian, Bart.

'*Nothing better than a rap about running numbers...*' William is certain he hears him say.

He stops singing and angrily lashes out. "This ain't a song about numbers running!" '*Asshole!*' he thinks.

Bart snorts a nasty laugh. "Who says it is? But now that you mention it..."

"If you didn't say it, you thought it."

"What if I did? You a mind reader? With the resurgence of socialism and political correctness, there may not be freedom of speech anymore. But I *think* there is still freedom of thought. And I think you're the asshole, not me."

No one has time to wonder how Bart and William seem to be hearing each other's thoughts. They do their best to mollify both men who proceed to air ancient, imagined grievance and invectives at one another with such escalating volume and vehemence that all performances of talent going on in the other groups cease.

Anton and Elaine both rush to intervene.

"What is going on here?" Anton demands.

The bickering stops. Everyone silently looks at each other.

George, from Group J, tries to explain. "Bart didn't seem to like William's rap about doing math when he is a kid..."

"I didn't say anything," Bart professes innocently. "He called me an 'asshole' and jumped all over me with bat-shit crazy accusations about what he thinks I am thinking. Can we have another vote on whether this guy should even be here?"

"Some spontaneous ESP is happening," says the ballerina, Lois. "I don't think any of us heard William call Bart an 'asshole,' although he certainly acted like one."

George jumps in again. "I don't know if it's telepathy, but Lois has a point. William never called Bart an asshole, but Bart thinks that he did. Bart did not *say* anything to ridicule William's rap, but William thinks that he did."

Barry throws in his two cents worth that everyone ignores. "I thought it was just me at first, but there seems to be a lot of ESP going on. Does that always happen at these seminars?"

"Look, I'm not interested in deciding who's to blame or whether somebody is reading somebody's mind. I suggest that the most experienced mediator in our midst sit down with Bart and William and help them work out this conflict without dragging everyone else into it." Anton turns to Elaine. "That would be you."

Elaine nods and, in one graceful gesture, takes each man by the hand. Bart no longer wants any part of this touchy-feely bullshit and brusquely drops her hand.

"I'm not doing it! This all started, Anton, when you broke protocol and allowed this man, Barry, to disrupt the proceedings and bring in a person off the street. I *demand* that we reverse that decision and restore our gathering to its previous constituency."

"Oh, you demand that, do you? Well, you can take your demands into your mediation session with Elaine and William. I leave it to Elaine to decide from that session whether we should revisit the decision to include William."

Anton's facial expression, posture, gesticulation, and tone of voice leave no doubt that the discussion in front of the entire group is now over.

While the rest of the seminar resume individual talents performed for the benefit of their respective group, Elaine has the two unhappy men grab a chair while she takes one for herself. They form a small triangle within the right angle of a far-off corner.

"Let's take a moment to breathe in silence." Elaine faces directly across where the two walls meet. She grabs the right hand of William on her left and the left hand of Bart on her right. She waits a moment to see if either make a move to take the other's hand and close the circle and then goes on. "Close your eyes and imagine a boat taking you across a smooth lake toward a peaceful sanctuary if you have one. Feel free to summon a higher power, a higher self, a higher intelligence to be with you now and perhaps serve as your guide..."

"I came to believe that a power greater than myself can restore us to sanity," William whispers to himself.

"Ha!" laughs Bart. "Step 2."

William opens his eyes expecting mockery, but Bart looks more like an interested human being.

"Been there. Done that. Going to meetings became for me like going to church," Bart explains. "Every Tuesday night for fifteen years. It is that one hour of the week when I could be honest and not such a prick."

"I am glad there has been progress," Elaine says. "And, glad that you two may have something in common. In that spirit, I would like to say a little prayer. I will feel more hopeful if we could close this circle with a gesture of oneness, if not oneness itself." She waits a second, but they do not seem to get it. "Could you hold each other's hand, please?"

Bart reluctantly offers his, but it is William who is reluctant. "I ain't touched or been touched much by anyone since before them pandemic days. For some reason, I feel like you aren't diseased, Elaine. But I worry about this guy."

"Pandemic has been over and done with for a long time, dipshit. I ain't going to cry if you don't want to hold hands. Do your prayer without physical oneness." He takes his hand away from hers and William does the same.

"Okay, then. The suggestion is as much for me, as for you. For my own peace of mind, I will imagine Oneness between the three of us." She prays...

Dear Spirit,
Allow us to see there is but One Spirit here,
Not three.
Allow us to let go of the fear that keeps us separate.
It is in letting go that we move on,
It is in wearing the shoes of who we think to be foe that we empathize,
It is in accommodating our adversary that we satisfy our own claims,
It is in striving for a settlement that we find peace.

When finished, Elaine turns to William. "I'd like you to go first, William..."

"Why?" Bart asks.

"Why what?"

"Why should he go first?"

"Someone has to go first, so I chose William."

"But why did you choose him instead of me?"

"Do you want to go first? It doesn't matter to me."

"I think it does matter. What I think is that there is bias."

"A bias? No, not at all."

"I can smell it and I can see it. Trump tried to turn it around but you liberal snowflakes hounded him. Now that he's gone, you liberals have gone hog-wild, in my opinion, bending over backwards to hand out any advantage you can to Black people."

William tries to tune Bart out by rocking back and forth in his chair and humming some old gospel tune of his mother's.

"What are you talking about?" Elaine says to Bart.

"He da' black man, so he gots to go first..." Bart spits out in what he thinks is a joking darky dialect. But he is the only one who laughs.

"So, William, what do you think about Bart's opening remark? How does it make you feel? Are you getting special treatment here because you are Black?"

William lets loose with a good laugh. "I ain't never felt that way—ever!"

"Alright, here we go!" Bart roars.

"Is this what you want to address, Bart? Racial resentment?"

"I see it everywhere I go."

"Okay. I am supposed to be mediating a dispute between you two. Bart, is part of your negativity towards William related to race?"

"I'm not a racist, if that's what you're getting at," Bart says with some hostility.

William cannot keep himself from laughing. "You're not racist? I heard plenty of racist shit including the N-word during your song or whatever that was during your showtime."

Bart's face turns beet red and fidgets in his seat but recovers when he remembers something. "You fucking liar. You didn't hear shit. No one could with all the screaming going on."

"You're right. I didn't *hear* you, but I could read your lips."

Bart scoffs and is about to taunt him with a challenge for him to "*prove it*" when William repeats word-for-word what he saw Bart say, complete with a pitch perfect imitation of his voice.

Stunned, Bart says nothing.

"Busted," Elaine mutters. Elaine puts a few more questions to both men and decides mediation is not necessary. Once Bart acknowledges that his grievance against William may be more racial than personal, she tells William he can return to Group J. Bart begrudgingly agrees to work on issues one-on-one with her. He looks forward to holding her hand. William can be spared the possibility of being re-traumatized by racist material.

As he walks slowly back to his group, William hears Elaine patiently, kindly probe Bart's complicated psyche and soul with some confidence.

"Bart," she says holding his hands, "Why did you come to this seminar? What do you hope to accomplish?"

William knows intuitively that Elaine's palpable compassion and love is not at all a tacit approval for Bart's bigotry. She has profound faith that Bart's abhorrent behavior is a mere defense mechanism, a shield of fear that hides vulnerability and more fragile qualities such as empathy, kindness, and love that she is determined to find.

William has no idea how this insight comes into his head. He wonders if Elaine's skill and warmth can melt Bart's ice-cold exterior. That she seems willing to do so in order to find some goodness within nearly breaks open his heart. If there is something worthwhile in someone a hell of a lot meaner than he is, maybe all is not lost.

He is not planning to cry. However, when he steps close to Group J, something about the way Lois, George, and two other people smile at him trigger a steady stream of tears. Lois says, "Aw..." and gives him a reassuring tug at the arm. They both join the others in listening to a man named Stan deliver a poem extemporaneously.

Everyone is appropriately impressed and cheered when he reaches a dramatic climax at the exact moment Anton hollered, "Time!" As for all other performers, enough time is provided to properly compliment, gush, and go on about how "great" and "wonderful", and "interesting" the presentation was.

William feels a bit sad thinking how it would have been nice to be on the receiving end of such appreciation at the conclusion of his own little rap about arithmetic, but he quickly recovers when he recalls it was he himself who never gave anyone the chance to applaud by jumping on the reaction he imagined or perceived from Bart.

The show of creativity and talent quickly turns to another person in the group, too quickly for William to get lost in the twists and turns of his own journey through the maze of impressions, sights, flights of fancy, and desires that this entire evening presents. What he maybe *thinks* about anything, while maybe important in some way, does not seem to matter.

William is in the swing of things. He can feel it and see it flow in and out and among all the other groups in the room. He and Group J are part of an impressive array of myriad expressions of energy and creativity. The song and dance of the next per-former in his group, Millie, takes his breath away. She leaps in the air and throws her voice toward the stars. In the space of just a minute or two, she manages to convey both jubilation and utter despair, hilarity and unending grief. He would later tell Barry and Hope that he had never cried and laughed so hard in such a short period of time.

Millie gets his vote and everyone else's when the time comes to choose someone to perform for the entire workshop. While Anton and Elaine organize her and the other chosen represen-tatives for the big show, Bart returns to the cluster of folks at Group J.

Except for one or two nods of acknowledgement, he does not receive what might be called a warm welcome. He looks a bit shaken and chastened. Had something momentous and life-changing occurred during his session with Elaine? William hopes so but is finding it hard to find (and much less act) on the spirit of forgiveness and magnanimity which his mother, God bless her soul, had tried to cultivate. It would be up to Bart to make amends if he were to be so inclined.

Before moseying on to look for his other friends, William exchanges warm, non-verbal connectivity signals with the others and somehow manages to look Bart in the eye to grant him the slightest, most neutral look possible.

William slides through the buzzing, excited throng all eager to see what comes next. He sees Barry at the front of the crowd standing next to Hope. The two of them along with the church squad, Jane, Mary, Ned, and Fred, turn simultaneously to see him, as if sensing his approach.

"William! You've made it this far!" Barry says with a strong hug. The three women follow suit with hugs of their own. Ned and Fred are happy enough to shake hands. It is as if he is back from the dead or some other long, hard journey.

"You look like you've been having a good time!" Hope exclaims.

"Damned if I ain't," he says.

"Mighty glad it worked out," Barry says with relief. "Thought for a minute there you'd be thrown back out into the street."

"You and me both. Turns out that woman Elaine knows what she is doing."

They all agree and seem keen to share with him examples of her wisdom, skill, and compassion when Anton takes the stage in yet another outfit. He is dressed as a mime with black pants and suspenders over a black and white striped shirt. His face painted white, a red kerchief around his neck, with white gloves and black beret completing the disguise. He does classic mime routines climbing a rope, going down an elevator, being stuck in a box, etc. He quiets all assembled. He finishes his act to applause and removes his beret.

"Has every group selected their shining star? Good! I've already told them they have another three minutes to shine. They can do what they did for their group or come up with something entirely new. Group A! Tell us who you got!"

The ten people from Group A lustily chant, "Ed! Ed! Ed! Ed!!" The person named Ed jumps up on the small stage. The fact that every other group had apparently experienced so many stunning creative performances that could be described as transcendent, ethereal, and remarkable in so many ways, every person not part of Group A watch Ed totally confused why he was selected from their cluster.

Is it that Ed has every appearance of a middle-age recluse too shy to even speak to more than one person at a time that it feels liberating for him to express himself in both the small and large group with a dance that features the removal of all his clothes? While one piece of clothing after another is removed and flung about the stage and into the crowd, he waves arms, pumps legs, and gyrates his hips all the while ululating nonsensical, garbled words and atonal simulacrums of melody.

Some of the crowd enthusiastically encourage him to the very end when whitey-tighty underwear is swung over his head and flung into the crowd. In what more than one person feels is a bit too much, he whirls and twirls his penis back and forth, up and down. Totally committed to the performance, Ed concludes the show with a bow to the left, right, and center. With just a few people still clapping, he faces away from everyone and ingloriously bows and moons his rear end to all who still have their eyes open. Whether intentional or not, a loud burp of a fart concludes the show.

No one applauds. Ed retrieves his clothes and in a far corner of the room shyly puts them on. A look of complete terror crosses his face. Elaine goes to check on him.

The assembly erupts with mixed reactions. Laughs, titters, groans, gasps, and some hostility fill the room. "Man! I wish I thought of doing that!" Barry says. Thankfully, his companions know he is joking.

"That is *not* the dance we all voted for!" Fred says in dismay. "When he performed the dance for our group, he kept his clothes on."

Anton jumps to the stage. "Next up, 'The Aristocrats'!" Only a couple people get the reference. "That is an unforgettable performance that I would like to forget. It is not the kind of inspirational creativity I am particularly fond of (sorry, Ed). But if it helps personal liberation, who am I to judge? I don't know why, but there always seems to be someone at our workshops who likes to take off their clothes. If anyone is terribly disturbed by what you have seen, Elaine is available to help process it." He looks her way, and she with her arms around Ed nods in agreement. "Next up is Group B. What do you got?"

Group B shouts in unison, "Julie!"

Julie shyly takes the stage. "How do you top that?" she says. She hums the stripper tune Ed had sung and pretends to take off her blouse. After the laughter, she gets serious.

"I made up this song just a few minutes ago and my group helped by singing along. I hope you sing along too. Be forewarned—it turns into a round."

Julie sings.

How to sing a song? *(Group B repeats)*
What do we want to say? *(Ensemble repeats)*
We can sing along
It's alright to play.
(she jumps an octave)
What's inside a heart
Is difficult to say,
The longing, the pain,
The hope, the joy,
When sung is no cliché`...

With love and fear
We are still here
To live another day...

Julie repeats the verses. Trained well, her group repeats each line midway through and leads all gathered into a round with three parts. Everyone heartily cheers Julie and themselves when the song fades and ends. The parade of talent continues with each performance seeming to outdo the song, dance, or poetic expression of the ones which precede them.

None of the group consisting of William, Barry, Hope, and the church squad had won the endorsement of their respective groups. Hope confesses she thought, due to the "pity vote," she might be selected to perform for everyone her "wheelchair cha-cha." However, she is just as happy not to be compelled to repeat what, to her, is strenuous exercise. Barry shares his theory that, although he thinks he did a "splendid job," he is not chosen because most everyone had already heard his rendition of Stevie Wonder's song out in the hotel lobby and most likely did not wish to hear it a third time. William relays the story about his rap song which met great acclaim plus some sympathy for the unfortunate reaction of Bart. Mary says she recited a poem which no one seemed to understand. Her husband, Fred, reveals to everyone's amazement that he has a long dormant facility for whistling! To demonstrate, he trills a rapid string of melodious notes that elicit a shriek from his wife, Mary, who gushes her sincere belief that he "should have won!" Jane confesses she took the opportunity not to perform, but to let loose with a speech to white supremacists she says she had practiced in her head for almost forty years. Ned is the last one of this group to describe what he called his "three minutes of fame." He says it is but a "mere snatch of a song" that rose out of the empty space in his gut where the "lump of fear" which is his tumor had once been.

"The pressure to perform is scary and it feels as if the fear is gathering down here." Ned jiggles the right side of his substantial belly. "I hollered, 'Oh, no!' and began singing those two words repeatedly. As I sang, I could feel the lump travel up my spine, like it did when you healed me, Barry."

"Uh-huh," Barry says uncertainly.

"I kept singing, 'Oh, no. Oh, no. Oh, no...' until it seems to hit my throat and I let out a blood-curdling scream." Ned screams so loudly not a few heads turn in their direction. "It felt pretty darn good."

Anton interrupts the post-performance murmuring of over 150 people for an announcement. "Thank you, everyone! That is a thrilling sample of the talent and energy possessed by this talented and energetic assembly. Speaking of which—our talented and energetic sound man, Kevin, is going to lead a dance for all of us who wish to participate, which I hope will be all of us. Kevin?"

Kevin leaps to grab the microphone. "Ladies and gentlemen, boys and girls, les dames and les hommes—let's make one big circle. Don't worry about a partner. You too, Hope! I've seen you whip that chair around faster than anyone else can run. Join hands please" He pushes a button on the remote in his other hand and music erupts. "Circle right..." With Kevin, Anton, and Elaine guiding them, they do a circle dance...

They dance a variety of moves together as One for more

than an hour before exhaustion, boredom, or other demands have individuals, couples, and small groups peel away from the group experience. Kevin announces, "You're on your own!" and changes the music to a tech-rock style popular with the under 30 crowd.

"Barry's Cult," as Ned likes to call it, goes through the motions of boogieing for the duration of one song and then, one by one, surrenders the floor to the "kids.'

Barry, probably twenty years older than anyone, is the last to call it quits. "Hey, what's the matter with you all? You aren't *tired*, are you?" He bends forward, grabs his knees, and pretends to gasp and struggle to catch his breath.

"That's enough dancing for me," Fred announces.

"Probably more than we've done in the past ten years," Mary adds.

"That was really fun!" Jane says. Ned laughs and spins her around one last time.

William smiles and silently bobs his head up and down in agreement. He cannot bring himself to say so, but he feels as if his heart is breaking. It suddenly feels terribly sad to feel as if, after 55 years of living, he is experiencing what it feels like to be happy.

Hope resists Barry's attempt to give her and her chair one last twirl around the dance floor and lets loose a sharp, "No!" All give her their attention. "I loved it, especially the Peace Dance. But you probably noticed the chair made it more than awkward. Although everyone is super-nice about helping me get around, twirl around, and dance a round or two, it is exhausting. I'm heading home to collapse. Ta-ta, y'all! See you tomorrow."

She glances at everyone staring at her as if in shock and propels herself toward the exit.

"Whoa! What? Huh? Wait a minute...etc." six voices ring out for her to stop in six different ways. She acts as if she doesn't hear them and keeps rolling. Fred sticks two fingers in his mouth and produces an ear-splitting whistle.

All business within the lobby, all conversation, all the coming and going, as well as Hope's progress in leaving—everything comes to a sudden stop. All eyes turn to the source of the whistle.

"Why don't we all de-compress and relax in the lounge for a drink before we have to part?" Fred says.

"Oh, good idea," Hope spits out. "Alcohol is just the thing I need while driving home very tired."

"Think I'll pass on a drink, also," Barry says. "Ten years sober now."

"Oh, for pity's sake," Jane cries. "Who says you have to drink booze when you socialize?"

"To stay on the wagon, you gotta keep away from the wheels," he explains.

"Would it make a difference if we all didn't drink alcohol?" Mary says. "I'd be good with juice and seltzer."

"Me, too," Ned offers. "I know that doesn't sound like me but being re-born a couple times today makes me want to start fresh."

"Now I feel like crying!" Fred says. "All that singing and dancing..."

"And whistling!" William throws in.

"Yes, whistling...I hadn't whistled in years. I hadn't danced since...I don't know, never! I don't know—just hanging out with you all I am thinking it would make me feel, what? Simply happy having a real drink, a hard drink, and not just seltzer with everybody. Doesn't anyone else want to have a drink?" Despite his best efforts to make a joke out of everything, to not show any vulnerability ever, Fred is unable to hold back a well of tears forming along the brim of his eyes.

"Damn! I'd like a drink!" William says.

"Alright! William. There's a jolly good fellow. Let's go! Beer drinkers! Wine sippers! Tea totallers, even, c'mon!"

After brief farewells, all but Barry and Hope follow Fred into the hotel bar.

"I'll go with you to the garage," Barry says. Hope nods and briefly struggles to turn her chair. He grabs the handles. "May I push?"

She starts to resist, then relents. "Yes, please."

Barry slowly rolls toward the elevator but pauses when he spots Malcolm at the front desk. "Are you still here?"

"Almost every day, all day, and half the night. Sounded like quite the party in there. Did you have a good time?"

"Quite the blast, wouldn't you say so, Hope?"

"I guess so. Yet, it is a grim reminder."

The glum tone of this remark does not encourage either man to inquire as to what she is reminded. Barry asks Malcolm a few questions about his day—about whether romantic prospects had improved, if there is a particular talent he would have shared had he been a part of the spectacle they experienced, or if he had any exciting plans for the near future.

Malcolm is clearly reticent about sharing. He responds nothing beyond a superficial description of a life with no prospects, no talents, and no plans or hope for the future.

"Nowhere else to go than up!" Barry says with exaggerated cheerfulness. He salutes Malcolm with his signature jaunty wave and moves on.

"That went well," Hope says drily. Barry pushes the button to go down to the parking garage. They wait in silence for a beat.

"Sometimes the magic works, and sometimes it doesn't."

The bell chimes, the door slides open. They enter and the door closes. Alone together within that shiny steel cube creates, for just a moment, what feels like a sacred space.

Hope breaks the silence. "What you said about magic sounds familiar. Where does it come from?"

"Like much of the wisdom I have been able to gather, it comes from a movie..." Forgetting to push the button to send them down two floors to the garage, Barry describes and acts out the penultimate scene from a popular 1970 film, "Little Big Man."

Barry is lying on the floor of the elevator delivering the final line of a scene for Hope's benefit when the bell once again chimes and the door slides open. A familiar looking young couple seem stunned to catch sight of the very same old man they happened to see lying on the floor in the very same elevator a few hours earlier in the day. The door slides shut. Hope pushes the button to open the door while Barry leaps to his feet.

The man and the woman exchange looks with Hope and Barry but seem unable to move.

"Welcome to the theater of the absurd, my dear friends." Barry bows and gestures for them to enter. As the doors close behind them and the car begins to descend, he continues. "May

I present to you the reigning monarch of this metal contraption, the estimable, exemplary, extraordinarily exceptional, Empress of Hope..."

He winks and nods at Hope who somehow grasps what he wants her to do. She elegantly offers her hand that the man, and then the woman, lightly kiss. The door opens and everyone disembarks. Before moving on, Hope turns to the couple still lightly dazed.

"It has been lovely being in the same space, the same time, as you. Would you give us the honor of knowing your names?"

The young woman looks at her partner, then speaks, "I am Rebecca and this one is called, Ralph."

"Rebecca and Ralph. Please go in peace and know that you are loved."

With that, Hope rolls away. Barry takes a step to follow but stops to turn around and offers them a solemn, reverent bow.

The young man named Ralph looks at his companion. "Weren't we going up?" he says.

With the sound of the elevator opening and closing behind them, Hope shakes her head and begins laughing. "Now, that was fun!" she says.

Barry tries telling her how earlier today these same two people had opened the elevator door while he lay on the floor tripping wildly from the effects of the drug she had given him. She does not believe him, especially when he attempts to describe his cosmic journey beyond the edge of the known universe. When memory fails to deliver more interesting material, he makes stuff up.

Hope stops her chair at a smart-looking SUV. "Elves, sure. Whatever..." she says. "This is my car."

The driver's door unlocks and opens with no perceptible action on her part. She reaches behind her, pulls out her plank, grabs hold of the steering wheel, and pulls herself onto the seat. Before Barry can utter even one helpful peep, Hope quickly folds up her chair with one hand, pulls it up and over her head, and swings it behind her seat.

"Wow!" Barry exclaims. "Nicely done!" He insists on a demonstration of the hand controls for acceleration and braking. "Pretty nice rig you got here."

"Unfortunately, hardly any disabled person who needs something like this can afford it. I cannot begin to express how grateful I was, and still am, for the crowdfunding efforts of family, friends, and co-workers. I cried and cried when they surprised me with it." She looks at him through a blur of tears.

"Very cool. Jane says you work on disability issues. Much government support these days for helping folks get a hold of equipment like this?"

"Oh, there is support but not for anything as expensive as this." She hesitates before saying "good night" and closing the car door. Ever since the dramatic re-enactment of the movie scene in the elevator, she could feel a subtle energetic buzz reminding her of their earlier embrace and the brief, exciting stroll during the workshop. Barry calmly looks at her without any apparent agenda, anxiety, or expectation. Whether originating from some hypnotic suggestion of his or from her own mind, this wordless expressiveness seems to say, *'I am your friend and would like to help.'*

"Where are you staying tonight?" she asks.

CHAPTER TEN

As Hope finds herself driving across Memorial Bridge into Virginia, she has trouble remembering exactly what was said but knows she had invited this old, rather strange white man in the passenger seat to come spend the night with her. She feels certain there will be no problem if she wants him to sleep in the guest room, but not as much certainty that is what she really wants.

He turns to look at her at the very moment she turns to look at him.

"Just to be clear," she says, "there won't be any sex."

"Between us, you mean, or for anyone?"

"You're so weird."

"Admit it. You're tired of normal."

"I'm just plain tired," Hope says. "I'm not sure why you are coming home with me. Did I actually ask you or did you use your hoodoo on me?"

"Hoodoo?"

Hope laughs. "You do..."

"I do what?"

"You do remind me of some man."

"A man with the *POWER*...?" The volume and creepy modulation has her laugh once again. In the ensuing silence, she glances his way again. Barry is counting off something on his fingers. "I forget. How many do I need?" Hope gets it and giggles helplessly. "Unless you've moved the goalposts on me, I must be over the limit by now."

"Definitely weird. Sorry, Charlie. You not tickling my booty no matter how many times you tickle my funny bone."

"Damn. I been thinking we were going for it since you asked me to get in your car and, I quote, 'Shut up!' In any case, I did not use any of my voodoo powers to persuade you. I was quite content to get in my own vehicle and sleep, as planned, at a friend's house in Georgetown. But, since I have become very fond of you, I could not turn down the chance to spend more quality time with you, with or without the 'booty', as you call it. I am curious to see your home and look forward to talking more, watching TV, playing Scrabble, or whatever you'd like to do."

"I'll probably just take a bath and go to bed."

"Fine with me. You need any help?"

"To take a bath? I don't think so, Mister."

Barry becomes animated looking out the window as Hope steers the car into an area of Arlington with prosperous upper middle-class homes. "You're not going to believe this, but I feel as if I've been here before."

"*Deja vu* kind of thing?"

"I don't think so. My grandparents lived in Arlington. My mother grew up here. I was just a wee lad while they were here during the war and soon after."

"What war is that? There has been a lot of them."

"There sure has. The big one, WW two."

"World War Two? That was over eighty years ago. You that old?"

"Born soon after the war ended."

"Okay, boomer..."

"You're okay yourself, Gen Xer, or whatever label your generation goes by." Hope makes a left turn. "22nd Street!" Barry screams in a high pitch voice. "That's where Pop and Grammy lived! I kid you not." Barry swivels his head from one house to the next as if some memory of his four or five-year-old self might pop out from behind a bush or emerge down a driveway. He gasps and points excitedly. "That's it! That's their house! I'm sure of it."

"Uh-huh," Hope says with little enthusiasm as she slows down. "Which one?" She pulls into a driveway and the door to the garage in front of them opens. Barry is suddenly quiet. She pauses before entering. "These houses have no doubt changed appearance many times in the last seventy years. Do you really think one of them is where your grandparents lived?"

"Oh, yeah!"

"Well, which house is it?"

"It is this house," he says looking at her dead serious. "Your house, apparently."

Hope pauses, too blown away and suspicious to be reasonable. "You are shitting me, man!" She jerks the car forward. The collision safety sensor stops the car before it crashes into the back wall of the garage. "That's it, that's it. I ain't playing with you no more. Get out the car!" As soon as he opens his door, she opens hers. Reaching behind her, she once again swings the chair over her head and expertly lands it on its wheels.

By the time Barry walks around to the driver's side, Hope is safely in her chair. With the push of a button or two, the garage door begins falling and a door to the house opens for them. Barry stares as if he never witnessed such magical technology. Hope commands him to grab a small bag from the back seat.

Inside the house, a voice activated mechanism responds to her commands for "Light" and "Music." She rolls to a table and, ignoring Barry, opens a laptop and starts tapping.

"Come in and close the door, please," she says. Barry is still standing in the doorway.

"Are you mad about something?"

"Oh, no, not at all," she says sarcastically. "You still think this is Pop and Grammy's place?"

He peruses a very modern looking kitchen complete with stainless steel appliances, beautifully stained cabinets, and a quite snazzy kitchen island.

"A lot of changes on the inside," he says. "The kitchen I remember was a lot smaller. This living room wasn't here. A lot more windows also. Nice. I should probably check out the attic to be sure."

"Oh, shut up. What kind of idiot do you take me for? You've been playing me for a fool since the unfortunate moment you tried to pick me up in the bathroom."

"No, no, no, Hope. Not at all. Quite the contrary..."

"Don't know what kind of advantage you think you'd get by pretending my house is your Grandpa's..."

"None! There's no scheme here. It is just a crazy coincidence,

I swear. I have a hard time believing it myself. Can I look in the attic?"

"This house doesn't even have an attic!" Hope screams. "Aargh. Look. If you promise to leave me alone, you can stay here for the night. I need to check on some things from work."

"No Scrabble?"

Hope lays her head on the table. "You need something to eat or drink? Help yourself. Can you bring me that bottle of white wine in the fridge? Glasses are to the right."

"You want anything to eat?" She doesn't answer and resumes work on a few email issues.

Barry grabs a pear and a glass of water and brings them to the table with Hope's wine. He starts to sit with her.

"Go!" she orders harshly. Then, more gently, "Thank you. The guest room is up the stairs and to the right. There's a bathroom all ready for the guests I never have. My bedroom is to the left. Stay away from it. See you in the morning."

Barry looks at her as if he has something important to say but realizes he has no means and no words to say it. He bends down and. with the gentlest manner he can muster, kisses her softly on the top of her head.

Hope feels *something* pass through her hair, latch onto *something* inside her head, and split into three directions. Two electrical pathways travel along pathways that shoot out and tingle the tips of her fingers while a third rushes down her spine and splits into two currents that work their way through her legs, feet, and toes.

"Barry!" she cries. Hope turns and sees that he is gone. "Barry? You there?" She calls him again, a little louder. Either he cannot hear or will not respond.

For the next few minutes, Hope struggles to pay attention to the relatively minor grievances of friends and co-workers. She feels her own observations and advice to be equally shallow and inconsequential. She keeps thinking about the man upstairs in the guest room. Could she trust, should she trust, his apparent affection and attention?

A folder on her computer holds hundreds of journal entries. Among other experiences, it documents nearly 30 years of relationship hopes and disappointments. Before typing up some of her impressions of the people, words, feelings, and events of this day, she briefly scans earlier stories of her life.

One ten-page document titled, "20 Disappointing Men," reminds her of those times when she trusted and loved men. Had she really been that naïve? Could she really believe all those lies? Is she still so gullible, so blind?

What is Barry up to? Is he one of those twisted fucks with a weird sexual attraction to cripples? Her antenna is up and alert to any hint of a man's lust for control and domination of the vulnerable.

Like so many women, Hope had been seduced, used, and abused. She did not know what strange psychic power this guy has to not only make her *think* she could walk but fool her limbs to do so. What is that? But part of her doesn't care. If she has to make a deal with the devil to perambulate on her own power once again, maybe she is willing.

She rolls toward the stairs and maneuvers herself into the seat of the lift. At the top of the stairs is Chair #2 to help her to her bedroom.

While Hope had read emails and ruminated over her past, Barry wandered around the rooms upstairs. Had this really been his mother's childhood home? Outside, it felt so certain. Remodeling might explain why nothing inside feels familiar, but the news that there is no attic threw a bucket of cold water on his certainty. Had he somehow remodeled his own memory to match this house on 22nd Street? Is he somehow manufacturing this "coincidence" to establish a deeper connection with her?

Nothing about the small guest room and its bathroom, the little office and library, the stairs, or the hallway strikes a chord. He stands in the doorway to what is certainly her bedroom and feels a natural reluctance to enter.

Yet, the way that the wall to the left meets the ceiling at a sharp 45-degree angle piques his curiosity. It reminds him of something. A large walk-in, or more precisely, a roll-in closet takes up about half the expanse of the wall maybe only five-feet tall. He hesitates a moment and then dares to enter.

Hope's dresses, pants, shorts, blouses, and sweaters hang on a rod about four feet off the floor. For additional accessibility, a dozen pairs of shoes rest atop foot-high wooden blocks. Barry feels a *frisson* of affection to be near such an intimate array of her things.

He thinks, for a second, it would be wise to stop this investigation right there and go to his room. But first, he needs to look behind the row of clothing.

And there it is! Where once was a door to a crawl space is now a faint outline of a two-foot square board, perhaps painted over several times. During visits to Pop and Grammy's, Barry would sometimes go through this Hobbit-like doorway with his siblings and cousins on days when the weather discouraged outdoors play. Games were played, scary stories were told, and taboo explorations attempted. He remembers quite clearly the efforts of his older cousins, Larry and Dale, to persuade his sister (and everyone really) to take off their pants.

Although not an attic, precisely, this had to have been the house once owned by his mother's family. He didn't have to wonder for very long what Pop, known to be a prominent racist in his time, would think of who now lived here.

"*Uh, oh!*" Barry hears Hope out in the hall calling his name. She rolls into the last place upstairs to look for him at the same moment Barry steps out from the closet.

"What the fucking hell are you doing?" she screams. To say that she is furious would be an understatement. Righteous anger over his snooping and the invasion of her privacy spills over into a fierce denunciation of "white entitlement, privilege, and supremacy." He, like so many white men she had known, betraying her trust, her vulnerability, her humanness…

"I am so sorry," Barry says when Hope pauses to take a breath.

Hope renews her attack in earnest. She tears into him with cuss words and expressions many of which were new to him. "Uncle Fuck!", for instance, sounds like a curse, yet amuses him. Feeling she needs to get her rage about racism and patriarchy out of her system, Barry calmly listens and watches. He strangely loves her more than ever.

"I know I should have asked you if I could look around, but can I at least explain why I was in your closet?"

"No! I don't want to hear your lies and rationalizations. Nothing you can say will smooth over this...this violation of *me*!" She holds her chest as if stabbed in the heart. She summons all the strength she can muster to keep from crying. "Please, just leave me alone. I'll call you a cab."

"Okay, if that's what you really want. But please listen to me for just a second. This...", he says gesturing at the closet, "is not about you. Come with me, I want to show you something." He starts to enter but she does not budge. "Come on, Hope, I am not going to hurt you. I would never want to hurt you in any way. Like it or hate it, you are very precious to me." He seems close to crying himself. "To have hurt you actually hurts me."

"Oh, poor baby..."

"You were, and still are, justifiably suspicious about the unlikely coincidence that this house in which you live happened to have been the house where my mother lived with her parents over half a century ago. You will just have to accept my word that I have no ill intent or bizarre manipulative plan in sharing what to me is a very astonishing realization. The exterior of this house somehow triggered a memory before we even drove into the driveway, and I discovered it is *your* home. I was less convinced when we came inside. Due to remodeling, or other reasons, the interior seems less familiar..."

"Is this recapitulation going to go on much longer?"

"Ok. Briefly—when you suggested this could not be the same house because the attic I remembered playing in when a child does not even exist, I chalked up the coincidence to my own wishful thinking. Yet, when I came up the stairs the layout of the walls and rooms up here again struck a familiar note. I just ducked my head in the doorway to your room and got another jolt..."

"Did you now?"

"It is a bit of a shock. The sharp angle where the ceiling and roof truss meets this unusually short wall?" Barry pats the wall, five feet high. "I remember it! It wasn't an attic we played in. It was a crawl space. And here's the door!" He takes a couple steps inside the closet and pulls back a handful of dresses. Hope rolls closer to look. "The opening has been nailed shut and painted over but you can still see its outline."

"So?"

"So, I'm not crazy!"

"Are you sure?" She rolls towards the doorway, as if she needing to escape. "That this house once had a crawl space doesn't prove it is your family's ancestral home."

"Maybe not," he admits. "But it sure feels that way, or at the very least, it could have been."

"Okay, okay. Whatever. Although I am very tempted, I won't call a psych hospital and get them to get you the hell out of here—if you don't get out of my bedroom in the next ten seconds."

Barry dashes out of the room. "This is not as amazing to you, Hope. I get it. But, finding myself in the house of Harry and Mabel Hicks after maybe sixty-five years just blows my mind. May you sleep and dream well, my dear sweet Hope!" He waltzes down the hallway.

"I am not *your* Hope, jackass!" Barry gently closes the guest room door before she can think of a few more things to call him.

Hope closes and locks her bedroom door. She slowly

recovers her equilibrium as she goes through her bedtime routine. She tosses into a hamper clothes thoroughly drenched after a long day and night of expressing grief and anger and fear. Years ago, she had honed the slow and deliberate skill of transferring her body from wheelchair to shower chair and back to wheelchair after spraying, soaping, and rinsing with the handheld showerhead. Still naked from the shower, she treats and ties up her hair, then brushes and flosses her teeth in the time it takes to recite to her image in the mirror her favorite poem—"Still I Rise!"

With great relief, she slides onto her bed, into her night clothes, and under the bed coverings. She picks up a book and tries to read, but her eyes and mind are still too restless. Uneasiness over the most recent exchange with the strange man, Barry, gnaws at her.

She *liked* Barry. Why is she so quick to attack and seemingly blame him for matters that have nothing to do with him? Okay, he really is a jerk for nosing around in her closet, but his explanation and perhaps genuine remorse tempers her anger some.

What if this house really was once in his family? She knows how to find who owned what property from when she once researched racial redlining. She grabs her smart phone and searches Arlington County historical records. The list of property owners for 622 22nd St. stretches back to 1936. She guesses Barry's grandparents would have lived there in the 1940s and there they are! Harry and Mabel Hicks, 1940-1956.

Hope leans back in bed and suspiciously searches her memory. Barry did duck into the bathroom as soon as they came in the house. He could possibly have looked up on his phone these very records and drop the name of the previous owners to do—what? Impress her somehow? Manufacture a connection with her that is not there?

She starts to Google search his name but realizes she has no idea what his last name is. She makes a note to her online "To Do" list—*Barry's last name*. In her journal, she writes fifteen pages about the events, words, feelings, and conjectures of the day.

For the final line, she types all in caps, in a large colorful font, I ACTUALLY WALKED!!!

Hope is exhausted enough to skip an Ambien sleep aid. She claps her hands to turn off lights, recites to herself the usual meditative instructions for recalling lucid dreams, and drifts slowly to the Land of Nod.

After a very full day of emotional highs and lows, Hope thinks her dreams might generate more chaos and turbulence than usual.

When she awakes, she grabs her dream journal and jots down what she could remember...

"...party scene, inside a grand ballroom. Lively conversations and songs! An enchanting young man stands close. We desire each other and begin to dance! I have never moved so gracefully. My waking mind creeps in to remind me I cannot dance like this. 'Oh, I am dreaming,' I think. 'This must be a dream.' Although such realizations usually wake me up completely, I allow myself to continue the dream which puts me alone at a beach. It is near sunset (or is it sunrise?). I walk and walk and walk, enjoying the breeze, enjoying the sound of the waves, enjoying the pressure and movement of legs and feet..."

Hope smells something and stops writing. *Bacon!* She throws back the covers and somewhat angrily transfers herself to the chair. Morning routines in the bathroom calm her down some. She wonders if maybe she had told Barry, like she would tell anyone, to help himself to breakfast, but decides she probably did not.

By the time she has dressed and rode the lift downstairs, she is more grateful to have breakfast ready for her than she is pissed he breaks a rule of common courtesy.

"Good morning, dear Hope!" Barry sings out with unbridled joy at seeing her. "I hope you don't mind that I made us breakfast."

"You could have asked first." She rolls up to the table. "But I'll eat it."

"Excellent. How do you like your coffee?"

"No sugar and, as my mother used to say, just enough cream to match the color of my arm."

Barry takes advantage of this instruction to take her hand and seriously study the light brown hue of her arm. She, once again, feels an electrical impulse throughout her body.

He turns to prepare cups for them both. "Eggs will be ready in a moment. Since you have some in the fridge, I assume you like bacon?" He faces her in time to see her nod. She takes a sip of coffee and a small bite of bacon.

"Mmm. Both perfect. Thank you."

"You are most welcome. My thanks to you." He toasts her with his cup. Focused on not screwing up, Barry dishes up what he calls his "famous" frittata with red pepper, onion, and mushrooms. He adds a generous dollop of grits plus a muffin to their plates and sits down with her.

"Wow. That looks and smells great!"

"Oh, the juice!" he leaps up and grabs two small glasses filled with OJ.

"Damn. I hope there's something left to eat in the house for the rest of the week," she jokes.

"We can stop at the store when we come back tonight." The remark makes her stop the lift of her cup in mid-air. "If there is a tonight, I mean."

She lightly chuckles. "You are very strange."

"Barry Strange."

"Pardon?"

"That's my name. Barry Strange, Universal Celebrity." He offers his hand to her. Hope takes it, wondering if she'd feel that electricity again. She does. Barry does not seem to notice it. He gives her hand a shake and releases it. "Barry nice to meet you."

"Your last name is Strange?" He nods. "Suits you."

"A lot of people seem to think so. What is your last name? Let me guess—is it something like, 'Neverending'? Are you 'Hope Neverending?' No. 'Hope Survives'? Oh, I know, something more conventional. Hope Good. You're good. Hope Good. That's your name, or it should be. That'd be the way Tonto would say it—'Hmm, Kemosabe, Hope good!'" The Tonto impression does not elicit even a smile.

"That's my name alright, Hope Good. And believe it or not, my sisters are (or were before they married) Faith Good and Charity Good."

"Wow. Something to live up to, I guess. Reminds me of a friend who named his girls, Molly, Polly, and Dolly. He also had two sons, Frank and Hank. A third son, the youngest and last child in the family is legally named Wilbur, but everyone called him, Tank."

"When I was a girl, I wanted an African sounding name, like Keisha or Shaquana. Hope seems corny and, oh I don't know, so white!"

"What were you like as a little girl? Smart and sassy, I bet."

Hope shuts down this line of inquiry. "I don't want to talk about that."

"What do you want to talk about?"

Hope quietly thinks about last night's fury and again wonders about his family's history with her house.

"Could I borrow your phone for a second, Barry?"

"No, sorry, you can't."

"Why not?" She feels her temper start to rise.

"You cannot borrow something I do not have. I stopped carrying a phone about four years ago. Can't stand the little buggers."

She does not respond and silently chews the last bite of her breakfast. Had she wolfed it down? Barry's plate had barely been touched. Although feeling reticent, she forces herself to speak.

"That frittata is really good! Thank you."

"My pleasure. The secret ingredient is mayonnaise."

"You're kidding!"

"Actually, I am. My mother used to say this whenever anyone praised something she made. Her actual secret ingredient was sugar! Depending on the dish, she might put a cup, a half cup, a quarter cup, or a mere teaspoon. The green beans or turnips at our house were always just a little bit tastier than anyone else's."

"Anyone in your family come down with the diabetes?"

"Everyone except me. I lost my appetite for sugar midway through high school when I tired of fat jokes, fat shaming and bullying."

"You damn skinny now. We probably should get going. You going to finish your breakfast?"

"One more bite..." He pierces a hefty bit of the egg dish and very deliberately chews while looking at her. Hope guesses he is waiting for her to talk but she will not give him the satisfaction. The last swallow of juice is downed so slowly it seems to her a disciplined mindfulness exercise for her benefit. She watches him grab the glass, raise the glass, tip the glass, empty the glass, and return the glass to the table as if in a trance.

Maybe Barry is a hypnotist! She looks away to break the spell. "I'm done," he says. "Would you like this, or should we save some for later?"

Hope does not like the emphasis he puts on the word, "we." '*There is no* we...' she wants to say. Instead, she says, "I'll finish it," taking his plate.

Barry can tell Hope no longer has an appetite for small talk and silently takes on the task of cleaning up.

"I'm not sure why everything you do seems to piss me off," she says as he takes the plate from her.

He stares at the empty plate and slowly returns it to her. "It looked as if you were finished."

"Not that, you idiot." She gives it back to him. "Doing things in *my* house without bothering to ask or communicate your intentions rubs me the wrong way. It is as if you take it for granted that you are entitled to look in my closet, fix my breakfast, and wash my dishes. Not sure where this sense of entitlement comes from—may be rooted in white privilege, male privilege, the perks of old age, or good old-fashioned ableism."

Barry drops into the chair and with big, sorrowful eyes takes her hands. "I am so sorry, Hope."

She pulls back her hand. "Also, is it not a sense of entitlement for you to think you can touch me any way or any time you want? We aren't lovers, soul mates, or really even friends."

"What are we, then? I don't know what the label should be, but I feel as if we are onto *something,* or could be something. Am I that off-base? There *is* something between us. Call it chemistry or electricity..." This word jars her. He raises his hands. "I will do my best to refrain from touching you and try to let you know when I want to cook or do anything else for you—especially in your house." He lowers his hands and sighs. "Jesus. How could I so misread or believe there is anything going on between us? Nothing extraordinary or real from our session in the workshop? Your brief walk afterwards? Or, that incredible embrace in the hotel room?"

This speech hits Hope hard and leaves her speechless. She is about to cry. Instead of answering Barry, she spins her chair, announces it is time to go, and leaves the room.

No words or even a significant glance at one another while they gather things, go into the garage, and prepare to depart. Hope seems to have more difficulty than usual with her chair, but Barry pretends not to notice.

'You want help, ask for it!' the petulant seven-year-old inside thinks to himself. Hope jerks her head as if he had said these words out loud. Perhaps, he had. "Damn Tourette's!" he mutters aloud.

"You say something?" she says while backing the car out of the garage.

"Not really. Occasionally, I say things not worth listening to."

"So, I have noticed, Mr. Strange."

They remain quiet until they get to the bustling traffic of Rt.1.

"May I ask you a question?" he says.

"If you must..."

"If you prefer I don't, I won't."

"Oh, go ahead. I may not give you an answer you'd like, however."

"Fair enough. You do not seem to like my company and attention all that much. Why did you ask me to come home with you last night?" He hates the rather pitiful tone and wishes he could take it back.

Focused on merging with the traffic on I-395, she does not answer right away. "If I told you I hoped to return to that intense connection with you that seems to get me on my feet and actually walk for the first time in ten years, it might encourage you to pursue even more interaction and connection."

"Which is something that at least part of you doesn't want?"

"Right."

"So, today, you are not going to tell me that last night you hoped for more connection..."

"Yes."

"But you just did."

"Stop talking to me while I drive, please."

"May I just say that you give me mixed messages?"

"No, you cannot."

"Well, I just did. So there!" He gives her a sputtering raspberry, just light enough to make her smile.

When they reach the hotel parking garage, Hope continues to discourage any further discussion. When the doors close on the elevator to take them to the lobby and ballroom, Barry turns to her as if they were strangers.

"Pardon me if I disturb your ascent, but you seem like an interesting person. Could I trouble you for your phone number? I want to leave a short message."

"Oh, yeah? I don't give my number out to strangers. Tell me now. What would that message be?" Her smile says the amenable Hope is now online.

The goofy version of Barry holds an imaginary phone to his ear and sings in his Stevie Wonder voice. "I just called to say, I love you/I just called to say how much I care/I just called to say I love you/And I mean it from the bottom of my heart."

Hope's friendly smile fades as the elevator chimes and the door opens to the lobby. "I know you mean no harm, but something about white men singing like Black performers rubs me the wrong way." She rolls into the lobby and towards the hotel ballroom before he has time to fashion any kind of response.

Barry walks slowly toward the front desk. Distraught that he may have caused offense, he examines his motivation and the emotional tone and inflection of the fragment of song he imagined might amuse and/or charm Hope. He *loves* Stevie Wonder's music and means no disrespect. Had she mistaken the lightness and fun in his voice for mockery?

"Mr. Strange!" a voice rings out. Barry looks up and away

from this gloomy self-incrimination to see the desk clerk, Malcolm, smiling broadly at him. "Very good to see you this morning!"

"Is it, now?" he responds with a hint of menace. "Forgive me, Malcolm. I just heard the most distressing news..." *'That I am still a racist,'* he adds to himself.

"Oh. You must have heard about the riot."

"What? What riot?"

"Right over there in the lounge. There was a bit of a row late last night. It involved people you know. Let me pull up the notes from the overnight clerk..." Barry steps closer to hear. The chatter of dozens of people in the lobby is overwhelming. "It says here that your homeless friend, William, was in the lounge with two couples apparently from the workshop you're doing..."

"Yes!" Barry shouts. "Jane and Ned, Mary and Fred. Nice people."

"That's right. Their names are listed in the report. They ended up vouching for William, maybe also known as Joe. There is some confusion about the name—the night manager got suspicious and thinks maybe the Black guy by the name of William is pretending to be the guy you checked in as Joe."

"Oh, for crying out loud..."

"Anyway, the real problem arose when someone else from the workshop, a very inebriated man by the name of Bart (no last name given), had engaged this group, also 'probably inebriated' according to the clerk making this report. William is almost arrested by the police..."

"Police!"

"Yes. This drunk fellow, Bart, stopped at their table and

proceeded to '*castigate*' Joe for some transgression earlier in the day." Malcolm reads the next part. "'*When he began to swear and use racial slurs, Ned and Fred rose and attempted to steer Bart away from their table. Bart resisted. According to their statements, Bart punched Ned in the face and Fred in the stomach. William or Joe Smith rose to help defend them. He and Bart threw punches and ended up wrestling on the floor, upending drinks and snacks not only from their table but also from a table nearby.'* The report goes on a little further describing how the hotel security man and others tried to break it up. Guests and staff, including the clerk who wrote up the report, started arguing with each other. Some sided with the Black guy, some with Bart, until it looked like a riot might erupt. Someone called 911 and six policemen, two in riot gear, joined the '*fray.*' Sadly, they put handcuffs on the Black guy and supposedly roughed him up a little. They were about to take him '*Downtown*' before the woman called Jane got everyone's attention and straightened out the entire mess."

"Jesus!"

"That's for whom she cried out for help. '*Help us, Jesus! Help us!*' The police eventually let Joe or William go and told Bart he is not under arrest, but would he like to go get a cup of coffee before he drives home?"

"What! They were taking him out for coffee? That's totally weird."

"And a donut they said. Maybe they wanted to make sure he'd be sober enough to drive. Exciting, huh? We don't often get riots in here."

"Sounds like it made your day. His real name is William, by the way. Street name unknown. Hope he's okay. Have you seen him this morning?"

"I have not seen him and not likely to. The night clerk notes that when he and his companions went their separate ways, Joe (or William) disappeared and returned a few minutes later with his loaded grocery cart. He told the clerk he would not be returning."

"Holy shit! Where did he go?"

Malcolm shrugs. He is not unsympathetic about the situation. He is about to say, '*I could have told you so,*' but refrains from doing so. "Would you like to cancel tonight's and tomorrow's reservation for Room 417?"

Barry thinks for a couple seconds. "Not quite yet. I'm going to look for him and maybe get him to come back. You would still welcome him, would you not?"

"Certainly, Mr. Strange," Malcolm replies in a very uncertain tone of voice.

Barry is about to run out the door and see if William is back at his place on the sidewalk where he had first met him. But someone across the lobby is waving at him. He rushes over to her.

It is Mary. "I guess you heard what happened last night."

"I heard what the official hotel version might be. Tell me yours."

"I blame Fred!" She had tossed and turned and thrown this thought back and forth all night long. Unreasonable as it might be, it felt good to say it out loud. "The five of us were having a jolly time in the lounge. William's stories had us all roaring! I told Fred I thought it was a mistake to be drinking so much, but he wouldn't listen to me. Fred kept buying William one drink after another to encourage him. And he got really drunk."

"William?"

"No! Fred! William held his liquor a lot better than everyone else. Fred gets incredibly loud when he drinks, and Jane and Ned were also boisterous. You know how grumpy and judgmental one can get when everyone else is drunk, uninhibited, and trying to outdo each other in jokes and cleverness? Well, that was me. I thought maybe our little group wasn't as loud as it felt to me, but it was definitely loud enough to annoy our fellow seminar member, Bart. I had noticed him sitting with two other men I don't think were part of the workshop. While William is laughing particularly hard at something Jane said, Bart came over to where we were sitting and just stands there silently watching. William stopped and nodded at him. 'You having a good time, William?' Bart says with obvious attitude. 'As a matter of fact, I am,' William says, not at all backing down in the face of what Jane later described as, '*White man disapproval*.'

"'Would you mind not having as loud a good time? My friends and I would like to be able to have our conversation without listening to so much 'shuck 'n jivin',' Bart says."

"He really used those words?" Barry asks.

Mary nods. "William quite calmly told Bart that he may not have the correct interpretation of what 'shuck 'n jivin' is. It almost ended right there, but Fred very quickly escalated the situation by standing up and demanding Bart apologize. Bart countered by saying he is the one needing to hear an apology. William, trying to end this before it got out of hand, muttered something like, 'Sorry if I offended you, Brother Bart.' Bart, as drunk if not more so than everyone else, threw back his head and spit out something along the lines of, 'I'm obviously no brother of some wino.' He obviously regretted the words as soon as he said them, but the damage was done. Fred called him an 'asshole.' Being furious and drunk, he gave Bart a little shove that Bart returned, which made Fred lose his balance. When Ned jumped up to catch him, he incidentally jostled Bart and got punched in the ribs for doing so. This horrified William and he leaped up swinging. Bart's friends then showed up swinging."

"Holy shit."

"Holy it wasn't. But it was some shitty scene. Jane and I were screaming like hell, trying to get them all to stop. Hotel security and another staff person tried stopping it also. Police showed up and, predictably, believed Bart's ridiculous claim that William was to blame. They put handcuffs on him, but Jane and I convinced them it wasn't all his fault."

"And the cops took Bart out for coffee and donuts..."

"We were probably too busy yelling at our husbands to notice that." Mary adjusts her skirt and pushes her bangs from her forehead. Does she need a haircut? She feels a little guilty to be so exhilarated by the incident. Life had always seemed one boring event after another.

The music of Edvard Grieg wafts from inside the ballroom.

"Shit," Mary uncharacteristically cusses. "Do we have to go in for more of this BS?"

"You think it worthless? I'm finding it quite stimulating."

"Getting your selfie improved, are you?" Mary thinks about reeling in her bitterness but needs to say one more sarcastic thing. "This self-improvement workshop works wonders with racists."

Barry reacts to someone walking past. "Well, speak of the devil... Good morning, Bart!" Bart halts his swift progress towards the music and stares at them. Barry lets his anger get the better of him. "Did you have a good time last night attacking a homeless Black man?"

"Fuck you!"

"No, fuck you," Barry says with disarming tenderness. "Are you finding this workshop helpful in getting hateful racial prejudice out in the open? Even if you may not be able to comfort and bring peace to the souls of anyone but yourself, I nevertheless pray you may find some measure of joy and peace within your own soul."

That Barry delivers these words with such palpable emotional warmth so stuns Mary that she nearly falls backward. Bart is also visibly jarred by the surprising timbre and carefully chosen words. His voice cracks and sputters before managing to revert to form and advise Barry to, "Go to hell, asshole!"

Fuming, Bart storms off.

"You sure told him!" Mary notes with a hint of sarcasm.

Barry shrugs. "I was a little hard on him, I guess." Mary smiles, deciding at that moment to like him a little bit more. "A guy like that can push all your buttons. Yet, somewhere inside of him is a real human being."

"You think?"

"I know a lot of people like that," he goes on in a serious tone. "You do too. Men, white men particularly, are frightened by their own shadow. They imagine and project their worst fears about themselves onto 'the Other'—the immigrant, the weak, the scared, the soft, the liberals..."

"Women..."

"Yes, unfortunately, yes. The compassion and wisdom of women, of anyone, definitely feels like a threat to the trembling tiny unreal ego that the man has learned to protect with the armor, shield, and sword of belligerence, contempt, and, as a final solution, violence."

"Jesus."

"Probably not Jesus. He may have been an exception to the rule of the insane dominance of patriarchy and privilege. But he also died a horrible death." He smiles his most reassuring smile.

"Yes, but then he rose from the dead," she says with sarcasm. "And you? Are you an exception? How do you know all this?"

"I'm a man, aren't I? A white man of some privilege, and by a stroke of luck, of some wealth. When I had the chance, I went on a journey to know myself. What I just told you is just a tiny slice of what I learned—about men trapped in their own minds, about what I learned about me, Barry Strange, Not-so-Famous Celebrity."

"Uh, oh. Sounds as if we're about to hit the final note of *'Peer Gynt.'*"

"You go on. I've got something else I have to do. I need to find William."

"Oh, dear. I almost forgot about him. He had a great time at the workshop. Maybe he forgot or overslept. Go roust him out of bed!"

They hug. Barry turns her by the arms so he can deliver this information face to face. "You haven't heard. William checked out of the hotel after last night's fracas. Sorry to spill it like this—tell the others. I need to find him."

Barry turns and dashes out of the hotel. When he had disappeared, Mary turns to see Fred *running* toward her. She had not seen her husband run as fast in an exceedingly long time.

"Mary! What are you doing? We should be in our seats." He pulls her toward the door being slowly closed by Elaine. She nods to reassure and invite them inside.

"I was talking to Barry. Did you know William checked out of the hotel? Barry went to look for him."

Fred stops and stares at her. He feels a convulsive reaction in his chest. He is not going to cry! He is not! "Maybe we can help sort everything out later. You coming?"

Mary looks toward a door as if it held a clue about what she should do. It does not. She follows Fred into the hall.

CHAPTER ELEVEN

Barry sees no sign of William where the two men had met the day before. He studies the sidewalk space between two units of an office building, remembering how William had made it his own. The two wings of the building jut forth leaving an inviting 12'x12' area protected from the elements on three sides. When rain or snow was forecast, William could stretch a tarp a few feet over his head.

Yesterday, the grocery cart had sat outside this niche while William sat inside it. The gray tarp had been spread in front of him with many interesting items. A rather artistically made flyer taped to the bucket informed passersby that the items (hand-made, found, purchased, or maybe even stolen) were "not for sale." They could, however, be taken home for "free" in return for a donation.

No cute little toys or figurines, no 5 or 6 pens wrapped in several rubber bands, no masks left over from the pandemic, nor a stack of blank index cards are available today.

Yesterday, Barry had barely glanced at the things arrayed on the tarp. He thinks it more than strange that today he clearly *sees* so many of them in his mind's eye—the broken tin whistle, a few unmarked pill bottles containing God knows what, some Christmas bows, a rusted tin water bottle, and abstract art sketched upon a set of brown coasters with colored markers.

This phenomenon might have felt too weird for comfort had he not been more concerned about William. *Where is he? Where could he go with a grocery cart full of stuff?* Barry walks around a few blocks. A search seems futile. He is returning to the hotel when some elemental mental constructions from within apparently collapse.

The doorman carefully watches him approach. "Everything alright, Mr. Strange?"

Although Barry sometimes has fun pretending to be famous, he often feels unnerved when strangers know his name. He's forgotten the previous acquaintance with the young Black man working the door. Barry sees the hotel and wonders why it looks so familiar.

"I'm Elliott," the Doorman says kindly. "We talked a little yesterday. I am glad to see you. You gave me a relatively extravagant tip, a hundred dollars to be exact. I thought it might be possible you slipped me a denomination higher than you intended." When Barry does not respond, Elliott removes the C-note and hands it to the obviously distraught older man.

Barry takes the bill and stares at it. He hated such moments when any sanity he once had disappeared. "I gave you this yesterday?"

"Yes, you did. In return, I think, for relatively minor assistance."

Barry does not move a muscle for several seconds. He looks up and down the busy avenue. He hopes it might soon return to him the knowledge of what city he is in—and why. He is touched to see compassion in the face of the bright young man in front of him. He hands the cash back to him.

"Don't think I need this where I'm going."

Elliott does not like the sound of this. "Where are you going, Mr. Strange? Back to the seminar, maybe?"

'*Seminar—that sounds familiar,*' he thinks. He has a sense of being somewhere doing something rather exciting with some other people. Calling this gathering a seminar seems about right. "I am going nowhere, Elliott. Don't you know there is nowhere to go but here, no time to be anywhere but now?"

"That's deep. You downing more edibles today?"

Barry has no idea what he is talking about. He is aware that he may have slipped away from vital connections, memories, and fundamental agreements about reality. Where it all went so suddenly feels like an unusual thing, but what did he know? The usual context for comprehending any experience has inexplicably vanished.

"I don't know what you're talking about," he tells Elliott.

"If you'd like my advice, you should go easy on the drugs. Would you like me to help you get to your room?"

"My room?"

"Yes. Number 417, if I recall." He taps his tablet. "Yes. It is the room you reserved for Joe Smith." The blank look on Barry's face sends him back to tapping. "He is also known as William Smith."

"William!" His face lights up remembering. "Where did he go?"

"Looks like he checked himself out early this morning but, according to the record, the room remains reserved in your name, 'Barry Strange.'" Elliott leans heavily on the appellation just in case it had been forgotten. "If you no longer need the room, you should perhaps let the desk know."

"I should find William—make sure he's okay." Everything is coming back to him. "You wouldn't happen to know where he might have gone. He isn't at his usual spot down the street near Wells Fargo."

"He might be at CCNV, the Community for Creative Non-Violence. It is the largest homeless shelter in D.C.. It's on 2nd St. NW. I'll call them for you…"

Elliott whips out his phone and asks it to call the shelter. He asks whoever answered whether they know if Joe or maybe William Smith is currently there.

"I'll wait," he says to the phone. He whispers to Barry, "He's there. They're getting him. You feeling better, Mr. Strange?"

"Strangely enough," he answers. It is all slowly coming back to him—the seminar, the woman Hope! The church friends, the sub sandwiches with William and Hope. The workshop variety show! The car drives to and from the house once owned by Pop and Grammy. His pitiful ploys to gain the affection and/or respect of Hope.

Elliott announces he is activating the speaker phone.

"Is this the William who was staying at the Regency last night?"

"Maybe. Who wants to know?"

"Relax, man. This is Elliott, the doorman. Remember me?"

"I remember."

"I got somebody here wants to talk to you…" He hands Barry the phone and shows him how to turn off the speaker, but he doesn't seem to care if Elliott and everyone else can hear his conversation.

"William! This is Barry."

"Who dat?"

"You know—Barry! The guy that got you that fancy hotel room. Why did you take off? Anyone tell you had to leave?"

"No. I wanted to go. I made enough trouble."

"From what I hear, it wasn't you that started it. Come on back."

"Thanks for calling, Barry. I'm just as happy here. More like where I belong. I got friends here and good folks helping me get through the day. I'll never forget what you done for me, though."

"I liked you being here. The whole gang did—Hope, Mary, Ned and Fred."

"And Bart. Don't forget Bart."

"I think they might kick him out of the workshop. If I don't kick his ass first. Whether he's still around or not, there are a lot of people who got your back."

"Just the same, Barry. I ain't going back there. Tell all those good folks good-bye from me."

William hung up the phone. Barry hands it back to Elliott while a terrible sadness comes over him.

"I thought we were going to be friends forever."

"Things don't always work out the way we think." Elliott looks away. He has mixed feelings seeing this old man cry. Part of him is touched by the surprising dramatic spectacle of a white man grieving about some homeless Black guy. But he is also glad to witness what sounds a bit like Black liberation. William, or Joe, or whoever he is, had apparently decided he is no longer part of a rich guy's pet project. "May I be of further assistance, sir?"

Barry stares at Elliott for a few moments. The tangible aura of caring compassion projected by the young doorman has been replaced by official, professional courtesy.

"No, Elliott, you have done more than enough." He gives the hundred-dollar bill back to him. "I seem to have recovered my sense of self, poor and limited as it may be. Wait a sec—I got an idea. Maybe you can help me with something. Can you find that homeless shelter on your baby computer? What was the name of it—CCNV, was it?"

"*Baby* computer? You mean my phone?" It takes Elliott about three seconds to find it. "Okay, Mr. Strange, I'm on their website."

"Is there a button or something to make a donation? If so, punch it!"

"Done. You want to donate something?"

"I'll put in the figure and a card number, if I can borrow your phone."

"Sure. You don't have a phone?"

"Can't stand the little buggers..."

In what seems an eternity to Elliott, Barry types in the necessary information for a donation to the Creative Center for Non-Violence in honor of his friend, William Smith. When the transaction is at last concluded, he hands the phone back to the doorman.

Elliott takes a peak at the screen and nearly drops the phone. "You donated a million dollars!!!"

Barry offers him a small smile. With a brief bow, he skips

across the pavement to the front door.

Once again inside the Regency Hotel, Barry finds himself in serious self-deliberation. He does not understand why he treasures it so, but the severance of the connection with William has shaken him deeply. Coupled with Hope's repeated determination to push him away, he thinks perhaps it is time to step away from this emotional, spiritual, and sociological mélange, step away from life, maybe.

It would be easy enough to take the elevator down to the garage, get into his smart-ass Tesla, and drive home or maybe just keep driving somewhere. No one would miss him, no one would really care. And, despite investing energy and insight, creativity and nonsense into the passions and people here, he himself would soon forget all the real or imagined significance of the moments they had together shared.

Such is the stuff of dreams. Such is life. Barry lifts his eyes off the mandala design of the tiled floor and sees the desk clerk, Malcolm, staring at him. He gathers what strength he can from the Universe as he makes his way towards him. He tells himself, not for the first time this weekend, it is okay for him to be friendly and to feign interest to someone, if not interest itself.

"Hello again, Mr. Strange."

"Malcolm...I started to wonder, as I walked over here, how's it going with the young woman with whom you were smitten." Malcolm tilts his head and assumes an expression of complete bewilderment. Barry plows on. "Juanita! That's her name, isn't it?"

Malcolm looks as if he is choosing his words carefully.

"There is a woman from the housekeeping crew with that name. But I don't know how you got the impression I was '*smitten*' with her."

"I believe you told me so yesterday."

"I assure you, I did not."

Why Malcolm dissembles on such a harmless matter, Barry cannot fathom. Perhaps, he fears management might frown on any hint of staff fraternization.

"Very well," Barry says. "'Tis no business of mine. Simply curious. What is my responsibility, however, is Room 417. I have talked with Mr. Smith and he will not be returning to the hotel."

"I am so very sorry to hear so," Malcolm pronounces with absolutely no hint of regret or sorrow. "Would you like to cancel the reservation for tonight and tomorrow?"

"I would."

Malcolm taps a few keys and shows Barry a printout of the charges for amenities William had accrued.

"Wow. He did a lot of drinking, didn't he? $320! That's a lot of mini bottles. Pay-for-View, $100! What did he watch? That's okay, I don't want to know. I told him to enjoy himself. I need to sign something?"

"Hope it was worth it for," Malcolm says. Barry shrugs.

While signing off on the room and the charges, the housekeeper Juanita strolls by. He notices but does not remark on the flirtatious smiles and winks Malcolm and she exchange. He flashes the grinning and beaming clerk a look of exaggerated innocence that produces another broad smile.

'*A smile from Malcolm!*' Barry thinks. '*All is not lost.*' He turns to Juanita. "*Buenos dias, senorita. La gente de aqui te trata bien*?

The people here treating you well?"

"*Muy bien. Mucho major de lo que sone.*"

Juanita lets show the most beautiful smile Barry had ever remembered seeing. She slowly, seductively even, shines an even bigger, wider, warmer grin upon Malcolm.

Barry thinks, for a moment, that he may be hallucinating once again when it seems as if Malcolm's face literally lights up as if a soft golden flashlight had turned on him.

For what is probably only a second or two (but seems so much more), the desk clerk, Malcolm, and the housekeeper, Juanita, barely move a muscle and say not a word. Barry (perhaps hallucinating again) would swear (if asked) that he could not only *see,* but also *feel* waves of loving energy vibrate back and forth.

Juanita smiles and projects strong emotional energy that gently reaches Malcolm who allows it to pierce and apparently dissolve his customary armor. Malcolm smiles back projecting some strong energy back at her.

'*Something definitely going on.*' Barry thinks. Out of a life that had witnessed many unexplained miracles and wonders, this exchange, this mutual simultaneous emittance and absorption of loving vibrations feels to Barry to be one of the best he had been fortunate enough to witness. '*How wonderful this is!*'

They both turn towards him, as if they heard or read his thoughts and emotions. Perhaps they had. The goodwill riding the frequencies floating back and forth between them now seems to be shining on him. For only a moment, three people totally, and unconditionally, love one another.

Barry recalls being transported like this at a couple weddings he'd attended—maybe even at one of his own! He accepts the loving energy they silently bestow on him and does his best to return it. A memory from his stay in a Tibetan vihara emerges. The round joyful face of the teacher, Chung-Li, reminds him that there is no *doing*, only *being*. *"End your mental battles with the stories of the past and future. There is nothing you have to do but allow your body—your eyes, ears, nose, and hands to be here. Close the gap. Be the light, be the love."*

Not sure what to say, if anything, Barry looks at the young couple and spreads his arms in a way might look as if he is blessing them.

"Ahora los declaro esposo y esposa." They simultaneously gasp and rush into each other's arms. To the small number of people who happen to stop and watch this impromptu dramatic/romantic scene, Barry explains in English. "I just sanctified their love for each other and pronounced them spouse and spouse."

The witnesses, which Barry notices includes Elaine and Hope, applaud and cheer.

He thinks maybe he'd get a small nod of approval from Hope, the one person from whom he most hoped to be judged approvingly. She has a slight smile on her face, but he cannot determine if this is a look of admiration or something else. It is both. The *something else* is not disapproval, exactly. More an observation, a creative critique.

Hope and Elaine had watched Barry bless the two hotel workers with the same total attention and loving kindness Hope had experienced with him. She admired the *chutzpah* and spirit of the scene but had to laugh when up popped the persona within herself that she recognized as the '*theater critic.*'

"A bit *schmaltzy*," she whispers to Elaine. "A tad over the top."

"Yes," Elaine replies with sweet innocence. "I love romantic weddings."

At that moment, a woman with an air of authority emerges from an office and Malcolm and Juanita cease embracing. Humans were caught in the act of loving each other. No one quite knows what to do.

"Are you the manager?" Barry demands.

"An Assistant Manager, but I am in charge today. What is going on?" This is directed at Malcolm, but being halfway in halfway out of a trance, he is having trouble. Juanita has an irrational fear she is about to be deported. The emotional reality of love is threatening to become overcome by the way too familiar unreality of the fear of authority.

Barry answers her. "What two fantastic people you have working with you today! I hope to have a chance to submit a very high-performance rating, indeed. I think I speak for everyone here when I say that they have gone out of their way to make us feel very, very welcome." Hope and Elaine join the others watching with them in applauding the sentiment. "Could you make a note on their work evaluations? In my opinion, they deserve 5-star ratings and substantial bonuses and raises."

"I agree!" Hope yells. She hopes no one would ask why she seconds that emotion. She had virtually no contact with either one of them.

"Whatever..." The Assistant Manager shrugs. "Juanita, dear, can I see you in my office? *Por favor.* Malcolm, your phone is blinking. Thank you for your recommendation, Mister?"

"The name is Strange. Barry Strange, Galactic Celebrity."

The Assistant Manager, Karen, wishes all a "Good Day" and escorts the trembling housekeeper out of the lobby. She is not sure what is going on with the two staff members or the guests.

Juanita is so young, so new to the city and country, so pretty. Is she naïve and easily seduced? Malcolm seems particularly good at his job, but it is difficult to read the person behind the aloof exterior.

Karen asks Juanita to sit and tries to reassure her that she is in no trouble. She gives her a cup of water and consults the Spanish app on her phone.

"*Te gusta* Malcolm?" she asks her. Juanita nods. "Is he kind to you? *Amable?*"

"Yes, Miss Karen. Truly kind. *Muy amable.*"

"*Por favor tenga cuidado*. Please be careful."

"*Por que?*"

"*Eres muy bonita, Juanita.*"

Wary and worried, Juanita waits a moment before responding. "Gracias."

"Men, young men particularly, are attracted to pretty young girls like bees to sweet smelling flowers. But, like bees, men often take the pollen from pretty flowers and do not return."

"I do not understand. *No entiendo. Amo* Malcolm. *El me ama*. He loves me."

"*Entiendo*, Juanita. Just be careful! *Tenga cuidado.*"

"Si, senora. No sex at work."

"That's not what I mean. But yes—no sex at work. I would be careful outside of work also. Don't let him break your heart." She consults her app. "*No dejes que te rompa el corazon.*" Karen is not sure she is getting through to the young girl at all. She can only think of one more last bit of advice and looks again at the app. "If you do have sex, make sure to use a condom—*condon, por favor.*"

"*Condon, si. Sexo en el trabajo, no. Si, senora!*" Juanita says. She patiently waits for any additional directives or words of wisdom from her boss. "I like working here very much," she adds with a little more accent than usual.

"You're a good worker. You are fast and thorough. Several guests mentioned your friendliness and thoughtfulness in their online reviews. I'll add Mr. Strange's opinion to your file."

Juanita is not sure she catches all these words fast enough but the words, "good worker," along with the friendly tone allow her to think she is receiving a compliment and that there is no trouble.

"Si, senora," she says.

When dismissed, Juanita sees Malcolm hard at work on a computer. She puts her hands on his shoulders and whispers, "Boss say, 'Use condoms but no *sexo* at work.' Is *bueno, si?*"

Before he can recover from this shocking declaration, Juanita runs off laughing. She looks incredibly happy. He had not thought it possible he could ever be as happy as she can make him feel. But suddenly there it is—rising out of a warmth at the bottom of his spine, spreading throughout his torso, then pouring out the top of his head.

Despite his own stern self-inflicted admonition to hold it in, hold it together, and keep it tight, Malcolm throws his head back and lets everything out. He laughs with utter abandon until some logjam within gives way. He cries there and then at his workstation.

Partly crying in total joy, partly in abysmal grief, he wails long and hard on behalf of all that that had been lost all that has been gained. Fellow staff members give him wide berth while hotel guests postpone their little questions and concerns until a better time.

Juanita disappears back to work and Malcolm turns his attention back toward his work duties. Barry is feeling such an overflowing abundance of love for all beings that he rushes toward what certainly appears to be the open and inviting arms of Hope.

Elaine, standing nearby, displays astonishment at the passion of this embrace by a slight tilt of her head. She softly whispers, "Good gracious me!"

This utterance reminds both Barry and Hope that there are more souls in the universe than the two of them and disengage. A tearful Hope reaches for Elaine's hand while Barry stands erect and wraps his arms around her.

"I know you also feel the love," he tells her.

Elaine feels something. She almost always does. And, if a label is needed, she feels it fair to label that unconditional affection and attention for other humans, '*Love.*' Ever since her first experience with the Seminar seven years ago, she not only allowed herself to have such positive reactions to most everyone she met. She considered it a type of sacred *duty*.

"Yes, of course," she says to them both. "To me, love is the most natural and even easiest way to be. Shall we return to the workshop?"

Elaine walks a half-step ahead while Barry pushes Hope across the lobby.

"Are you licensed to marry people?" Hope asks Barry.

"Heavens, no! I merely offered them my blessing."

"Sometimes a couple needs *permission* by someone, a stranger maybe, to tell them it is okay to love each other," Elaine says.

"Nobody as strange as this guy," Hope jokes. "What is *your* story, Elaine? You have a day job? Boyfriend? Wife?"

In the space of about 30 seconds, Elaine shares a narrative about what she calls, "full human emergence." Born into poor white working-class squalor with all its grievance, ignorance, and bigotry, Elaine is rescued from what seems a likely path of teen-age pregnancy and marriage, alcoholism and depression.

One high school teacher, who took the time and energy to care, steered her into community college and certification as a nursing assistant. Another mentor then encouraged her to become an RN in a psychiatric facility which stimulated interest in various "human growth" movements such as the "You Be You Seminar" in which the three of them found themselves this weekend.

"I have no partner or spouse," Elaine tells them, "But I could tell you about the true loves of my life—the hundreds of people from these workshops I have loved and helped steer onto paths for their own emergence."

For a brief flash of a moment, Elaine silently demonstrates with her eyes and the pure vibration of her emotional being what Joy and Love feel like to her.

She smiles and opens the door to a workshop scene erupting in full, terrifying chaos. Four strong men restrain each of the four limbs of a troubled and furious Bart. An actual muzzle spares all those assembled from hearing whatever vile and hate-filled words come out of the man.

"What the fuck!" Barry blurts out.

Although certainly not fans of the writhing figure that the handlers let drop to the floor, Barry and Hope both express strong disapproval of what is apparently meant to be a therapeutic technique.

Elaine grabs both of their hands. "It's not as bad as it looks," she whispers. The three of them watch from the rear of the room. Anton, now attired in a leather jacket festooned with chains, begins singing a soothing lullaby calling for all races, genders, and cultures to live and love each other in peace. This sets Bart off in another furious flaying of legs and arms. The muzzle blurs the words but not the emotion.

Elaine explains what is going on. "Anton only resorts to muzzling when someone needs to work on anger issues but can't seem to do so without using offensive racial slurs or other material that easily re-stimulates the distress in others. We weren't here to see the run-up, but the muzzle and other restraints are only deployed when a severely disturbed client agrees to their use. "I worked one-on-one with Bart. Despite vile things he may say or do, I believe there is still a human being in there hungry to be free of fear and anger." She stares at the pair of humans before her to make sure they are listening. "And Bart believes that also. There are some people who need to say out loud the awful things they feel inside in order to be rid of them. The muzzle is not there to prevent Bart from expressing vile feelings. It helps him express them more fully if he thinks others can be spared any harm his words might cause."

"Strange..." Hope mutters.

"I should help," Elaine says as she heads to the scene down front. Bart's emotional fury intensifies when he sees her come near.

"I don't think I can watch," Hope says. "Guess I'm not a very kind and forgiving person." She spins her chair and rolls quickly to the door. Barry pushes open the door and follows her out to the lobby.

"Thanks, Barry. I'm okay. You can return to the action."

"I don't really want to. Frankly, there's nowhere else I'd rather be right now."

"In a hotel lobby?"

"If that's where you are, yes."

"Oh, brother. You got some suave cornball moves." She rolls towards the plush stuffed furniture. "Come sit if you want. My neck gets tired looking up at people."

Barry sits in the chair nearest where she stops. He so wants to just hold her hand but dares not suggest it. '*Talk first, touch later,*' he tells himself. Her small smile hints that she perhaps catches the sentiment if not the thought.

"That is one strange scene in there," he says aloud.

"Indeed, Mr. Strange. Some people go out of their way to soothe and understand racists, but I just want to wring their necks," she hisses with pure venom.

"That's what I like about you. You are *so* sweet!"

"And you are so goofy! That's probably what I like about you."

"That you like anything at all feels like progress."

"Oh, yeah? Towards what?"

"Oh, I don't know. Friendship maybe? True love?"

"Dream on, Mr. Strange." The way she stresses his last name is a strong indication how Hope sees him. Though definitely weird, Barry is nevertheless someone to whom Hope feels she can talk straight and true and still feel safe. "Although there is support here for me also, this workshop is obviously created by and for privileged white people…"

"Obviously…"

"I get that the effort to help someone like Bart might also include the intention to help free him of racism…"

"Let's hope so…"

"But can I tell you what worries me?"

"Absolutely!"

"I wonder if all this therapeutic work on Brother Bart will only make him a more effective white supremacist. I understand the process—it's why I'm here. The loving attention from Anton, Elaine, and each other makes it safe for us to see and possibly rid ourselves from emotional and physical distress…"

"Yes. I think it possibly does that…"

"Crying heals grief, laughing and shaking heals fear, pounding a pillow can heal anger, and even yawning is supposed to do something… I forget what."

"It relaxes you…" Barry yawns.

Hope allows a huge, wide-mouthed inhale to fill her lungs and then loudly exhales.

"(yawn) Right!" Hope cannot stop. "*(yawn)* It supposedly *(yawn)* works on *(yawn)* physical *(yawn)* tension *(yawn)*…Shit! *(yawn)*"

Barry reaches for and delivers the longest, loudest yawn ever heard or seen by anyone anywhere. All chatter and movement in the hotel lobby cease.

A yawn from the front desk turns heads in Malcolm's direction. He sheepishly shrugs.

"It's contagious," Hope says while another champion-sized yawn takes off.

Barry and Hope continue exchanging yawns with Malcolm and another person or two in the lobby throwing in their yawns with seeming abandon.

"That is certainly fun," Hope says when the yawning session finally ends.

"I'm exhausted," Barry sighs. "What were we talking about? Seemed like it was important."

"Oh, I don't know," Hope takes a deep breath and exhales. "Does it really matter?" She feels so relaxed her entire body is tingling. And were her legs tingling? Or is it another phantom limb illusion?

She cannot stop her body from trembling. She is not sure she even wants it to stop. She seizes Barry's hand resting on the arm of the chair next to her. It is warm to the touch with a slight surge of energy. What seems odd to her is the near certainty that the vibration she feels is also her own. As people keep saying, cultural conditioning and delusion convince us that we are all separate, very lonely beings.

"Can you do me a favor, Barry?"

"Yes, anything."

Hope rolls to get as close to him as she can. "Can you hold me, please?" She holds out her arms, her face betraying a mixture of excitement, grief, hope, and fear.

"Gladly." Barry positions himself for an awkward, but relaxed, side by side embrace.

Hope feels the tremulous and contradictory urges and tensions within her suddenly calm. The energy is still there but the vibrations no longer collide with each other. It is as if the oscillation of diverse physical and emotional/spiritual frequencies had discovered and joined with respiratory rhythms and the beating of her heart and soul.

If Hope allows herself to admit it, she will have to say all the sensations running through her are also operating through the person embracing her. Every pulsating wave inside her flows on—past the apparent permeability of cells and organs; blood, arteries, muscles, and skin.

Whatever this energy inside of her is, it flows out of her and into the conglomeration of tissue and energy next to her. And whatever it is that flows inside him, this strange man named Barry, flows back into her. They are not two beings, but one.

And whatever energy that melds these two beings is not a closed system. All flows through their chairs, through the floor, throughout the room, and beyond...

"Wow..." Hope says as they disengage.

"Wow...is right," Barry agrees. The walls and ceiling of the lobby continue to shimmer, buckle, and connect them to the Cosmos... "Was that OJ in your fridge spiked with some very special ingredient?"

"Not unless you added something. I usually have a little bite of inspirational medicine in the morning, but I forgot today. You know what I'm thinking?"

"After that hug, I feel as if I should know what's on your

mind. But I don't. Could it be we should get a room and see what happens?" He arches his eyebrows up and down in what he hopes is a light comical touch.

It isn't received as such. Hope exhales hard and in disgust turns her chair away from him. "Jesus. You really know how to spoil a mood, don't you?"

"Do I? Huh, guess I misunderstood. I thought we were One with the Universe."

"That doesn't mean I want to go to bed with you."

"Did I say the word, 'bed'? I don't think so. I was joking, sort of. Sorry. Let's rewind. What are you thinking?"

"Oh, never mind. Let's go back to the seminar. Maybe Bart is now woke." Not eager to see what that looks like, neither budge. Hope's flurry of annoyance at Barry's attempt at jest fades. She closes her eyes as a sense of peace swiftly arises and quietly re-connects them—not only to each other, but to the entire room and, if the truth be known, beyond...

CHAPTER TWELVE

Hope feels as if she could stay wrapped within blessed silence and nothingness for a long time. When she recognizes she is dreaming, she slowly awakes and senses a stirring close at hand. Reluctantly, she opens her eyes and sees the desk clerk, Malcolm, standing over her.

"Are you well, Madam?" he wants to know.

"Quite well," she whispers. The way he tilts his head lets her know that he has not heard. She repeats herself and then adds, "Mr. Strange, where is he?"

"Madam?"

"Where did he go?"

"Mr. Strange?" he asks. "I am afraid I do not know who that is..."

"That's preposterous!" she spits out. "You know perfectly well who he is. Why are you pretending you don't?"

"Is he a resident here? I apologize for not recognizing his name. We have so many clients coming and going. It's hard to keep track..."

Hope feels this highly unlikely. "Barry Strange, a real nutty guy who calls himself a Famous Celebrity. He is a participant in The Seminar going on in there." She points to where was once a ballroom door but is now a wall with two floor-to-ceiling mirrors!

This cannot be. She begins to panic but stops herself to summarize some of the interactions between Malcolm and Barry of which she is aware. "You must remember him—he rented a room for our homeless friend, William, and let me take a nap there when I grew tired from the workshop that has been happening there for the past two days." She points once again towards the room which is no longer there.

What Hope sees in the mirror sets off further alarms. It is her reflection, certainly, her hand rising to cover her mouth agape in astonishment. The image is her, but in a different hairdo, different clothes and, most unusual still, the reflection has her sitting not in a wheelchair, but in a stuffed armchair.

Her legs twitch nervously. *What! Her legs move!*

The man with the nametag, 'Malcolm,' tries a lighter approach.

"There is a workshop going on in the mirror? How very strange, Alice!" Malcolm decides she is toying with him for some reason. "I believe I did see a March Hare darting in, saying something like, 'I'm late, I'm late for a very important date!'" He can see she is not at all amused and appears very distressed indeed. "I am so sorry, Madam. Can I help in some way? Call a friend, relative, or someone else? You have been quietly sitting here for a couple hours at least." When the woman doesn't, or can't, answer right away, Malcolm pulls out a rather odd-looking electrical device that he quickly taps. "Might I have your full name, please?"

"You don't remember me?" Hope looks around the space that no longer bears any resemblance to the hotel lobby she had been in and out of several times in the past two days. "This doesn't look like the hotel!"

Malcolm sits in the chair next to her and finds within himself, among several possible disguises, his *'compassionate face.'* "This, my dear, is not a hotel. We are in the 'Capitol Help Center'. Whatever help is needed, can be found." He hands her the small device.

Hope carefully studies the thin, stiff rectangular object a little larger than an outstretched hand. It is of a substance completely foreign to her eyes and touch. It is not cardboard, nor plastic, metal, or some new plant-based material. It seems *alive*, glowing and reacting to her touch with subtle vibrations.

The press of fingers leaves diversely colored afterimages. A bit enchanted by the results, Hope spends a few moments creating hand-sized works of art that genuinely lift her spirit. How and from where all this creative inspiration arises, she cannot say.

A splash of red reminds her of the cardinals she loved to watch at her grandparents' bird feeder. As if by miracle, her fingers produce an image of the red bird that touches something deep and magical inside.

"This is so beautiful..." she murmurs in ecstasy.

The elation, however, is short-lived. One exquisite work of art after another disappears whenever she lifts her touch from the device. To see a cardinal or flower or abstract design vanish like this sends her down a spiral of grief and loss so profound she feels she will go mad.

She looks at the person sitting near her. Forgetting that she is familiar with him, she reflexively studies the name badge affixed to the shirt. The six or seven black letters there lose their individual shape and form a solid black line that rises and falls, animating up and down like a wave.

She again looks at this person's face. *It is a man, isn't it? She knew his name, didn't she?* Once more her eyes rest on the rectangular badge on his shirt. The black wavy line within slows its undulation and assumes the look of words written in cursive...

Malcolm...at your service

Hope waves the artistic device in his face. "Malcolm! This is so weird! Can I save what I draw somehow? Send it to my email or printer?"

He furrows his brow as if deep in thought. "Hmm, no. I don't think so. I'm not sure I know what those things are. You do have an account, don't you? A Zee device? No? You must have some communication device."

"Ah, my phone!" she cries. She reaches for the small bag which contains all her most vital stuff. It is almost always stashed in her wheelchair which also, alarmingly, is nowhere in sight. "I don't have my phone or the bag which contains my phone and my wallet and my keys and my medications and a pack of tissues and cosmetics and a dozen other things I need!" Her voice rises in tone, volume, and emotional panic with each mentioned object. "And my chair! WHERE'S MY FUCKING CHAIR?" she screams at the top of her voice.

Malcolm (or whoever he is) calmly looks at her, completely unfazed by her distress. "Uh, aren't you sitting in it?"

"Not *this* chair! My wheelchair! It is a chair with wheels, you know for *cripples*, people who cannot walk under their own power?" she explains in that withering condescending tone of voice that her mother, and others, despised so. *'I will not absorb any words soaked in sarcasm,'* were the words Mom often spoke just before walking out of a room.

"You cannot walk?" Malcolm says with mock astonishment. "I believe you can."

This statement sends a chill up and down her spine. Hope feels very real, non-phantom impulses throughout thighs, calves, and feet. Although expecting serious unsteadiness and almost certain collapse, Hope feels a surge of strength and stability and slowly stands up and walks towards the big mirrors.

The image seems to be her, but younger, stronger, *livelier* than she is used to seeing. The reflection (or is it the mirror itself) appears charged with the same type of vibrating energy of the colorful, arty *'Etch-a-Sketch'* Malcolm handed to her. And this shimmer of sparks and light surrounding her own image? *What the hell is that?*

Hope turns to Malcolm. "What is going on? I've lost my chair, the workshop I was in...Barry! My stuff! The hotel has turned into a 'Help Center'? I am wearing new clothes, have a new hair-do..."

"And you can walk!"

She steps closer to him. *Were lit sparks shimmering around him, also?* "Yes. I can walk when three or four minutes ago, I could not. This is all disconcerting to say the least."

"And you need help?"

"Yes, I need help."

"Help is in your hands." He points to the warm, vibrating gizmo still in her grip. "Instead of creating pretty pictures with your fingers, place it between both hands for a few moments. Help will be on the way..."

She does just that with the pad and her hands parallel to the floor. This seems a bit awkward, so she twists and holds the pad in front of her chest in a way that feels, and looks, prayerful.

Hope looks toward Malcolm to maybe check if she is doing this correctly, but he is no longer there. Like almost everything else in her life from a few minutes ago, he too has vanished.

Deep confusion and wide-spread panic are close at hand. She quietly sits down and closes her eyes. The warmth of the pad still pressed between her hands reassures her somehow as she slips into a peaceful, meditative state.

Later, she might not know for what she is praying, but she definitely prays...

Once again, she finds herself aware and comforted to be at *One* with the great sea of Everything which paradoxically feels *full* yet entirely empty of material things. She has no body, no thoughts, really, other than to remind herself, *'This is okay.'* "If this be death," Hope says aloud awaking from her meditation. "It won't be so bad!"

From somewhere in the darkness, she hears a soft laugh. With some surprise, she remembers she has eyes! And opens them!

In a chair sits a familiar white man with a wide grin. Barry Strange, Infamous Doofus. She groans and lifts her hands to the arms of a chair—a wheelchair.

"Oh, dear God! Back here again?" She wails in pain and grief.

"You that glad to see me?" Barry cries out, in high spirits indeed.

Hope looks his way, relieved to see him smiling. "I actually am!" She grabs his arm. *'She actually touched me!'* Barry thinks. "I disappeared..." Hope continues.

"Oh, I know. Believe I went into a trance myself. When I emerged from my little nap, I checked your pulse to make sure you were still alive." He taps two fingers to her wrist but resists the temptation to prolong the contact. "Where did you go?"

"I'm not sure. I think I might have gone where you go when you're gone."

"Really? You woke up muttering something like, 'Death's okay!' You okay now?"

Before Barry can suggest it is time to return to the workshop, Hope jumps in with a full description of what she had been through—the immersion into Oneness, Emptiness, and the silent cosmic field of creative Potentiality followed by a very real encounter with a version of Malcolm who did not recognize her and handed her a kind of I-pad on which she drew lovely pictures and connected her with Oneness that seems a likely destination for the Soul or Mind, once the Body ceased to be.

"Quite a... what, dream? The Afterlife?" he suggests when she winds down and tires out.

"No! Not a dream," she says emphatically. "This was real, very, very real."

"Whoever said dreams weren't real?"

"I know I sound crazy. You are probably dying to provide an explanation, but there may not be one. How long were we out?"

"Not long, really." He looks at his wrist, but his watch is no longer there. 'Might have been a minute, maybe two tops."

"Seemed way longer than that."

"Dreams are like that. And maybe death also. I'm thinking this whole thing is just a weird Life-After-Death charade, maybe a sneak preview of what's to come."

Hope feels a need to put some distance between them and pushes herself towards the wall in front of her. In her Vision, two huge mirrors hung there. At this moment, a large video screen displays a loop of photographs and paintings depicting the people and events bordering the Potomac River stretching hundreds of years.

There are crowd scenes and marches that seem familiar, some hero's welcome perhaps for someone, the construction of unfamiliar buildings, and other unnamed gatherings and events. There are also photos of thousands of ordinary Black citizens doing ordinary things. Black families smiling at picnics and in churches, going in and out of shops, or playing ball in parks.

Although the neighborhoods, vehicles, clothing, and signage all suggest the style of the 60s, the 50s, 40s, 30s, and earlier, the photographs seem *new* somehow. Had they been digitally created to envision a happier milieu that never was? Where was the rampant racism, Jim Crow, and slavery of the past?

She suspects that the entire panoramic historical display is a contrived, photo-shopped concoction put together by a New York or L.A. dream studio. This hypothesis seems confirmed when the production begins to show "photos" of the Native tribes which once hunted, fished, and lived a relatively peaceful and indigenous existence long before the invention of photography.

Hope turns to see Barry watching her with serious attention.

"Can you believe they did this?"

"Did who did what?" Barry says with a smile.

She turns to look back at the screen. "Wait a sec…I want to see if they have bucolic images of happy slaves on Maryland and Virginia plantations."

Barry gets up and stands beside her. "Is this new?" he says pointing at the screen. "Don't recall seeing this yesterday."

"Neither do I."

"Let's ask the desk clerk, Malcolm," Barry suggests.

"Ask me what?" says a voice.

They turn to see the hotel desk clerk halt his passage behind them. He had an enigmatic grin on his face.

"We were wondering about this video," Hope says. "Is this new? Neither of us remember it being here yesterday." She stares hard, trying to adjust and compare this Malcolm with the Malcolm she had encountered in her one or two minutes of meditation, or whatever that was. This Malcolm in front of her lacks the powerful energy and sense of spiritual depth emanating from the Malcolm of her *dream vision*. He has different clothes! And the name on his badge no longer resembles an acid hallucination.

"No, not new at all," Malcolm says with a laugh. "This vid has been running non-stop every day, every minute, for as long as I've worked here. Over three years now. You both may have been too busy doing whatever it is you've been doing to notice."

"You sure about that Malcolm?" Barry stares at him. Sometimes he is able to tell whether someone is telling the truth or just misinformed by squinting and tilting his head just so...

"Yep. Positive about this one. Someone put it together when D.C. became a state."

Barry and Hope stare at each other, both with the same thought. *Should they correct him?*

"Malcolm, dear," Hope says gently. "Congress has been talking about making this city the 51st state, but they haven't done it yet."

"What are you talking about? I was living here when it happened and danced in the street myself." He laughs thinking she is pranking him.

"Don't know how you got the impression, Malcolm, but Hope is right," Barry says. "It still has taxation without representation."

Now it is Malcolm's turn to be concerned. *How could they both not know?* He looks at Barry, then at Hope, expecting to see some sign that they are kidding. But they look back at him as if *he* is nuts.

"Good grief, you both live under a rock?" He pulls out his phone and quickly finds a passage on the internet describing what to many was a momentous historical event seven years ago.

"Is this some kind of weird fake news campaign?" Hope says. "Can I search something on your phone?"

Malcolm hands it to her and gives Barry a helpless shrug. Hope panics with every swipe at the screen.

"Where have we been for the last seven years?" she asks Barry. "There is no way we could have missed this."

Malcolm takes back the phone. "I gotta get going, folks. I don't know what to say—at least it's not something really serious, like a war. Oh, look! There it is on the big screen."

They all watch scenes of a president signing the bill for statehood, of happy D.C. residents hugging and dancing, of banners and signs and parades all proclaiming, "Happy Statehood Day!"

"Here comes my favorite part!" Malcolm says. He pushes something on his phone and the stream of historical images pauses at a celebration on Constitution Avenue. "Look there!" He points a red laser at a group of people with huge smiles. One happy young man, especially, seems to beam right at them.

"That's you!" Hope shrieks.

"Fun, huh? I don't know why I was so happy that day. I'd only been in the city a little bit and doubt I would even have voted or paid attention to the news. People were really having a good time. Maybe so many folks passing joints and popping edibles had something to do with it."

"Could be..." Barry says as he steps closer to the screen. "It seems weird, but I feel as if I know a lot of these people. Wait a minute! I know *this* guy. We all do!"

Hope rolls near for a closer look. "Is that William? Omigod, it is!"

"I believe that is the same coat he wore yesterday," Barry says with wonder.

"It sure is," Hope says. "A little less shabby then. Is that his cart full of stuff behind him?"

"Could be." Barry is surprised by how strongly this image of his new friend from the street moves him. It is as if he can feel what William feels standing there among jubilant people but not really connected to them. He is glad people are happy. But, aside from a few smiles and a couple of '*Hi, how are you?*' comments, not many promising connections. William had that look of being '*alone in a crowd.*' "I think we should find William," he says to Hope.

She doesn't answer right away. Malcolm re-starts the video and with a wave returns to his post at the front desk. He cheerfully banters and flirts with another staff member there, a vivacious young blond woman Barry had not seen before.

This brief flirtation inexplicably unnerves him. Does he feel it unfairly betrays the housekeeper, Juanita? Although he and others had felt momentarily enchanted by the unofficial marriage blessing only a few minutes old, Barry intuitively senses Malcolm's apparent interest in someone else entirely is not the source of his very real unease. He does not really know Juanita and cannot discern whether a romantic attachment to Malcolm would be to anyone's benefit.

No, there is *something else* about the body language and exchange of words between Malcolm and this woman. A *strangeness* about it, a displacement maybe. It is as if the familiar characters of a play suddenly appear within a new and foreign scene divorced from the prior narrative context.

Barry turns to ask Hope if she has a similar impression, but she is not paying any attention at all to him, to Malcolm, or to the person with Malcolm. She is leaning forward in her chair in rapt attention to the historical presentation. Without looking, Hope senses Barry watching her.

"This video is not some white man's whitewash of white supremacist history," she tells him over her shoulder.

"No?"

"Nope! All the pictures are very real images of very real events."

"Is that so?" Barry says uncertainly. "Does that include the depictions of Native Americans before the invention of photography?"

"I can't say how, but yes. Sit down and look closely and you'll see what I mean."

Barry does sit and tries hard to keep an open mind, but some instinct to hold onto rationality will not allow him to believe for one second that such a thing is possible.

The presentation again goes through lovely photos of the culturally and ethnically diverse citizens of the small 51st state now known as "Columbia." Here in streets, parks, offices, theaters, and homes are Black & White people working and/or enjoying life together. Here are Muslims, Christians, Jews, and atheists playing games, dancing, laughing, talking, listening, and simply meditating together in peace.

One large circle of adults and children holding hands and joyously singing falls so out of focus that the various colors of their outfits, skins, and surroundings begin to fade and bleed into one another. The distinction between the forms of life and the objects on and around them fade.

One beautiful circle of myriad shades of light fills the screen that softly vibrates and beckons at the viewers. All imagery fades to what seems infinite emptiness.

"Very far-out," Barry whispers in that stoned hippie tone of voice which amused people fifty or sixty years ago.

"Hush!" Hope barks. She feels the story told with these images touches her deeply. Whether the man next to her is genuinely awed by the same story she sees or sarcastically poking fun at it is not important to her. "Watch the next part," she urges him.

From out of the black nothingness emerges a spark which spews forth like the light of stars. Lines of light become shapes, which turn into waves that resemble water that breaks upon land that produces trees and other vegetation that nourishes recognizable life forms such as insects, birds, reptiles, amphibians, mammals...

A four-legged furry mammal springs up erect to reach the high fruit of a tree and frolic with others of its kind. As the camera point-of-view pans the broad and fertile savanna, Barry cannot help but vocalize the music of Strauss..., "Thus Spake Zarathustra."

Although Hope is impressed by Barry's ability to reproduce the sound of various orchestral instruments, she shrugs off his performance.

"Where's the monolith?" Barry demands.

Hope does not know what he is talking about and ignores him. Probably another obscure cultural reference from before she was born.

Once again, she becomes enthralled by snapshots of indigenous families and tribes impossibly captured before the appearance of technology capable of capturing them.

"You know these images were created by modern cinematic techniques," Barry insists.

"No! They're real! I know it!"

"And how do you know they're real?" Barry gently asks.

"These pictures are of a different reality, one in which many indigenous societies were not exterminated, where slavery and racial oppression did not traumatize millions of people. It is a different history where the District of Columbia becomes a state." Hope pauses, realizing she is incapable of adequately explaining the unexplainable.

At that moment, the doors to the ballroom swing open and people pour into the lobby, all chatting excitedly with one another. Jane and Mary see Hope and Barry and rush happily toward them. They are followed by a remarkably thinner and healthier-looking Ned.

The astonishment and glee the women shower upon each other seem way out of proportion to the circumstance. When the hugging and kissing at last cease, Barry looks toward the more reserved countenance of Ned.

"Where's Fred?" he asks. "Gone to the bathroom?"

"Who is Fred?" Ned replies. "Have we met him?"

Hope and Barry exchange a brief glance of panic and simultaneously look at Mary.

"Mary, I thought you said something about a guy named Fred," Barry says. She helplessly shakes her head. "Maybe I got you mixed up with someone else here. No old boyfriend or husband named Fred?"

"Heavens no!" she laughs. "Whatever made you think that? I did know a guy named Fred in high school who was kind of sweet on me. He kept insisting we'd be married someday, but I was not interested—at all. Like I told you last night, I knew I had too much living of my own to do to surrender at least half of my dreams for the sake of one man!"

Jane and Ned laugh hard and long at the remembrance of this oath from the night before. Hope and Barry can see how they expect both to join in.

Barry looks at Hope. "You want to tell them, or should I?"

"I'll do it." Hope grabs Mary with one hand and Jane with the other. "Mary—Barry and I were not part of that discussion about not wanting a husband."

"You certainly were! It is in the lounge where we went for a drink after the workshop ended." Jane and Ned agree.

"We did not have a drink with you last night," Barry says solemnly.

Hope continues. "Barry and I went back to my place." The three of them react in shock.

"What? You two together? No way!" Jane says.

"Nothing happened. Barry slept in the guest room."

"The most remarkable thing is that I think Hope's house used to be owned and lived in by my grandparents. My mother grew up in Hope's house."

"Incredible," Ned agrees.

"That's not important," Hope quickly says.

"It is to me..." Barry says.

Hope continues. "What is remarkable is that when we left you were going to have a drink with two other people—William and Fred!" She looks for some recognition or confirmation of her memory.

"Not Fred again! Who, in the devil, is this Fred?" Ned says.

"Or William! Who is William?" Jane says.

Barry picks up the thread. "You might want to sit down for this." They sit. "William is a Black gentleman I met yesterday when I went for a walk. He joined the seminar last night and hit it off with nearly everyone."

"Except for Bart," Hope jumps in. "After the seminar, when you were having a drink with William..."

"And Fred..." Barry adds.

"And Fred..." Hope continues. "Bart apparently stopped at your table to complain about the noise and became confrontational and aggressive..."

"Bart? You are talking about that really sweet guy, Bart, from the workshop?" Jane says.

"He's from the workshop, but hardly *sweet*! At least, that's not how we think of him," Hope says.

Mary is shaking her head, eager to say something. "There was no confrontation with Bart, no William, no person named Fred." She points to each of them in turn. "Jane, you were there. Ned, you were there. Hope, you were there—you had the biggest margarita I'd ever seen. And, Barry, you were there. You had a non-alcoholic beer. The five of us talked about an hour, maybe an hour and a half. No Fred, no William, no Bart, no confrontation.'

Ned and Jane agree with the description.

"Listen," Hope says slowly. "Something has happened. Barry and I seem to have different memories than you three do about what happened. Before we get into that, I want to ask you something which may seem a bit silly..."

"The previous discussion isn't?" Ned jokes.

"How many states are there?"

"Pardon?" Jane asks, not sure she heard the question right.

"The number of states. How many are there in the United States of America?"

"Seriously?"

"Yes," say Barry and Hope in unison.

"Fifty-two," Mary says, "Duh." Jane and Ned provide the same figure.

"Are we within the 51st state right now?" Barry asks.

"Of course," Ned laughs. "Did you miss that little news item, old man?"

"Maybe. How long ago did this momentous event take place?"

"Six or seven years ago, wasn't it?"

Mary and Jane agree it is seven. Barry and Hope explain that they both had been aware of the possibility of statehood for D.C. but absolutely no knowledge that it had been passed.

"We just found out by watching this production." Hope points at the screen just as the street celebration comes into view.

Barry runs up to the screen and points at the Black man standing near a shopping cart. "And that's William there. And the guy next to him is our desk manager, Malcolm."

The photo is not as significant to Jane, Mary, or Ned.

"Oh, yeah! That photo is famous," Ned says. "Won a Pulitzer, I think."

"And you all say there were now 52 states?" Barry asks.

"Yep. Puerto Rico came on board at the same time," Jane says.

"I didn't know that, either. Did you, Hope?"

She shakes her head. "It is more than a little strange this

statehood thing seemed to pass us by. I live in Arlington and work in the city and just could not have missed it."

"That is strange," Jane agrees. The others are also puzzled but not wildly so. Just another little quirk in a wild and turbulent world.

"But the statehood thing is not the only thing that's bugging me." Hope looks up at Barry standing nearby. He seems as helpless to understand as she is. "It is one thing for a hotel public relations media presentation to gloss over such horrors as slavery, racism, and war, but when I look online it shows me a version of history I don't recognize at all." She shakes her phone as if trying to pound some sense into it.

Hope struggles to say the words out loud. Her voice shakes, her body shakes, a world she had known all her life is shaking. She points to her phone. "According to sources of information I previously considered reliable, the period of Black chattel slavery in colonial America existed for only a few dozen years and not for 240 something years." She looks at the screen on her phone and re-reads what she sees in disbelief. "'In 1676, a widespread blight brought an end to the cultivation and export of tobacco in the American colonies. Because it no longer seemed profitable or necessary to use enslaved labor, the practice was officially abolished throughout the British Empire in a decree from the King of England, Charles II, two years later.'"

She pauses and looks for any hint of astonishment. Only Barry appears disturbed about what to her is a historical anomaly.

"And your point is...?" Mary asks.

"My point is—I'm freaking out!" Hope shouts. "My point

is I have lived my entire forty-eight years of life under the ponderous weight and burden from the horror of the enslavement of my ancestors, of my people, *our* people, Jane! This enslavement, in my understanding and knowledge of history, lasted not fifty-seven years but 244 years. And the legacy of racial bigotry, oppression, violence, and disenfranchisement of my ancestors, my parents, my brothers, and sisters, *our* people, Jane, went on and on not just for a few decades back in the 17th century—it has lasted over 20 generations of our people, more than 400 years of racial injustice, indifference, cruelty, poverty, and despair."

A heavy silence ensues.

"Wow," Mary says. "Jane, do you share Hope's racial grievance? Is the slavery of Black Africans four centuries ago a burden for you also?"

"Not really. How I feel about that short-lived period of slavery is analogous to the way I look at the slaughter and oppression of Christians maybe 2,000 years ago. They are both sad and sorry chapters of history." Jane places a hand on her husband and her best friend, Mary. "But, if I hear you right, Hope, the history you and Barry know includes hundreds of years of not only slavery but a type of racial oppression that lasted hundreds of years after?"

"And has not stopped yet..." Barry sadly adds.

"That's right," Hope agrees, glad he is there. "We could go into the many examples from the horrible history of racism—the Tulsa riots, lynchings, Jim Crow laws, segregation, the fucking Civil War, for God sakes..."

"A civil war?" Ned exclaims. "Over race?"

Barry answers. "A dispute between the Northern and

Southern states over slavery. More than 150 years ago. It ended slavery but over 700,000 people died."

While the three close friends try to absorb this news, Hope continues. "You three have a different history from the two of us. Barry and I came out of the workshop during Anton's session with the white supremacist and die-hard Trump supporter, Bart (whom you think of as a 'Sweetheart') ..."

"Who is Anton? And who is Trump?" Mary asks.

"Anton is the workshop leader and Donald Trump was a president of the United States," Hope says.

Mary, Jane, and Ned roar in laughter.

"You talking about Donald Trump the wealthy TV star and con man? He was convicted of tax fraud twenty years ago and died in prison, although some conspiracies say he's still around," Mary says.

"The workshop leader is a woman named Elaine." Ned laughs and shakes his head in apparent disbelief in this entire narration. "Alright, Hope, you really had us going. You can stop this little fantasy you and Barry cooked up for some reason. Unlike some former colonies, the leader of the U.S. has never been called 'President.' Don't pretend you don't know we call the leader of our country, 'Prime Minister.' We have a parliamentary system, like every former colony of the British Empire."

"Not in the world and country we know," Barry offers. "The ancestors we were taught to learn about fought a revolution to gain independence from the British Crown about 250 years ago. You ever hear about our famous founders, George Washington, Thomas Jefferson, John Adams, and Benjamin Franklin?" They all shake their heads and indicate, '*No, they had not.*' Barry forges ahead with the lessons about a history completely foreign to everyone but Hope. "Although half the founders were slave owners themselves, they patched together a nation supposedly based on freedom. They scribbled together a constitution and government with two legislatures, a panel of judges, and a president that made and enforced laws supposedly for the benefit of the people and by the people."

Hope picks up the thread. "This morning, in a very short period of time, we now find ourselves in a world that seems highly different, in some ways, from the world we know—not only was there a relatively short period of slavery, but no civil war, and no racial discrimination..."

"We didn't say there was *no* discrimination," Jane says.

"Less bigotry and less trauma in any case," Hope continues. "Something happened to us here in the lobby, am I right, Barry?"

"Something did..."

"I meditated or maybe napped and had a kind of strange vision of the future with Malcolm..."

"Yes...I had a little meditation also," Barry agrees.

"Barry thinks it was just a dream. If so, it was very real and perhaps I am still dreaming. You all have memories and knowledge of a different world altogether. Your world (or is it my dream of your world?) has had no devastation from a civil war, no centuries of soul-destroying slavery and racial trauma. Why, this world, your world, doesn't even have a Fred!"

"Fred again!" Mary cries completely exasperated. "Who in hell is Fred?"

Hope, still feeling reluctant to say, allows Barry to step in with a final bombshell. "Up until a few moments ago, Fred was a curly-headed jokester who was married to you!"

Mary rocks back and forth while laughing at this ridiculous notion.

"We all liked him, Mary," Hope says. "Especially you, Ned. You guys had been best friends for years."

At this moment, a stunning attractive woman shows up and announces that the workshop would be re-starting soon.

"Do you know who this is?" Jane asks Hope and Barry. They look at each other.

"Elaine! You somehow look 20 years younger," Barry says.

"I wish!" Elaine says. "Hope, you and Barry seem a bit distressed. Has something happened?"

Jane politely asks if she can explain the situation before diving in with a full account of how the world of Hope and Barry, how reality, diverges from the world the rest of them knew.

"How very interesting," Elaine says. "What do you say we go in and look at this? There may be an innocent explanation. Unusual perhaps, but not terribly alarming. You two okay with that?"

"Not sure what else we can do," Hope decides. They all move toward the ballroom. A pleasant piano tune invites them from within.

"We're no longer 'In the Hall of the Mountain King', eh?" Barry jokes. No one except Hope has any idea what he is talking about. "I'll be there in a minute. I want to check on William."

"Who is William?" Elaine asks.

Barry rushes up to the front desk. Malcolm and the young staff member with the nametag, "Joy," are still playfully bantering.

"Mr. Strange!" Malcolm says cheerfully. "You are well-met."

"Yes. Thank you, Malcolm. I wanted to ask if you happen to recall renting a room to my friend, William, yesterday."

There is a moment of silence. "Sure, go ahead," Malcolm replies with a smile.

"Go ahead with what?"

"Go ahead and ask."

"Do you remember?"

"A friend of yours named William?"

"Yes. Do you remember him? A Black homeless fellow I met on the street. I rented a room for him, Number 417, I believe."

"Someone else may have handled that. Allow me to check." He taps the image of a keyboard that appears beneath the glass countertop. "There is no record of that transaction, sir."

"Are you sure?"

"As sure as one can be about anything these days. I was here all day yesterday and have no memory of that. And the computer...well, the computer is hardly ever mistaken."

"Something strange is happening..."

"You should know..."

"I beg your pardon?"

"That is your name, is it not, Mr. Strange?' Malcolm is all smiles, smirks really, but Barry is not in a mood to be amused.

"You do not remember?"

"I am so sorry, sir. It is so easy to be confused about which way is up these days. What has been where, along with who and what is real—everything changes so quickly now. It can be a little disconcerting. A lot of people say there was a mass extinction event and we are all trapped in various versions of reality in the

Bardo. But I do not believe that for a second."

Barry feels a seismic shift deep in the core of his midsection that feels a lot like pure terror.

"No William has been here?"

"Not as you described him."

"No civil war back in the 1860s?"

"First I've heard of it."

"Can you call the homeless shelter for me? I would like to see if William is there."

"I am not familiar with such a place. Do you have a number?"

"I do not. But it is called the 'Community for Creative Non-Violence' on 2nd St. NW, I believe!"

Malcolm searches all the information resources at his disposal but can find no mention of this shelter, or any shelter. "Mr. Strange, you may not be aware of this, but as far as I can tell there are no homeless shelters in this city."

"Are you nuts!" Barry explodes. "There has to be. Every major city in this country has thousands of homeless people. Where do they go?"

The young staff member watching Barry and Malcolm steps in. "I studied this in college. Homelessness and poverty are a problem in a lot of big cities in Asia and some in South America, but never here in the U.S.," she says smiling. "The emergence of large, profitable corporations at the beginning of the last century created a vast safety net where every citizen was guaranteed not only a safe place to live, but ample income for basic needs like food and health care."

"You're kidding me. Health care?"

"Sure! All but the most primitive nations in the world provide universal health care for its citizens."

"That's right," Malcolm says. "Where in the world have you been?"

"I'm not sure. In a different world altogether. A world with wide-spread poverty, disease, death, war, and a legacy of divisiveness, hunger, and despair. Where did that world go and how did I and Ms. Hope get here in a different reality?"

Malcolm shrugs. "Who knows? Stuff happens."

"You've seen this happen before? People popping up from what seems a different time and history?"

The young woman, Joy, places a reassuring hand on Barry's arm. "I personally have not seen a lot of it. But we hear it happens more and more."

"But why? How?"

"No one knows. But there are places to go, people to see who try to help folks who get disoriented and freak out."

"Joy is right, Mr. Strange," Malcolm says as he shifts his eyes toward some distraction on the screen below him. "As a matter of fact, that workshop in the ballroom right behind you is supposed to be helping folks adjust to whatever reality is happening. They probably have more answers than we have."

Barry turns to stare at the door to the ballroom, then turns back to face the two hotel staff members. "You think there are answers there?" he asks Joy.

"Hard to say," she says with a smile. "As my grandpa used to say, 'You never know!' Good luck, Mr. Strange!"

"You never know…Why do I not find your grandfather's words reassuring?"

Joy shrugs while Malcolm indifferently waves a hand in farewell.

Barry realizes it totally unfair for him to feel disappointment that two members of a hotel staff were unable to explain the disturbance and anomalies in the field and fabric of the reality to which he clings in desperation. In the world he had been used to, for over seven decades now, there seemed always a predictable, almost alphabetical order to everything.

This current unexplainable distortion has him teetering upon the edge of a kind of mad chaos that is not just a threat to his personal ego. The world itself threatens to turn upside down.

He needs fresh air and charges out of the building.

CHAPTER THIRTEEN

What greets Barry outside is a vastly different street scene from any scene he ever saw. Yesterday (or was it just a moment ago)—cars, buses, trucks, and motorbikes flowed up and down New Jersey Avenue at a brisk clip. Today, there are no motorized vehicles at all. Some men, women, and children walk, run, and bike while others look as if they *float* up and down the street.

Barry's amazement at this parade intensifies when he realizes that the offices and government buildings that were across the street the day before have been replaced by a large park with ballfields, tennis and volleyball courts, plus wooded nature trails and a playground for children!

"What the hell is going on here!" he cries.

A gentle hand on his shoulder makes him jump. "Are you well, Mr. Strange?" Barry stares at the man next to him in wide-eyed alarm. "It's Elliott, sir. We talked several times."

"Yes, I remember. The doorman. You're not in uniform today."

"Um, no sir. I am the manager and do not feel the need for uniform."

Barry examines his handsome and stylish tan jacket, blue

shirt and slacks that say successful and unpretentious.

"You're the manager? You get a promotion?"

"I was promoted from Assistant Manager years ago."

"You were not a doorman yesterday?"

"No, I was not. You appear a bit upset. Is there something I can help you with? Are you hungry? Would you like a drink of water?"

"The street seems closed off to vehicles. Is there some kind of parade or festival going on today?"

Elliott looks at the elderly man with gentle concern. "You must be experiencing a time displacement or quantum superposition. No need to worry—it happens all the time. Vehicles for individuals may have been a huge part of the reality or time you accepted as real. Non-polluting public transports help people get where they need and want to go but none of them travel on this street. If you're looking for a shuttle or another means of transport, there are entry ports on the other side of this building or in the Underground as well as trustworthy souls quite happy to assist you at every corner..." He nods to one of these souls on his left and then one several yards away to his right.

"Time displacement?"

"Yes, Mr. Strange. The way I understand it—it's like dreams in which many people find themselves. The mind travels to different times or realities. You may be from a reality when it is normal for cars and trucks to clutter and pollute the street. It is a reality that is, in so many ways, unreal. Sometimes, with intentionality, one can project oneself into a different, alternate reality. Sometimes one finds oneself elsewhere with no intentionality at all."

"Reality... In my reality, people don't float through the air."

A man and a young child notice they are being watched and happily wave as they float by about a foot off the ground.

"Pretty cool, huh? That's a recent innovation. Special foot-wear required! There are also anti-gravity insoles to put into shoes which are cheaper but, from what I hear, do not seem to work as well."

"Anti-gravity! How does that work?"

"Although it has been explained to me a dozen times, I don't really know how it works. There is a bit of a learning curve just turning the lift on and off. The boots or shoes have a tiny switch in the heel. The insoles are trickier—your big toe has to flex just so to turn it on."

"You expect me to believe this?"

"You see those people flying around, don't you? I'm just tell-ing you what I know, which is not much. I've done it myself but am waiting for the price to come down before getting my own. You get a strong electrical vibration in the soles of your feet. If you just stand still, you don't go anywhere, and the vibration eventually fades. As you begin to walk, however, the vibration grows larger and with each step you feel lighter and lighter. It is as if your shoes emanate waves of energy that you simply and slowly walk upon. It requires some concentration, both to lift off and sustain the flight, if you will. It is a bit like ice-skating if you ever have done that."

"They're walking on air?"

"It *looks* as if they're walking on air because we can't see the waves of positrons and antiprotons between their shoes and the ground."

"Positrons and antiprotons…"

"That's what they call the basic ingredients for not only these anti-gravity boots but the buses, trains, and cars that go back and forth and up and down the whole world now."

"Holy shit."

"It is all part of an anti-matter, anti-gravity revolution no less miraculous than the ones which brought us electricity, the internal combustion engine, nuclear power, airplanes, and computers. Scientists discovered how to introduce anti-matter into gravitational fields and, *voila,* a new non-polluting source of energy emerged. They are still working out the bugs for anti-gravity planes and spaceships."

"I don't get it," Barry says after a long pause.

Elliott leans back and laughs. "Neither do I. No one does except for some engineers and scientists who are so excited to have something to work on."

"I mean, I don't know why I'm in a different world with sci-fi technology and utopian social and cultural miracles like universal health care and the elimination of racism, hunger, and homelessness."

"People everywhere one day just decided to stop fucking around and get their shit together is how my grandpa described it."

"And what day would that be?"

"I don't think he literally meant one specific day. It may have taken a little longer than that to turn things around. You feeling better now? Folks in the workshop looking for you?"

"I am feeling better, Elliott. Thank you!" Barry searches but his pockets are empty. "Sorry, I seem to have lost or misplaced the cash I usually carry. I want to leave a tip to show my appreciation."

"Oh, please! The improvement in your disposition and a smile are more than enough thanks for me. Besides, cash has almost been entirely eliminated in the world you are in now."

"How do I purchase or rent things? I don't seem to have any kind of card, or even a wallet...anymore." He performs another futile search in clothes that he notices, for the first time, are totally unlike anything he had ever worn. A diversity of bright day-glow colors—bright red for the left sleeve and right pants leg, sky blue for the right sleeve and left pants leg. The vest portion of the shirt between the sleeves is bright gold that shimmers and shines like the sun. He feels like a court jester or a circus clown. Panic is about to ensue.

Elliott shakes a turquoise wristband. "This has replaced plastic cards." He points to Barry's left wrist where Barry notices, for the first time, a similar band there. "Everybody gets one of these when they finish their free education and their two years of public service. You want to have food, clothing, entertainment, or anything really, just shake your wrist." He again vigorously shakes his fist. "You need to make other financial arrangements if you desire something extravagant like a boat or levitation boots, but for basic day-to-day necessities, the wristband is more than adequate."

"I can't give you, or anyone else, money, or financial credit of some sort?"

"There is no money to give, or credit... And why would you want to? You can, of course, use your wristband to obtain a hat or scarf or gadget you think a friend or family member might like, but to give them monetary 'credit' or a means to obtain something that they can readily obtain by shaking their own wrists, has become pointless."

"Are there limits to the number of things you can obtain with this?" Barry shakes his wrist and feels a slight electrical vibration that startles him.

Elliott smiles. "A shake of the wrist activates a transaction. Just about every object or service subject to a transaction carries a minute byte of data. When you checked into one of our rooms yesterday, one of our staff members activated a digital agreement that you accepted by shaking your wrist."

A clear memory pops into Barry's head. He remembers, as if a dream, flashing his wrist at somebody. Yes, it feels as if he had done this hundreds of times. But he mentally remembers nothing.

Elliott continues patiently. "In theory, you could reserve a room at every hotel in Columbia by a shake of the wrist, but such behavior would soon violate the 'reasonable threshold' for temporary shelter. So, yes, there are limits for the things and activities you can obtain within acceptable periods of times."

"Wow."

"Not everyone loves the system. Those who feel it their God-given right to be obscenely wealthy hate it but, for most of us, we are happy to give up our very slim chance to be rich in return for *everyone* being fed, being sheltered, and being cared for when sick. And, you know what?"

"What?"

"Long ago, when humans learned to pool resources to make sure all were kept safe and fed, we discovered we didn't have to waste a good third of our time on Earth just trying to 'make a living' and making fortunes for others. We found ways to really *live*, to connect with one another, share our creativity and love, and not shrink from each other out of fear and resentment.

"I could just be a bum and shake my wrist every day to get enough food and shelter and alcohol and drugs, but I learned just by looking around me that life is better when I have something meaningful to do, when I help people like *you* find a room, be entertained, learn, live, love, and connect."

Barry takes in this little speech and silently watches the endless promenade of people walking, biking, and floating by.

"I don't know why I'm here," he tells Elliott in a shaky voice. "This doesn't seem to be too bad a location, but do you know where I am supposed to be?"

Elliott takes a moment to think about this. He subtly shakes the apparatus on his wrist and mentally asks for the most beneficial options and suggestions for the man in front of him. Mr. Strange does not seem ready to absorb much more information about the multiple uses of the wristband or other features of the modern age. Why confuse him further by suggesting he himself could ask the worldwide web for information by a clearly formed intention and a flick of the wrist? The messages one receives in this manner are not to be construed as the final word, as 100% accurate, or even in some cases at all reliable, but they can with practice become useful.

A response to Elliott's request for favorable advice pops into his head. "Can't say for sure, Mr. Strange, but I know you were part of the work taking place in the ballroom. I'd say, look in there."

Barry takes one last look at the promenade on the street and the activities taking place in the park beyond. He supposes that should he venture into the street or into the park he could very well, in time, get used to the uniformly cheery dispositions, broad smiles, and the indisputable positive vibrations he is experiencing from a distance.

But he has a terrible feeling that he simply does not *belong* here. He has a terrible feeling that he is way used to, inured actually, to a "reality" way more numb, far more lifeless, more spirit-less than this one.

Of course, there had been smiles and moments of happiness where he came from, but nothing so prominent and per-petual and obvious as this. In the streets where he grew up, in the schools and workplaces where he studied or toiled; in homes and churches, in bars and gatherings where music was played and jokes shared; where speeches were made, time wasted or treasured; human beings from time to time might *look* joyful, might even laugh and sometimes put on a happy face, but the genuine stuff was always short-lived. The love near non-existent.

Barry could feel the dull weight of decades of sorry conditioning and patterns. What was it all for? Not caring if anyone listens, he feels a need to describe his world to the folks in the park in a stentorian tone of voice.

"In no time at all, the smile vanishes, the laughter fades, the spirited joyful connection and love recedes. Like a turtle, we stretch our necks a moment here, a moment there, and experience a spark of real joy but the smallest thing can send us scurrying back into our shell so we can feel nothing at all..."

Barry Strange, Timeless Celebrity, speaks loudly,

passionately, and deep from his heart. Since part of this oratorically unusual meditation is performed with eyes closed, he is unaware that a small crowd of people in the street, those inside the park beyond, and the few adjacent or behind him on the sidewalk are all listening.

"Well, hello, Everybody! Just what I need—an audience!" And, for another five minutes, complete strangers from an alternate reality happen to enjoy an old, retired wannabe comedian's most reliable routine. They laugh, they cry, they walk or float away in deep thought and/or confusion.

Behind him, Elliott had shaken the multi-purpose band on his wrist in order to record Barry's performance. If he thinks about it, he might wonder where or how the Web would file or use the information. Like so many words or events submitted without explanation or context, the speech could merely appear on the bandwidth or channel presenting occurrences in the Capital State of Columbia for this date. It may link with thousands of other utterances or writings in line with such keywords as, "smile," "laughter," "love," or even "turtle."

Why anyone might be interested or care enough to watch and listen to the words and songs of a person they may or may not know, Elliott is unable to say. Like so many things, the recording of the event as well as the memory soon after would simply disappear.

Barry simply stares at the people staring at him. What has he to do with them? And vice versa. A few people come near. Barry is sincerely touched by their curiosity and interest. Although tempted to give them a few more minutes of "The Act," Barry picks up on a concern that all assembled seem to share.

'Are you okay?'

Much of what he says and sings seems utter nonsense to them.

"Have these people never seen a blithering idiot before?" he says turning to Elliott.

"They may never have seen one," Elliott says in a light tone. He stands closer in order to take his hand. "May I?"

"May you what?"

"Take a reading. It is something a lot of us have learned to do." He holds Barry's hand palm up with one hand and lightly brushes it with the other.

"You read palms?"

"More like a reader of qi, your vital force." Since he does not resist, Elliott proceeds to sense Barry's pulse with the fingers of one hand and gently pass the fingers of his other hand over his palm and fingers. "Breathe with me—in and out. Good. I am hearing your energy with my hands. Your qi, your flow, is exceptionally good especially for an old person, but let loose of this block here...and this one here. Genuinely nice, indeed!"

Elliott releases his hands. Barry continues to breathe deeply and slowly opens his eyes. He had not realized they were closed.

"I don't think I ever felt so relaxed." He lets out a huge yawn. "What did you do?"

Elliott smiles. "Not much. You know that we have more than five senses, don't you?" Barry shakes his head. "I know for a fact that it is possible to become aware of at least a dozen more senses. I used a couple you may not be aware of to sense the flow of your essential qi, your life energy. Simply put, when I become aware of a couple places where your energy is blocked, a part of you becomes aware of them also and simply unblocks them."

"Cool."

"Bye, Barry!" Three or four voices yell. Barry scans the crowd of people walking and floating past him. A group of young teens laugh and wave at him. "We love you, Barry!" they shout and walk and bounce along.

"How do they know my name?" he says to Elliott with some astonishment.

"I'm not sure. They probably heard you announce quite loudly that you were, 'Barry Strange, the Celebrity's Celebrity'!"

"I said that?"

"More like sung it..." Elliott repeats a couple bars of the song Barry had very recently sung, with a spot-on impression of his voice...

"Oh, yeah," Barry says. "I did do that, didn't I?" He starts to move away. A small step by Elliott is enough to stop him.

"Before you go your merry way, Sir, I want to make sure that you will be alright... As the manager of this institution, I want you to know that I and all the staff here will be glad to assist you in any way." Elliott again makes eye contact with other people dressed just like him. There are two tan and blue helpers, one on each corner, plus a couple others on the sidewalk in intense conversations with help seekers not quite ready to come inside. "Any issue at all, any question, any concern at all, do trust that Juanita can be a reliable guide...."

Elliott gestures once more to one of the corner guides. A bright-eyed, eager, ecstatic, and easy on the eyes young Latina turns and delivers the smile which had won her a top prize in the

Mayan International Smile Contest.

"Juanita! I know her!" Barry yells.

"Maybe she has already helped you?"

"No, or maybe she has… memory has been tricky lately."

Juanita tries remote reading the old white man who seems to recognize her. He looks familiar, someone from long ago and her home village. That could not be. She had not known many white men until arriving in this country.

The person she is with thanks her for the directions and Juanita decides to dance her way towards Elliott and his companion.

"You are in a peppy mood!" Elliott greets her with a smile.

"Hearing you guys sing did it," she sings happily.

"I was singing?" Barry says.

"You sure were! Both of you." Juanita heartily laughs and holds onto Barry's arm as if to keep him from rolling around on the ground.

Elliott puts out a hand to still her. "Juanita, this is Barry. Have you had the distinct pleasure of meeting him? He thinks maybe he knows you from somewhere."

"I don't think so. I believe I would remember someone so distinguished."

Barry falls back for a second. "You mock me, Miss…"

Juanita halts and redirects this train of thoughts. "Not at all, Barry. You have substantial inner strength. So solidly grounded yet so ready to fly!"

"I am not sure I know what that means but thank you! I think." He studies her for a second.

Confident the rattled old man is in good hands, Elliott

exchanges a look with his co-worker, smiles at Barry, and moves on to a different person and task.

"Do you know a guy named Malcolm?" Barry asks Juanita.

"The Malcolm who works the front desk? Sure, I know him."

"None of my business, but did you and he ever have a thing? You know—a romance?"

Juanita stares hard at this strange little man and then bursts out laughing. "Me and Malcolm?" More laughter. "No, never. Sorry, but that is hilarious to me. How did you get that idea?"

Barry studies the face before him. Is the notion about she and Malcolm from a scrap of memory or a brief slice from a dream? This woman with the prize-winning smile is familiar.

"We did not see each other yesterday?" Barry says in a weak, frightened voice.

"Lo siento," she says gently. "I am sorry, but no. I was not even here yesterday."

"If today is substantially different from yesterday, that doesn't necessarily mean one is losing their mind..." Barry pauses and looks at Juanita. "Does it?"

"How would I know? I tend to believe the mind is never lost. It can feel misplaced sometimes but never lost." Without saying so aloud, she asks and receives permission to touch him. She holds his wrist and performs a reading of his qi.

His panic instantly subsides. He feels relaxed and at peace. Barry weeps.

When enough weariness and ancient grief passes, he opens his eyes to see Juanita and two others surrounding him with loving attention that veers close to being too much.

"Jesus Christ! What the hell is going on here?" he cries.

"We are trained listeners," says someone named Pete.

"We are here to help," says Juanita.

"But we'll need more cues from you to know how," says the other person, name unknown. Barry feels oddly reassured that this third person delivers their statement in a somewhat testy manner. Such impatience is a prominent feature of the so-called real world he knew.

Barry notices all three wear the same non-threatening color scheme, a uniform perhaps with tan jacket, blue shirts and slacks.

"I need to be in the world in which I belong," he says at last. "I appreciate your kind help but think I should look for the folks I know from that world. I believe they are in there!" he says pointing at the façade of the Regency Hotel.

However, the building indicated no longer seems to be a hotel at all. It lacks all the ornate frills and splendor of the Regency. Also, a small sign near the door announces that this is the location of the "Recovery and Replacement Center".

"Certainly, Barry! We have every confidence that you will find your way," Juanita says. "A group working on similar issues is in the first big room to the left."

Barry has no response to this. No one says a word or moves a muscle for several long moments. A major spiritual vision seems at hand. Although all pause in anticipation, for once Barry is shy about sharing. A little movie plays in his mind. He thinks if he had pen and paper or some sort of recording device, he could at least make a few notes. Maybe the story should be told and maybe it should not; maybe it would be told, maybe it would not. Only he could tell the story, he told himself. After all, it is his vision.

Barry thinks it curious that Juanita and the others continue to stand so close to him while he experiences this "vision." He is not about to expose himself to almost certain evaluation, concern, or criticism by describing the pictures in his mind or soul or awareness, or whatever this process or mechanism may be.

The vivid image of dwellings, perhaps thousands of years old, embedded on red canyon walls becomes more real the longer he looks at it. Is he imagining the cluster of families he sees living there? Two or three figures look as if preparing a meal. They stop what they are doing and stare back at him across the narrow geological chasm between them. More than a dozen people dressed in simple indigenous garb raise their hands to welcome him warmly.

Across an expanse of thousands of years or on a bridge to different dimensions, Barry raises a hand and waves back. Impossible as it seems, he knows these beings to be his family. This cave on the side of a mountain is the habitat for a community of humans who have loved and took care of each other for hundreds if not thousands of years.

The sound of someone standing a few inches away startles him. He turns his head and the image of the desert cliff dwelling vanishes.

Juanita, Pete, and the other observer exchange looks.

"Fascinating, Barry!" Juanita says. "Are we seeing an image out of your memory?"

"What do you mean, senorita? What image?"

"The one you just had, beloved one; I believe we all shared in the lovely vista you visited, did we not, Pete and Svetlana?" They shake their heads in agreement. "A beautiful sunset upon red hills warmly illuminating a peaceful domestic scene inside a large cavern cut into the side of a cliff. That is what you see, is it not? You do not need to talk about it if you do not want to. I only wonder whether this is a place you have been to before, perhaps your home?"

"Yes, Home," he whispers.

Barry looks around his immediate vicinity. He is outdoors next to an avenue devoid of all motorized vehicles. The edifice he thought was a hotel is now a "Recovery and Replacement Center." He had a peek at a wildly different era or reality altogether. The three people surrounding him can apparently read his mind.

Nothing to worry about here!

"Not sure what to say," Barry admits. He looks steadily into the faces of the three Helpers hoping to reassure them, as well as himself, that he has not totally lost his mind. "I think I will go inside. Friends, from the olden days, may still be in that big room, I hope."

He heads in the direction where he thinks is a door but stops short. He notices there does not seem to be a door anywhere. A pale green panel stretched twelve feet from the ground runs the length of the building with no discernible opening. He looks back at the Helpers observing his departure. Juanita gestures for him to keep going.

As Barry comes within a foot or so to the green wall, he sees it is not at all solid. It is a tight arrangement of vibrating waves and particles. The wall *bends* inward at his approach and gives way as he thrusts one hand, and then his entire body through the permeable layer. He steps away and turns to see that the vibrating green wall resumes its appearance of solidity.

'What a strange new world that has such things in it...' he thinks to himself. He closes his eyes and allows his breath and blood pressure return to normal.

Barry opens his eyes and makes his way towards the big room on the left. He is momentarily surprised to see that it has a door. The handle on it is oddly anachronistic, as if from an older more primitive age before people were able to walk through walls.

He glances toward the front desk to his right. The clerk Malcolm stands there happily flirting with a young Juanita, a different version entirely from the Juanita he had just left on the sidewalk outside.

Momentarily at a loss for doing anything else, Barry Strange, Famous Multi-Dimensional Traveler, pushes down the brass door handle and enters the hotel ballroom.

CHAPTER FOURTEEN

It feels as if he has been gone a long, long time. Here were the familiar wall hangings and art prints redolent of the ostentatious 21st century. There, in the cluster of blue chairs, are the 150 or so people of the self-improvement workshop to which he had been banished for some reason. The leader (Anton is his name!) dressed in a flamboyant costume is turning out one poetic phrase after another as he paces back and forth in front of the attentive throng many of which Barry recognizes!

There in the aisle, at the end of the first row of chairs, sits a black-haired Black woman in a wheelchair.

"Hope!" he shouts spontaneously. Anton stops talking and all heads turn towards Barry as he tosses caution aside and speeds down the aisle. With more effusiveness than most everyone cares to witness, he embraces and kisses her head, her cheeks, her hands... He pauses to take in her astonished and perhaps slightly appalled expression and then slowly, gently, kisses her lips.

"Whoa! Down, Boy!"

"Hope. I apologize if I offend, but I am so happy to see you!"

She pauses and looks around her. "Okay...".

A man two seats down the aisle from her stands and gestures.

"We saved you a seat, Barry."

"Ned!" Barry shouts. "How good to see you!" He works his way to the empty seat while enthusiastically embracing and kissing him. Fred, Mary, and Jane are also embraced and kissed. "How good to see all of you!" he cries while throwing a big-hearted air-kiss to all.

The snickers and buzzing of the crowd fade with a loud throat-clearing from Anton.

"Well..." he says drily. "I'm sure I speak for everyone in saying it is very good to see *you*, Barry." An audible outburst from one man seems to disagree.

"Got to be Bart..." Mary mutters.

"Where you've been and what you've been doing has got to be an interesting story, Barry..." Anton says.

"Oh, it is..."

"But, with your permission, I would like to finish my thoughts," Anton says.

As if a king granting dispensation to a loyal subject, Barry stands and bows.

"Jesus, save us..." Anton says raising his head toward invisible deities. "Before your glorious entrance, Barry, I was sharing thoughts about seemingly miraculous and unexplained phenomena some participants are having. As we get to know each other we build trust, we create safe havens to express our fears, frailties, hopes, and dreams. Some internal struggles are more difficult to hear than others. The more we listen and understand each other, the more we intuit and anticipate feelings and reactions." Anton pauses as if waiting for the slow ones to catch up.

"I have heard a lot of you say that you think you are reading the minds of others or others are reading your minds and that these workshop exercises are inducing telepathy. Others are saying that they experience alternate realities. I have not experienced such things myself, but I do not doubt for a moment that it can *feel* as if telepathy and parallel universes exist. I look at Barry, for instance. He has shown me enough of how he thinks and what he feels that I might be able to anticipate, or *intuit*, what he might say, what he might feel, and what he might think.

"It could very well be that this anticipation, this hunch about Barry, this *sense* of what is going on with him can, on a deep, personal level, *feel* to me (and to him should I express it) as if I am reading his mind."

There is a moment of silence while everyone absorbs this analysis.

"Okay, Anton," Barry pipes up in the manner that all recognize as one of his comical personalities. "What am I thinking?"

(Laughter)

"You think I'm a stuffed shirt compelled to explain away wonder..." Anton says.

"Wrong! That's not what I think at all!" Barry says. "I think all here would agree that you are absolutely brilliant. That you care enough to caution us all about the risks of investing too heavily in what might be fantasy is an admirable trait. You have a unique ability to both inspire and ground us." He stands and with a dignified air toasts with an imaginary glass. "Anton, may Dame Fortune ever smile on you, but never her daughter, Miss Fortune. I salute you!"

He claps loudly. Mercifully, almost everyone stands and warmly applauds with him. Anton, somewhat embarrassed, puts a stop to it.

"Thank you, everyone! I appreciate the sentiment but neither crave nor deserve acclaim. I'm here to work, not get my ego stroked. Like a janitor, I am here to help clean up some of the mess." To Barry's astonishment, Anton has lost his gay apparel and is now dressed in green overalls, a janitor's uniform. When did that happen? "Speaking of work, let's get to it. Who has something to say?"

As had been done many times before, the microphone is passed to Elaine who quickly delivers it into the hands of one person after another. The shy landscape worker, Manuel, rises to his feet first. He walks to where sits his *querido amigo*, Shirley, and *con un corazon pesado* thanks her for listening to him during the session they had together.

"I come to this country twelve years," he explains. "I work. I raise *familia*. I go to church. I play soccer. I pay taxes and do what I can to help other people. Today, Shirley listen to me with her *corazon*, her heart, and I realize this be first time any white gringo American ever truly listen or show they care about who I be, what I feel, how I think or dream. This sad to me but Shirley helps me see she will not be the last."

Manuel, shaky and tearful, returns the mic to Elaine. Shirley stands and hugs him. All applaud.

Betsy takes the mic and announces, "It feels as if I have been afraid or angry every day of my life..." Betsy is at least seventy years old. "Today, in my session with Bart of all people, I allowed myself to feel loved for the very first time."

"Bart?" Barry blurts out in astonishment.

"Loved not only by Bart," Betsy continues, "But loved by

Elaine, Anton, Felix, Billy, Mary, and everyone here. The most remarkable thing is—I feel love from the person I most needed to feel loved by—myself."

All applaud.

"Bart?" Barry repeats.

"Yes, Bart!" Anton says. "Where have you been, Barry?"

"I'm not sure..."

"It took a lot of work, but Bart bravely took a deep look at his own anger and inner dragons. He decided to no longer attack humanity. He sees it is better to join the human race. Do I interpret your journey fairly, Brother Bart?"

Bart takes the microphone. "It is a fair description. I have apologized for being a complete asshole and bully to everyone but you, Barry." He hands the mic back to Elaine and walks across the room to stand at the end of the row of chairs where Barry sits with a stunned look on his face. "I am sorry, my brother."

"Brother..." Barry whispers. The man standing there by the name of Bart looks like the person who, from the first moment of the workshop sneered and despised everyone and everything, certainly looks sincere. The goodwill and kindness he currently projects could not be fake, or could it?

"Yes, like it or not, we are brothers. That is what happened to me in my sessions—brotherhood! Or, more precisely, I became aware of how my own fear kept me from seeing that we are all one family."

"One family? Really?"

"Yes, really."

"And is my friend, William, also part of your new family?"

"Yes, of course," Bart answers quickly. "Although I do not

know who you are talking about."

Barry scoffs, near certain now that Bart's transformation is an act. He looks at his friends sitting next to him for confirmation. "You all know William," he says to Hope and Mary, Jane, Ned, and Fred.

They did not know William. No one in that room would admit to knowing William. No one had any memory of the homeless man Barry befriended and gave shelter. There is no recollection of the quiet soul who shared a song at the talent show, who had a run-in and later a small brawl with Bart. Unlike Barry, they could not mourn the fact that William had abandoned his hotel room and returned to life on the Street, because none of them knew William. Barry's narrative, to most everyone, seems some type of dream.

"Hope, did you not take a nap yesterday in the room I rented for William?"

"I did not have a nap anywhere yesterday. I wasn't even here. None of us were. This is the first day of the workshop, Barry."

"There is no yesterday. There is only today..." Barry's mind drifts away.

As sure as he is about the reality of events no one else remembers, Barry is now certain that nothing he thinks of as real is real to them. Not William singing, not Hope walking, not himself spending the night at Hope's house, not their breakfast nor the rides in her car, no statehood for D.C.—not any memory real to him is real to any of them.

'Now is not the time to panic,' Barry tells himself.

Everybody in the room is poised and apparently waiting for Barry to come to his senses. He would have liked to offer reassurance that his insistence on a different version of the recent past is not a sign of insanity or senility, but he cannot come up with any plausible explanation.

The meditative silence continues for several minutes. At long last, Anton breaks the spell. "Barry..." he says.

"Yes?"

"Are you OK?"

"Not sure, actually..."

"For a second there, I thought I'd have to call in the stroke unit. Barry, join me up here, please," Anton says.

Although the last thing he wants to do, Barry works his way down the row and past the line-up of friends with whom he thinks he had shared so much the day before.

Hope stares at him as if he were a lunatic. Jane looks compassionate but afraid. Mary holds an enigmatic smile, amused about the whole thing. The men, Ned and Fred, both evade his glance. Perhaps, they are afraid of catching some disease.

Head down, shoulders slumped, his short walk to the front of the room stilted, Barry projects the manner of someone on the way to the gallows. He avoids Anton's intense gaze as well as an open-armed invitation to embrace and stand rigid beside him.

"Hello, Barry!" Anton chirps brightly. "What is going on with you, dear friend? Could you look at me, please?"

Barry gives Anton a glance but quickly returns his attention to a spot on the distant wall over the heads of hundreds of eyes staring at him.

"Don't hide from us. We are here for you. What do you want? What do you need? Look at all these lovely people caring about you! Go on. Let them see you seeing them."

Barry closes his eyes for a second. He hears someone cough. He opens his eyes and scans each row. Somehow, he *knew* these people. For many, there is no memory of an actual conversation, no clue of their name or story. Yet, he has a strong intuition that he knows them somehow.

His eyes rest on Hope and the others that he feels he knew quite well. Ned smiles at him, as if in mind of a joke. Mary winks, Jane looks puzzled. Fred seems distracted and somewhere else.

Among those paying attention to Barry at that moment, Hope appears the most affected. Did he and the wild memories he shared a few short moments ago seriously disturb her?

Of course, it did! His yakking about Hope walking out of the room under her own steam clearly upset her. He had been forced to admit that she, and everyone else, did not share his memories. In fact, Hope, Anton, and all of them seem not to share the same reality he does. They might forgive his alternate version of recent history, the one he thought was real yesterday. '*Leave him be,*' they think. '*He is no danger to himself or anyone else.*'

Barry restrains his impulse to totally freak everyone out with tales from in front of the building at a different time and reality altogether. They might be excited to hear about flying people and cars, thrilled to know that in some reality somewhere or somewhen walls become force fields that humans can walk right through.

While Barry silently thinks about such things, all assembled are inclined to give him their full attention. After what to everyone (but Barry) seems ten minutes or more, Anton breaks the spell.

"How's it going, Barry?"

Barry jerks his head towards him in surprise. "Hmm, what's that?"

"What are you thinking about?"

Barry looks at him, then at the large expectant throng in front of him. As he often does when unsure what to do, Barry sings.

In a kind of dancing/strolling/show-off style he liked to think of as worth sharing, Barry sings the first verse and chorus while circling once around the circumference, then down and up the two aisles of chairs.

For verse two, Barry notices he is but a foot away from the wide-eyed attentive Hope and directs every word and note to her.

Can you remember who I was
Can you still feel it?
Can you find my pain
Can you heal it?
And lay your hands upon me now

Hope places a friendly hand into his outstretched and trembling palm.

And cast this darkness from my soul;
You alone can light my way,
You alone can make me whole
Once again

As he pauses to take in a breath, Hope jumps in. "That is a lot of responsibility to put upon one person. '*Only I can light your way*?' Don't think so, Bubba. Light your own damn way, Fool!"

The blast of laughter from a hundred or so souls sends a thrill of shame down and up his spine. Instead of taking a seat while taking care of his own humiliation, Barry double-downs and jubilantly sings the third and final verse to the entire crowd.

When finished, Barry looks at everyone, notes their stunned silence, and returns to his seat.

"Did you just make that up?" Hope says.

"Oh, no!" he says loud enough for all to hear. "That's a Don McLean song." No one seems to recognize the name. "The composer and singer of 'American Pie'?" He sings a line or two that receives the same non-reaction. "How quick we forget..."

Anton claps his hands twice, more to stop the singing than to applaud it. "Lovely song, Barry. Something like that would be good for the 'Variety of Talent Display' we have planned for tonight. Everyone, and I do mean everyone, will be encouraged to sing a song, do a dance, make a speech, pray, whistle...whatever your talent, you get to show it off this evening."6iv'

Barry is unnerved by everyone's exclamations of surprised delight

"Didn't we do that last night?" he says.

"Uh, no. That's tonight!"

Barry leans back in his chair. He is not crazy. He *knows* the talent show was yesterday, knows William was there to participate, knew he went home with Hope last night, knows that Bart did not go through any kind of transformation. He *knows* these things, did he not?

Barry Strange, Famous Delusionary, is willing to entertain the possibility that he perhaps merely *thinks* these things are true. After all, what were memories, anyway? Fragments of realistic dreams? He looks up from what he thinks were silent musings to see Anton, Hope, and everyone staring at him.

"Was I thinking out loud, again?"

Anton slowly nods. Hope, from a few feet away, mutters, "You sure were, Crazy Man."

"Just curious. Did you happen to notice if my lips were moving?"

"I didn't notice. Anyone see Barry's lips moving?" Hope asks in a tone of mock seriousness that draws more laughter.

"Am I imagining things, losing my mind?"

No one answers Barry. For a moment, everyone is unsure what to say, what is real.

Suddenly, a door opens. Anton's face lights up. "My god! You're really here!" Heads turn to look, then erupt with a roar of excitement. A tall Black man enters the room and spreads his arms as if to hug everyone all at once.

"Welcome, welcome to our seminar!" Anton gushes and flies across the room to embrace him. "I am certain you all recognize the brilliant mathematician and physicist and the winner of not one, but three Nobel Prizes, Sir Hugh Ever!"

The deafening applause goes on for several minutes. The well-known celebrity scientist and peace ambassador either shakes every hand or hugs every person in the room. The rapturous response goes on until Sir Ever stands before Barry whose serious demeanor quickly quiets the room.

"I am sorry," Barry says. "You are not Sir Whoever." His voice cracks with emotion. "I'm not sure what play this is, a comedy skit to mess with me maybe, but I am glad to see you, William!" With that, Barry throws his arms around the Nobel laureate and helplessly weeps. "I thought we'd lost you, forever, Willy Joe!"

"I am glad to see you as well, whoever you are and whatever reality you happen to be in. But I am pretty sure of my name— not William, not Willy Joe. My name really is, Hugh Ever." He smiles and gently disengages from Barry's trembling arms.

"You are Hugh? You are...Whoever? Perhaps William Smith is not your real name any more than was Joe Smith. Were you just pretending to be homeless and destitute?"

"You do look familiar, Barry. You say you knew me when I was homeless? That was a long time ago, another time and place and reality I barely remember. Someone did help me out of the hopeless mess I was in—oh, maybe forty years ago. That couldn't have been you, was it?"

"No, that was yesterday."

"If *you,* thank you for caring." Sir Hugh hugs Barry.

"Uh, this is too weird." Barry takes a step back. He turns to Anton. "Was this whole thing some kind of set-up? You were in on this hoax from the beginning, weren't you, Hope? Pretending not to walk so I could miraculously 'heal' your affliction. Ah, I get it now!" He paces twenty paces away from everyone to restore his bearings. "John, and everyone in Charlottesville who signed that ridiculous 'court order,' somehow arranged the entire prank maybe. But why? I don't see how you arranged for people outside to look as if they were floating down the street or how you created the illusion that I could walk through walls. Or, to nearly convince me that Washington D.C. is a state and that there wasn't a Civil War and there was only a few years of chattel slavery. Maybe there was some crazy chemical mechanism in that gummy..."

Sir Hugh Ever looks to Anton for some hint of an explanation, but the seminar host can only shrug and throw up his hands.

Barry takes a moment to study the looks of concern upon every face. If it is all one big joke, not everyone is in on it. He takes his emotional outburst down a notch and tries to recapture his equilibrium. "Maybe I am truly going insane, a form of dementia, a series of hallucinations and other self-created fantastical visions," he tells them. "Elliott, outside, called it 'time displacement' and 'quantum superposition.' Maybe, I'm just nuts..."

Laughter at this eases his anxiety. Maybe it is time to disappear. He blows a kiss to Hope and to a few select others. Jane and Ned, Mary and Malcolm, Anton, and even Bart have less of an idea what was happening than he. With a small smile, he heads out the room with a final goodbye wave.

Before he goes through the doorway, Sir Hugh emerges from a short chat with Anton and stops Barry's exit with a sharp, loud whistle through his fingers.

"Were you harmed by any of these unusual experiences? Did you come away from them with desires to harm yourself or others?"

"Uh, no."

"What's the problem? From the sound of it, you had some

incredible adventures. Besides being freaked out, there may be intimations of truth and beauty you might take with you no matter what paths and realities you find yourself. Some of my work in the fields of mathematics and quantum physics have shown there may well be an infinite number of universes, as this Elliott noted. Sometimes, it is said, one may choose the universe in which to live. Perhaps, you stumbled into a couple." Barry nods a couple of times and turns once again to depart. Sir Hugh continues. "The world you think exists is just that—something you happen to perceive. God be with you, sir! Share your love and your wealth of spirit wherever you go. You know you have all the love you need. Keep sharing that and you will be okay."

Before Barry makes his exit, he reaches into a pocket and hands a plastic card to Hope. He kisses her softly and whispers, "Pin number 1020." He winks at her. "Do good, Hope Good".

As he heads for the door, he hears Kevin's choice for his musical exit, the Beatles tune, "All You Need Is Love." He thinks he'll take a walk and discover some other things to do. A million worlds beckon but a familiar voice lures him toward a familiar path. Out of a billion hallways, at least one door was made just for him.

After all was said and done, there really was no place like Home.

ABOUT THE AUTHOR

BILL DAVIS has spent the last 55 years imagining and starting many novels. He is glad to have finished one. He also imagines plays, screenplays, poems, essays, and other flights of fancy at his home in Central Virginia.

ACKNOWLEDGEMENTS

I genuinely appreciate the expert edits suggested by my good friend, John Ruemmler. Bob Pavior, Lenny Carter, Susan Scofield, and my very significant partner Millie Fife also read this novel and encouraged its production. Special thanks to the Managing Editor of Lightfoot Press, Proal Heartwell and his colleagues C.J. Green and Laura Roseberry for their help in the interior and exterior design. Some of the depicted counseling and workshop practices are lifted from personal worthwhile experiences from Re-Evaluation Counseling and Insight Seminars. I also borrowed ideas out of Michael Brown's remarkable work, "The Presence Process".